Gwyneth Finally

Also by Reg Quist

The Church at Third and Main

Hamilton Robb

Noah Gates

Terry of the Double C

Danny Series

Just John Series

Mac's Way Series

Reluctant Redemption Series

The Settlers Series

Gwyneth Finally

FRONTIER DREAMING

BOOK THREE

REG QUIST

Gwyneth Finally
Paperback Edition

CKN Christian Publishing
An Imprint of Wolfpack Publishing
1707 E. Diana Street
Tampa, FL 33610

cknchristianpublishing.com

This book is a work of fiction. Any references to historical events, real people or real places are used fictitiously. Other names, characters, places and events are products of the author's imagination, and any resemblance to actual events, places or persons, living or dead, is entirely coincidental.

Paperback ISBN 979-8-89567-869-5 eBook ISBN 979-8-89567-868-8

Gwyneth Finally

Acknowledgments

Much thanks to my good friend, Dr. W.D., MD, FRCSC. TX.

Chapter One

El Paso, Texas, THE SIGN ON THE STATION HOUSE wall appeared proud to announce.

After having held to their seats to allow others to vacate the railcar first, Cob, followed by Gwyneth, stepped to the pine-planked station platform. As Cob held out his hand in assistance, they were welcomed by a single shot that sounded to Cob like a .44, followed by another short volley. People started screaming, running every which way, seeking shelter. Cob turned to Gwyneth. "Go Back. Stay inside. Stay low."

Ignoring that good advice himself, he drew his belted .45 as he scurried along the side of the passenger car, hoping to see where the shots were coming from, and what the danger might be. If asked, Cob would describe himself as a simple cattle rancher. But that didn't mean he would stand by where danger loomed.

The action appeared to be centered around a heavy, high-sided wagon drawn by a four-up team of strong mules. The well-experienced teamster had the rig backed up to the baggage car door. The train had come to a stop only moments before, indicating that the attackers had knowledge of where the baggage car would stop. The heavy car door was slowly moving, was almost closed, as if the attendant had opened it on their arrival in El Paso, before Cob had heard the first shot, but was now frantically attempting to close it.

Even as Cob watched, a big-hatted man rose from the wagon bed, rifle leading the way, as he placed one booted foot where it would prevent the closing of the car access. He transferred the rifle to his left hand, rested his right shoulder against the leading edge of the door, and pushed back against the efforts of the baggage clerk. Even as he held the door, two men who had jumped past the opening were lugging a heavy, iron-strapped box out of the car, squeezing past the half-closed door. They dropped the box onto the bed of the wagon and returned to grab another.

Riders coming to the assistance of the thieves raised their Colts. Hot leads slammed through the thickness of the car door. A sharp cry and then a morbid groan rose from the baggage car. When the wounded clerk who was holding the door collapsed to the floor of the car, all resistance to its opening was removed. The thief who had been holding the door against its closing easily slid it back, creating an opening wide enough for Cob to see the unmoving attendant.

He appeared to have skittered away a few feet and was now lying on the floor with his back leaning against other cargo and baggage. He was holding his shoulder with his one good hand. Blood dribbled through his fingers. But when the two men who had removed the heavy box leaped from the wagon back into the car, the wounded attendant rolled onto his side, facing the daylight with a double-barreled express gun aimed. The whoomph of released lead from one barrel was followed quickly by the same from the second death-dealing ten-gauge Remington. The two raiders were smashed back, crumpling to the floor of the baggage car, in a pile of blood and gore. Fools, Cob thought. Brave men dying for nothing.

The raider who had held the door open was the next to fall

when a rifle shot from somewhere in the crowd ripped through his throat.

Determined to still make something of their deadly raid, in spite of the from the rail crew and a few passengers, three men dropped from their saddles. Using the wagon's tailgate as a step, the three leaped into the car. They emerged almost immediately, dragging another heavy, iron-strapped wooden box as the clerk was fumbling with the Remington, trying to reload with blood-soaked fingers.

The same three men had time to drag out the third and then the fourth box before the firing became too intense for their liking. They ducked down below the wagon sides, hollering, "Go. Go. Get out of here," to the teamster. Through the shouting and the constant hammering of shots, the teamster responded to the command. The prancing mules, at first, wanted to run off in four different directions. It took precious seconds for the experienced driver to pull them into a team.

A rider on a big black was hollering orders no one could either hear or obey.

The platform had almost cleared of people, leaving just Cob and two others who had cautiously approached, guns drawn. Four more mounted men, out of a total of perhaps nine or ten by Cob's reconning, holding either Colt six-shooters or carbines, were attempting to steady their riding animals as they surrounded the wagon, ready to escort it out of danger. The car door lay fully open, an invitation no one bothered to take up.

Men had been shot. At least two, perhaps three, lay dead. The riders breaking into the baggage car had clearly shown themselves to be thieves and murderers. Now, with the wagon moving into its getaway, there was little for Cob or the others to do but bring down as many escapees as possible. Cob chose to hold steady on the one rider who appeared to be the leader, shouting instructions over the tumult that no one was heeding.

Two of the men standing beside Cob on the platform had opened fire, with the result that one rider was down, while two others were sending wild shots toward the platform. Recently alighted passengers who were crowded together at the far end of the plank floor ducked ricochets and clambered over one another toward questionable shelter. Hoping to stave off more shooting, more injuries, or deaths of the rail riders, Cob leveled his weapon. With a single shot, he took out the leader.

As the leader fell from his saddle, his cohorts leathered their Colts, tucked their hats down tight, as by habit, and spurred after the speeding wagon.

The teamster riding the seat of the wagon appeared to have taken a bullet. Where he was hit was unknown to Cob. He was awkwardly holding the reins with one hand while also pressing his other hand and arm against his chest. Shock and pain distorted his face. He still held his Colt, forgotten and useless, as blood soaked his shirt and the hand that held the weapon.

GLANCING back to see several of his pals either down or trying to hold in terrified horses and finally picking up on the voices of the men huddled behind him in the wagon, with a shout and a curse, the teamster gave up on the robbery and shouted the mules into all-out action. The riders who were still a-saddle decided the fight was over. The attempted theft had been a partial, but not complete, failure. They had four boxes, if they could keep them from the crowd gathering on the busy street of El Paso.

LEAVING three men on the ground, and with loose horses getting in the way of their escape, the miserable affair turned into a shambles. The teamster was now lying almost sideways on the seat, with the mules running free. Whether he had been hit and mortally wounded or was hoping to duck further lead was a mystery to Cob.

Cob turned his attention back to the station platform in time to see an old man, white-haired and be-whiskered, lift his Sharps Big 50. Cob and Gwyneth had visited with the oldster, who called himself Reb, as they traveled south from New Mexico into Texas. Reb was a storyteller and an altogether interesting fellow to travel with, shortening the dreary miles as he regaled them with claims of a long life of adventure and battle.

Now Reb leaned his shoulder against the corner of the station, took careful aim, and squeezed off a single shot. The *ssst* of burning powder, snuffed out by a boom that threatened to loosen the shingles on the station roof, overshadowed the noise on the platform and knocked over the near-side lead mule. The animal collapsed, but the momentum of the rest of the team dragged it along for a step before it fell. With the animal's fall, the wheeler behind stumbled, the wagon tongue tipped, dropping the end into the dirt of the road. The tongue dug in, stopping the wagon almost instantly. All four mules went to the road, the wagon rose into the air, turning at an angle to its previous travel, while the teamster flew over the heads of the mules, landing in an immobile heap on the road.

The wagon continued rising to a half-vertical position before tipping to the side and crashing into the horse droppings and detritus that had gathered on the road over the years. The four heavy wooden boxes flew out, raising dust as they hit the road and then rolled a time or two before coming to a rest. The two men riding the wagon hung on until it was too late for escape. They rose into the air along with the wagon, crashing to the road in a broken, dusty pile. The entire raid hadn't taken more than a bare minute and a half from the time the baggage car door first opened. In that short time, several men had died. Others had been wounded and needed medical assistance.

The following raiders, giving up on the heist, made a dash for freedom, but by that time, riders from town were heading toward the depot. The escapees were either shot out of their saddles or rounded up within minutes.

Watching from his shooting position at the depot, the grizzled old timer stood surveying the results of his one shot, his Big 50 held like a walking stick at his side. To no one, and to everyone, he said, "Hated to do it. That there mule didn't do no wrong. But that runaway was likely as not to take out women or kids. Had to be stopped."

Cob turned at the sound of footsteps behind him. Gwyneth was hurrying along, carrying her black leather medical bag. She walked past Cob without a word and fell to her knees beside one of the wounded thieves.

Cob said, "Best you see to the baggage clerk. He took lead. I don't know how much. I'll sort out these ones. One might still be alive. A couple are beyond human fixing. But the clerk is the important one right now. Judging by the shouts, there may be a second man in there."

Wordlessly, but seeing the wisdom of Cob's thoughts, Gwyneth rose to her feet. The railway conductor had just placed a set of steps beside the baggage car door and climbed in himself. As Gwyneth put her foot on the bottom step, the conductor held his hand out, palm forward, to stop her. "You mightn't wish to come up here, ma'am. This here ain't no pretty sight. Nowhere for a lady to be just at this here particular moment."

"I am a doctor, sir. I'll appreciate it if you step aside and let me do my work."

The two who had been the recipients of the shotgun blasts were clearly beyond help. The baggage clerk was alive, now crunched into a half-sitting position against two more of the steel-banded wooden boxes. Gwyneth didn't yet know where he had been hit, but his mouth was clearly working, even if the words coming out of it weren't meant to be to the betterment of women or children, nor the faint of heart.

Gwyneth again dropped to her knees. "Sir, you're looking

at the only doctor likely to be on this train. You close your filthy mouth and keep it closed until you have something proper and worthwhile to say. But first, tell me where you're hit."

"I'm right sorry about offending you, ma'am, er, Doctor. Took a piece of lead in my upper arm, right here," he said, nodding with his chin to his left arm. "Took another off'n m' hip. Feels like all the fires of perdition 'r a-eat'n away at it. Taken all in all, this ain't that good a job fer to justi-fy eat'n that much lead. Dang'd old railway. Cheap baa...sorry, ma'am. Fools should know better than ta tak'n on a shipment of gold bars with jest the one man in the car. Although I'll allow as that useless piece o flesh standing off there to the corner come along, ta enjoy the scenery I'm guess'n. Cain't say as he done noth'n else much. Anyone could have told em—"

"All right, you can talk to the railway later. Right now, let's get you out of that shirt and pants."

"Outta my? You'll be doing no such a thing."

"Fine. I'll go see to the others."

"Now wait jest a gol derned minute. All right, if'n I ain't got no choice, let's get 'er done."

Gwyneth reached back to draw her medical bag closer but touched nothing but air until the feel of cold metal landed on her open fingers. She immediately knew the feel of the scissors. Turning her head over her shoulder to see who had passed her the instrument, she stopped in mid-movement at the sight of Summer, also on her knees and with the medical bag open beside her.

"Summer? What in the world are you doing here? I left you nursing at the clinic in Pueblo."

"Yes. Yes, you did. And an almighty ungrateful move it was, too. What ever made you think you could go traipsing off to Texas without me? You need me. Now get to fixing the man up. There's a couple more outside that will be needing some help. And a couple that don't."

"I'll cut away the shirt sleeve. You drag those pants off after you get his boots loosed."

~

THE TWO WOMEN stepped down from the baggage car after plugging up a couple of holes in the clerk and went to where Cob was standing over one of the fallen thieves. The man was going to need more care than Gwyneth felt comfortable doing on the station platform under the blazing sun and with folks crowding around. Speaking loudly, she asked, "Is there a hospital in town?"

A woman standing close by answered, "Yes, just down the road a bit."

Gwyneth said more quietly, "Cob. Find a wagon. These two men need to get to the hospital. I'll come along in case the hospital doctor needs help."

~

IT WAS LATE THAT EVENING, with the sun drawing its light away from the West Texas town, when Gwyneth and Summer stepped from the hospital door. Both were exhausted, as much from the heat and the lack of nourishment as from the work.

Cob was seated on a bench under one of the rare shade-offering trees in town, waiting for them. He rose to his feet, reached for the black bags each was carrying, and said, "Come on. I have rooms reserved for all of us. And the dining room is open and welcoming. You can tell me about your afternoon later."

Chapter Two

NIGHT HAD FALLEN UPON EL PASO. THE STREETS HAD quieted down. Whatever activity remained had moved inside the bars and cantinas. Nurse and doctor, both, had taken time for a hot bath. Dinner had been the always-welcome beef steak, carved into small pieces and carrying with it a strong hint of Mexican spices, Picadillo style. The side dish was a delicious, if spicy, Mexican fried rice with finely chopped onion, red peppers, and whole black beans, along with a mixture of available vegetables. A small bowl of refried beans and a large slice of cornbread rounded out the meal.

Summer was the first to speak as the waiter was clearing away the dishes.

Wiping her eyes for what seemed like the hundredth time and quietly blowing her spice-initiated, constantly runny nose on a napkin, she offered, "That was delicious. The taste and the spices were new to me, a bit of a challenge, and I suspect some kind of an initiation into Texas culture. If I survive this night, I will consider myself thoroughly Texan."

Gwyneth laughed as Cob said, "There's a bit more to it than that, but I will admit this was a good start."

As Gwyneth lay in her bed, wondering if the spices that were very much active in her system were eventually going to allow her to sleep, or if she would lie there through the night, seeing in her mind strings of chilis hanging here, there, and everywhere in the restaurant, she rethought the day. And the couple of weeks leading up to that day.

Beyond losing Trent, her husband, to a bad horse, probably nothing in her life surprised and shocked her as much as looking through the rain-darkened evening to see Cob standing on her veranda, dripping rain from his hat brim and running down his oiled-canvas outer coat. Although she thought of him and her Texan friends and family from time to time, she hadn't seen him in years. Nor did she have any reason at all to expect him to arrive unannounced in Pueblo. Then, to have him confidently announce that he was there to take her home to Texas, when she had never in her life been south of Colorado, and had no reason to think of Cob's home as her home, left her stunned. Still more stunning was Cob's declaration that they were to be married, as if his simple, one-sided announcement had decided the matter.

She admitted to the truth that she had been going through a lengthy and difficult time of introspection and some mild depression, but leaving her beautiful home and the medical clinic she had worked so hard to establish was more than she had ever considered. Having two of her nurses leave her to marry the men of their choice had been the beginning of her melancholy. Or to be truthful, not quite the beginning. It was more probable that those two acts had brought her inner thoughts to the surface, where she had no choice but to face them. She had thought of Trent less and less over the years of study and work, but now it had all come back in a rush. Marriage, love, adventure. She had known it all. But no matter how much she and Trent had loved one another, the truth was that there was no comfort to be had from a man long in his hillside grave in Southern Colorado.

Gwyneth was confident that she would snap out of her days of melancholy and get on with her life and her doctoring, but Cob had turned up before that could happen. And now here she was, lying alone in a hotel bed in El Paso, Texas, with Cob in the next room. She had sold her home and clinic. She had bid farewell to the few friends she had made in Pueblo. Pushing thoughts of marriage into the future, she had boarded the train with Cob, having made no promises one way or another about their future, together or separately.

Having Summer, her young and beautiful Pueblo nurse, show up unannounced during the chaos of the gold theft that morning was a total surprise. When she had asked how Summer managed to remain unseen on the train, the girl, somewhat smugly, replied that she had sweet-talked the conductor, saying that she didn't wish to interfere in the growing love affair between her boss and her Texan. Gwyneth had objected that there was no growing love affair, but Summer had simply smiled, saying no more.

Sleep did finally come, followed by a tasty breakfast that the dining room had somehow found reason to pack with chilis. Then train time, and onward to the Texas hill country that Cob never seemed to tire extolling over. The hill country itself mattered little to Gwyneth, but she admitted that she was anxious to see Abe and Helen, her former in-laws. Over the years, when she had thought of Texas, Abe and Helen were in the center of her thoughts. The travelers managed to book three sleeping rooms for the two nights they would be eastward bound.

~

THE SLOWLY MOVING MIXED FREIGHT, cattle, and passenger train arrived only four hours behind schedule, a feat considered by the locals to be within the bounds of reason, considering the many stops along the way.

Cob assisted the two ladies as they maneuvered the three movable steps to the plank-floored platform at the Burnt Lake station. They moved together until they were free of the crowd. Summer took a few additional steps, casting her inquisitive eyes over the low cactus- and pine-covered hills. As if by a written script, both Cob and Gwyneth stretched, arms over their heads, wagging shoulders from side to side, with Gwyneth taking in the grim landscape and the adobe and wood structures making up the single street. Cob, ignorant of the fact that Gwyneth was emulating his unseen actions, was considering their next move as he stretched this way and that while he looked over the town. Both were hoping to work the stiffness out of their beaten and battered bones.

Riding the cars. That was the term used to describe the railway system stretching across the vast landscape. Riding the cars. It was luxury. It was restful. It was fast. It was the way of the future.

In truth, with endless hours on the wooden seats, in the insufferable, trapped heat of the car, it was none of those things, not in total, in any case, although Gwyneth could see the beginnings. See the potential. She had seen the potential in her earlier rides across the nation, too, but the advancement toward the promised future was slow indeed. Now there was to be a full day's delay before the eastern leg of the trip could proceed. She did have to admit that the northern routes, with their cushioned seats and adequate bedrooms, were somewhat ahead of this Texas misery.

Here in Burnt Lake, the rail workers would top off the coal supply, fill the water reservoir, offload eight cars of cattle, giving them the opportunity to water and feed, before reloading them for the long trip to market the next morning. Here too, the rail workers would end their shifts, sleep over for the night, and begin again the following morning.

Dr. Gwyneth Wycome stood in the shade at the side of the station, away from the crowds. Cob had suggested she and Summer should wait while he moved through the town seeking hotel accommodations and a good restaurant. There was a bench to rest on, but for now, the freedom to stand was not to be missed. Cob had warned that he could be gone for some time. Time to wait. Time to study her surroundings, as temporary as they were to be. Time to think. Time to reminisce. Time to allow her mind to catch up with the realities of her life, comparing it to this dreary town and the future the area held on offer.

She smiled a small smile as she thought how Gwyneth May Scanlon, nurse, had so easily fallen in love and become Mrs. Gwyneth May Wycome, wife to Trent Wycome, cowboy, cattleman, dreamer of big dreams, smiler of big smiles. In a flash of time, as only the human mind can accomplish, she envisioned herself driving the team and wagon across hundreds of miles of the west, establishing the ranch, the Mirrored W, and so suddenly and painfully becoming a widow.

She saw herself as, later, she looked at the big oak doors of the medical college, anxious to get to her studies. So much. So many things happening. And now? Now to Texas. To Texas with no firmly established plan ahead of her. Cob, an old friend that she had liked and admired during her marriage and after, while he stayed to assist her in handling the Mirrored W as a widow, had made it clear that his plan was for them to marry and for her to rely on him for her future, her financial well-being, her safety, her every comfort. She found herself loving how Cob, steadfast and firm in his cultural beliefs, was prepared, no, insistent, really, to care for a wife as if she were unable to care for herself.

But Dr. Gwyneth Wycome was not in any way helpless. If, in the future, she somehow found herself growing in her thoughts of Cob, from liking him as a friend to loving him as a potential mate, they would have to work out their independence.

Chapter Three

FOLLOWING ANOTHER AGONIZINGLY SLOW DAY moving eastward, the trio of travelers stepped to the ground and bid farewell to the train. While the ladies waited in the shade of the small whistle-stop station wall, Cob walked over to the livery.

"*Muy buenos días*, Ramone, you still got my team and wagon?

With a sad voice the liveryman answered, "No, *Señor* Cob. My little family, they get hungry. Mama, she look at goat. She look at horse. Goat give milk for *niños*. Horse give no milk. What was I to do?"

"Well, *Mi amigo*, run that goat out here. We'll see if it can pull a wagon."

Smiling and leaning on his shovel, he said, "It is good to see you return, *Señor* Cob. I trust all is well with you."

"Well enough, Ramone. Well enough."

With no further discussion, the hostler went for the team. Cob crossed the road to the general store to pick up the mail. Within an hour, the trio had loaded their baggage, eaten in the little café, and headed north. There was no further time to waste. The well-worn trail to the Sombrero Ranch, known for years as the Hat, was a full twenty miles. Even with the team pulling at a steady clip, daylight would be gone by the time they spotted the lighted lanterns hung from the house veranda and the bunkhouse eve.

As a general practice, in preparation for the unpredictable Texas weather, the wagon was kept loaded with blankets, warm coats, a supply of water for both horses and humans, and a few other items to make travel less onerous. In addition, the wagon bed was layered with a good thickness of hay. A tired rider could lie down with a blanket covering and continue in some comfort. Cob was at first insistent on holding the reins for the entire trip, but after the first three hours, Gwyneth, showing the forcefulness that Cob would have to get used to if their one-sided romance was to generate a life of its own, simply took the reins and told him to climb over the seat and lie on the hay for a while. Summer jumped at the opportunity to join Gwyneth on the spring seat.

The day's run was shortened, in a sense, as Cob described the country they were traveling through. There was a single ranch off to the west that they could see as they topped a rise in the trail. Cob nodded his chin in that direction, saying, "Monty's place. Good guy, Monty. Him and that skinny woman of his. Young, the both of them, but learning. Small claim. Only a few cattle. One thing I'll give him, he's growing by natural offspring. That and the few head he can afford to purchase each spring. He's not a rustler or a maverick hunter.

"Now you take the old Hat, down south and east of here, near onto the Mex border. We've had a constant run-in with both land grabbers and rustlers down there. Quieting down a bit now, but the boys still have to be alert. The Hat, she's too big to fence and too wild to trust to luck and good neighbors. Takes a goodly number of riders to hold it together. We've lost a couple of riders over the years. Men who gave their all, defending Hat interests. It's a big price to pay for the wages offered, and the guarantee of horses to ride and a bunk to throw your sougan on. Lays heavy on the last generation of Flemings."

Summer was quiet as she made her comment. "We've had nothing like that on the family's holdings in Colorado, but when the subject of Texas comes up, Father gets quiet and says something meaningless like. *In the past* or *best forgotten*."

"That's not meaningless, Summer. It's his way of saying he remembers well enough and has no desire to discuss it."

"I'm sure you're right, Cob. But what about here and now? There's all this land. The grass is spotty at best, and the waterholes even spottier. The cattle must get spread out and hard to find. Isn't that an invitation to rustlers?"

"It is, but the country has settled down a lot after the big cattle drives. All the animals are branded now. Everything else went to the eastern markets. It's that eastern market and the big drives that saved most of the ranches. Saved the Hat, that's for sure. Put money in our bank accounts and allowed me the time and freedom to drive cattle and see a bit of the country. We claimed our share of the thousands of loose animals after the war. And it was those drives that made the way for Gwyneth to meet Trent. Otherwise, you and she wouldn't be sitting here today."

Gwyneth had no response as the wagon rattled on for another few miles, when up ahead there was a small dust cloud. Cob studied the land from horizon to horizon, attempting to determine the source and direction of movement. There was only one possibility. The disturbance was indicating that cattle were on the move. Two other things were clear. The first was that they had entered the Sombrero Ranch holdings some miles back. The second was that the cattle were being pushed. The afternoon was too hot for cattle to be doing anything but lying up in the shade.

The women, both knowledgeable of ranching matters, watched the dust as keenly as Cob had been doing, but saying nothing, asking no foolish questions.

Summer was the first to speak. "They've turned. They've come onto the trail and they're coming this way. They're not far off either. Stop the wagon and stay here. I'm going to climb that rise off there to the side. See what there is to see."

The action fit with Cob's slowly forming plan, except he saw himself climbing the knoll, not Summer. But it was too late to object or call her back. She was scurrying like a cat closing in on a mouse, quick but not careless. As she ran, she reached under the waistband of her split riding skirt and lifted out her .38. She dropped to her knees behind a large prickly pear and lifted her hand to tilt her hat brim, blocking out the waning sun. She lifted her other hand and pointed down the trail. Cob and Gwyneth quietly remarked as they could see Summer's hand rising and falling just a bit.

"Counting," said Cob, as he counted along in time with Summer's hand.

Gwyneth had no comment.

The hand movement stopped when Cob reached thirty. At that same point, Summer whirled on her heel and ran bent over until she was well below the crest of the rise. Coming to Cob's side of the wagon, puffing just a bit, she said, "Thirty cows, three riders. Got them bunched on the trail. Not far away. Be here in ten minutes. I'd suggest you pull the wagon ahead until you're just shy of the top. I'll go up again and tell you when to pull ahead. We can get the surprise on them and hold the high ground at the same time." Without waiting for agreement or disagreement, she again turned, heading for the knoll.

Grinning at Gwyneth, Cob said, "She didn't leave much room for discussion."

"No, she didn't. It's a good plan though. I can see her father coming up with the same gritty idea. If you're going to do it, now would be a good time, before they have the high ground and the surprise."

Mumbling something about women, Cob gently put the team into motion. There wasn't far to go, and the timing was near to perfect. As the team and wagon neared the crest of the rise, Summer lifted her hand and dramatically dropped it before hurriedly waving the wagon forward. The plan worked out near enough to perfect. The horses dropped onto the slight downward slope with the wagon sitting level on the top of the rise. Cob pulled them to a halt. Gwyneth reached for the reins as Cob lifted his carbine. Gwyneth had her pistol out of its hiding place, lying on the seat, held in place by shoving it just a bit under her leg. Summer remained in her squatted position, staring back at Cob to see what his next move would be.

The three strange riders, at the sight of the wagon and Cob standing, with his Henry pointed menacingly at the nearest man, pulled to a halt. The cattle sensed immediately that they were free and began drifting off the trail. The two groups were close enough together for normal talk to be heard.

Cob shouted, "Hold steady, boys. You see what we got here, don't you, fellas? We got us a problem. A dilemma, you might say. Them there are all Sombrero animals, meaning that they're mine. The problem comes up because you're not, any one of you, Sombrero riders. The other problem for you is that I don't remember the last time I missed a shot with this Henry. If you boys have any knowledge of the damage a 44.40 round does to human flesh, I know you're going to be very careful when you drop those Colts and your saddle weapons onto the ground. One at a time, starting with you, here in front. To do anything but what I tell you will have a poor outcome, I promise."

A tall, rail-thin rider holding up the rear of the little cavalcade spoke, "You appear to be miscounting. What I'm seeing is you're just the one while there's three of us. That there lady a-sett'n there beside you don't count for noth'n."

A single, totally unexpected shot from Summer's .38 tore a strip of hoof off the speaker's horse. The animal went wild, dumping the rider onto the trail and running off into the brush. After landing with a scream of pain, the rider was scrambling to remove himself from under the hooves of the other two horses, while their riders were attempting to pull them down to a stand. Surprising everyone, Summer stood to her full five foot four and said, "My father taught me to shoot before I learned my numbers and letters. You wish to try me, why you just have right at it."

Silently, and one by one, the riders dropped their weapons. As Cob had them dismount and back away, holding their horses, Summer moved in quickly to scoop up the hardware. The unhorsed rider went into the scrub brush to retrieve his animal. Gwyneth watched him walking, limping and holding one arm with the other hand. When he returned, she said, "Mister, I expect you'll heal of whatever is causing that limp, but tell me the truth, is your arm broken or simply sprained?"

"Don't know why you'd care, but it's broke all right. Felt it snap. It's my gun hand too. Just one more thing to hold against the Sombrero."

"Tie that horse and come to the back of the wagon. You have no way of knowing, but my name is Gwyneth Wycome. Dr. Wycome. And this sharpshooting young lady is my nurse. You take off your jacket and shirt. I'll do what I can for you. If it's broken too bad, perhaps I'll just have Summer shoot you, like she would a horse with a broken leg."

With Cob taking a long look at his hoped-for bride, and then a quick glance at the beautiful young nurse, he got to hogtying the other two rustlers, binding them hand and foot. With that done, the men were directed to roll further into the wagon to give the doctor room to work.

There were no materials to form a cast from. The materials were in the two big wooden boxes of medical supplies Gwyneth had packed to bring along. It simply wasn't worth all the trouble to open the boxes and dig around to find the plaster and such. Without a cast, the best the girls could do, after Summer somewhat roughly scrubbed down the broken arm, was to pull it together and bind it with a couple of splints. With that done, Gwyneth formed a sling out of a roll of bandage gauze. It was the best anyone could have done in the conditions and with what materials were available.

Cob had no sympathy. Allowing the broken arm to rest freely on the man's chest, he bound the other arm and his two legs together, rolled him into the wagon, and closed the tail gate. With Summer now mounted on the rustler's horse, and having the carbine to supplement her own .38, the rig was ready to roll on toward the Sombrero.

Gwyneth and Summer had used the rustlers' own saddle ropes to tether two of the horses to the wagon. The third, Summer was determined to ride. The securely tied men in the wagon were of no concern. Their weapons had been unloaded and put out of reach under the seat. Summer had carefully looked over the carbines, choosing the best for herself, as she did with the horses. She had dropped the weapon into the offside scabbard and mounted.

Again, sounding just like her father, Summer said, "We've lost us a whack of time with this little go-around, Cob. You get them going. I'll keep a close eye on our guests."

Again, Cob mumbled under his breath, something about women. But he moved out, saying nothing Gwyneth could hear or understand. Summer gave him a short but exacting study before breaking out in a grin. They arrived at the Sombrero in full darkness. Summer had found no reason to shoot a rustler, although Cob was convinced that she wouldn't have hesitated or shown much remorse after the fact.

The Sombrero crew took charge of the rustlers while Trinity Castillo, ranch foreman, pulled Wally Tibbs, the cook, away from his poker game with instructions to rattle some pans *rápidamente*. Although Tibbs wasn't Mexican, everyone on the mixed-race ranch had picked up enough of each other's language to get by. With the boss and two pretty ladies involved, there was no time for arguments or wisecracks.

A hot, late dinner was shortly laid before the travelers. The fact that the dinner looked a great deal like a breakfast of ham and eggs was received with no complaints. The foreman took a coffee and sat down near Cob. Interested in what his foreman had to say but too tired to listen, Cob said, "In the morning, my friend. You could help if you were to see that Juanita gets a couple of rooms ready for the ladies."

"Sending me to do that is to send me into a cougar's den. I can't remember anyone ever being very successful instructing that woman on matters involving her house. You need to remember, Boss, it's your home, but it's her house. I'll go see her, but you know I'll be wasting my time. Juanita had rooms ready the day after you left. I'll check to make sure, but if she takes exception to my inquiry, I may need the doctor before she even gets a chance to settle in."

"Live dangerously, Trinity. Life is full of risks."

As always in ranching country, the new day started early. The sun was still trying to find the energy to climb over the eastern horizon when Wally Tibbs was splitting kindling from the pile of firewood behind the cookhouse. He would light the fire before dipping water from the still-warm reservoir on the big cast-iron range. While the fire readied the stove for its day's needs, the cook would remove his shirt and have a good wash with soap and water. Failure to follow the pattern laid down on the Sombrero would be cause for hunting another job. Cob was a stickler for cleanliness.

Wally emerged from the cookhouse with the bucket of warm water, thinking he was alone. When a feminine voice said, "Thank you, that's just what I need," the cook came near to stumbling over his own feet. It was only when Summer reached and took the bucket from him that he realized he wasn't dreaming or being put upon by haunts. He stood scratching his head as he watched the girl disappear back into the semi-darkness toward the big house, with his bucket. He muttered a surprised *dang* but didn't complete the thought.

The breakfast iron was rattled at seven. Coffee had been ready before that time, so most of the crew had already been fortified with at least one cup as they lounged around the cook-house porch. Horses had been saddled and tied to the outside of the corral, ready for their day of work. The prisoners were released and allowed to care for their own needs, including washing in the water trough, before being retied. A meal would be brought to them by and by.

As the men took on their morning nourishment, Trinity would lay out the day's work. On this morning, a pair of cowboys were commissioned to ride to where the rustlers had been running Sombrero cattle. They didn't expect to find anything, but they would give it a good search anyway and push back any animals that showed a tendency to wander south.

Juanita prepared breakfast for the ladies at the big house, as it was referred to. It wasn't really that big, but the title signified that it was the ranch owner's dwelling. Except that on the night just passed, the owner had rolled onto an unused bunk in the crew quarters, leaving the house for the women.

With breakfast and the first couple of hours of the morning behind them, Cob walked up to the house. The women, including Juanita, were sitting on the covered porch visiting. When Juanita made a motion to stand as Cob approached, Gwyneth laid a gentle hand on her arm, wordlessly bidding her to remain seated. She covered her actions by saying, "Good morning, Cob. I hope you had a restful night. Juanita prepared a wonderful breakfast for us and was just telling us what to expect during our stay on the Sombrero."

"And good morning to all of you, as well. Let's talk about your stay. I'd be in favor of a day or two of rest before we go on into town. The railroad is fast, compared to team and wagon. No one would argue that. But restful it ain't. We could do with an easy day or two. I know Abe and Helen will be anxious to see you, but another day or so won't hurt. Two of our riders have taken the rustlers into town. They'll leave those boys with the sheriff. Let us know if there's anything out of the ordinary happening when they get back.

"Everything on the ranch appears to be normal. We can take our ease until you're rested and then go on into town ourselves. Town is only three miles from here. We ride the trail regularly. You'll want to see what the town has to offer and what's already there before you make any decisions. When we moved this portion of the Hat up here and renamed it the Sombrero, there was no town. Abe and Helen had their general store up and running in a town about fifty miles to the east. When they heard the Sombrero had bought out the original settler and taken over this place, they came down for a visit. It was them who suggested building our own town.

"That's coming near to five years ago. There's three, perhaps even four hundred people in town now. And as I told you before, Gwyneth, old Doc Shultz followed Abe and Helen. Came down at their invitation actually. He's served our simpler needs for broken bones and such. But he leaves a lot to wish for when it comes to more complicated medical matters. In truth, he ain't really all that old, but he sometimes acts old, as if he's seen all the pains and misery of the world and doesn't care to see any more.

"I talked with him before I struck out for Pueblo. He's recognizing his age as well as his lack of knowledge on more modern practices. He would welcome you as a partner or associate, or whatever medical people think of yourselves as."

Summer fixed her eyes on Cob as he talked, expecting some mention of her nursing abilities, but finally turned away, disappointed.

~

Two days drifted by slowly. The restful time was welcome, but it wasn't in either Gwyneth's nor Summer's nature to sit overlong. Finally, when Summer was examining the barned animals for at least the fifth time, she glanced away from the gelding she had been admiring to see Cob walking her way. She stepped from the stall, closing the door behind herself, and said, "Cob, I'd take this gelding off your hands for use in town if you wanted to rid yourself of him. He doesn't look to be of much value, all gaunted-up and such. I'm pretty sure he's become a burden to the wrangler, caring for him every day. I might be able to get a bit of use out of him."

Her slight smile was her acknowledgment of the sarcasm.

"Why, that's a generous offer, Summer. And it shows that you have an eye for a problem animal. I'll have to think on that after you get settled, wherever that takes place."

His returned grin supported the little game wrapped around what might have been the best animal on the Sombrero.

Chapter Four

The move into town and the location of a pleasant cottage to rent was welcomed by Gwyneth and Summer, while it saddened Juanita, who had come, in just the couple of days since their arrival, to consider the guests as her special responsibility.

The welcome from Abe and Helen came close to overwhelming Gwyneth. Of course, for Abe and Helen to welcome their daughter-in-law after so many years had to bring up memories of Trent. Abe and Gwyneth held back their tears at first. Helen showed no resistance at all to weeping as she hugged Gwyneth, all the while whispering words in a voice no one else could possibly hear. The two women held their embrace until Abe finally joined in, wrapping his arms around the two of them, as far as he could reach. The verbal welcomes would come later, along with the rehearsal of the events of the past few years.

Abe managed the trading post while Helen fussed over every detail in settling the ladies into their new home. Two more days were lost, in Gwyneth's mind, frustrating her and raising her anxiety level, before she made her acquaintance with Doc Gabriel Shultz. She finally suggested that Helen and Summer care for the cottage while she moved on to her first love—caring for the sick and injured. She was most anxious to assess the medical needs and possibilities in and around the town of Sombrero.

The doctor wasn't as old as Cob had led them to believe. That's not to say he was a spry youngster, but he certainly had some life and drive in him yet. Gwyneth quietly let herself into the doctor's examination room and stood by while he treated a little girl with a rash on her neck and chest. Gwyneth found herself in agreement as Dr. Shultz said, "Young lady, I'm going to suggest you've simply succumbed to a common Texas summer ailment. If we don't see the sky cloud over and bless us with a pour a bit of rain soon, we may all have the same problem.

"I believe we can safely suggest this itchy nuisance is a heat rash. If it's something more, you will see changes in the next three or four days. If that happens, why you just get yourself back down here and we'll see what's to be done. In the meantime, you go home, have a warm bath, carefully and thoroughly cleaning around the rash area, stay out of the sun, and keep as cool as you can. And don't scratch, no matter how much it itches. On your way out, lift the lid on that jar over there and help yourself to a sweet. It's just the thing to enjoy while you're lying in the shade."

The mother and girl were soon gone. Smiling, Dr. Shultz turned to Gwyneth, inquiring, "And what say you, my good doctor? Is the diagnosis correct, and is the sweet treat going to help? Or have I misidentified you? Few people would walk into an examination room so comfortably. I assumed it was you, or I would have evicted you forthwith. News came to me yesterday about a mysterious lady doctor residing at the ranch, as everyone calls it, in our attempt to not mix up the ranch and the town, both of which were identified by someone much wiser than I, no doubt, using the exact same English letters, which would have been all right if they had placed the letters for one or the other in a different order. Are you, in fact Dr. Gwyneth

Wycome or do I seek elsewhere?" Grinning, he added, "Why, my dear, that's almost biblical. But we shan't fuss over deeper meanings right at this moment."

Gwyneth held out her hand in greeting. With a smile, she answered, "I believe I would have come to the same diagnosis, Doctor. And the sweet treat is definitely a help in recovery. It's good to meet you, Dr. Schultz. I am indeed Gwyneth Wycome. Lately of Pueblo, Colorado. Previously of Chicago. Our mutual friend Cob, master of the Sombrero Ranch, has suggested we may have common interests, further suggesting that our meeting may be timely and of benefit to both."

"I know of no other patients due for arrival, Doctor. Let us take ourselves into the shade of the north wall, where I have had a small roof added, along with some reasonable comfortable seating."

THE NEXT HOUR was spent with the two doctors exchanging details of their training and experience along with their plans and hopes for the future, both near and further in time. Dr. Shultz had immediately insisted that Gwyneth call him by his given name, Gabriel.

In discussing the future, Gwyneth inquired, "Cob tells me there are currently somewhere between three hundred and four hundred residents in Sombrero. He seemed a bit unsure of the true number. Now I'm wondering what has brought those folks here. Surely there aren't enough ranches around to demand that much servicing. The country we traveled through, coming in from the south, was bare bones at the very best. I'm not sure how many acres it would take to feed a cow and calf, but it would be considerable, I'm thinking. There would be little room to expand even an established ranch. What else is there nearby to pull folks this way?"

"That's a good question, Gwyneth. Prescient. To come in

from the south, you arrive at the ranch before you've hardly even seen the rest of the country. Cob might have you thinking this is all cattle country. And it is for him. But not for everyone. Escaping the hills, which are lovely and picturesque in their own right, to the north, as well as both to the east and west, for that matter, there is considerable farming. And more land opening every year. There's a major thrust toward irrigation, although the concept yet remains in its infancy. In terms of cash importance to the town of Sombrero, farming and land development far exceed ranching. That's not to say that cattle are not still an important part of who we are, but the future belongs to farming. Especially irrigation farming."

"I'll have to take a ride around and see for myself. I've worked too hard getting the training and experience that's brought me this far, to spend the rest of my life in a small town. Now, please understand. I have experience with small towns too, and I recognize their needs and how often those needs go unsatisfied. But I long, some days, for the pace of Chicago General, where challenges, both surgical and medical, were the order of the day, stretching my mind and satisfying something within me. I thought I was on my way to developing that situation in Pueblo, where I have most recently hung out my shingle, but my plans didn't exactly work out. So, at Cob's invitation, here I am."

There was a quiet pause in the conversation. Gwyneth could see Dr. Shultz's mind working through his thoughts, searching for the right words. Finally, cautiously, he turned his eyes full onto Gwyneth's with a bit of a grin. "Mind, my good doctor friend, Cob has never spoken to me about anything beyond medical matters. Still, I find myself wondering if there is more to the story than what we have, so far, discussed."

Gwyneth was equally slow in responding, having no idea what, or how much, was being whispered around town. Cob was a very well-known rancher, still reasonably young, strong and vibrant, attractive. A prize for any young lady. She could easily see that, although Cob would express no private thoughts publicly, people might sometimes be led into the temptation to gossip. Then there were Abe and Helen to consider. She was less sure of their discretion.

When she did find her words, she said, "Rumor, gossip, facts. Sometimes it's not easy to sort one from the other. I'll lay this much truth on you, Gabriel. Cob and I go back many years. Cob was best friends with my deceased husband, who was the son of Abe and Helen Wycome. Stood up with Trent while we were being married. During our marriage and all through our ranching years, Cob was a stalwart, the knowledgeable rancher and cattleman helping the son of a small farmer learn the cattle business. Of course we became close friends. And we still are, I hope. Anything further is yet to be discussed.

"Just exactly how that matter is to be reconciled with my practicing of medicine will be dealt with in due time. In the meantime, I'm looking forward to a fresh start clinically. Whether for the short or longer term, well, who knows at this point? It is that matter that I believe you and I must dig into, leaving other matters aside for now. I feel, Gabriel, that I must further say that all of this is confidential. I'm sure you understand that we would not be having this conversation were it not for the question of us working together or not. Not one word goes beyond this spot of shade we find ourselves in. We do both understand that, don't we, Doctor?"

"You have my every assurance, Gwyneth. Now, although we have barely begun our introductory visit, I must break off. I have a patient schedule within the next few minutes."

"Thank you for your time, Gabriel. I'm looking forward to our next meeting. Before I go, you mentioned one other doctor in town. What is his name, and where could I find him?"

"Good for you, Gwyneth. It is well that you should meet him. His name is Diego Esteban. You will find him in a small adobe close to the church. You can see the steeple from here. It is but a short walk. I believe you will like him as a man. How you think he sizes up as a physician, you can judge for yourself."

"Are you suggesting—"

"I am suggesting nothing at all except that you make your judgments based on fact and evidence, not on what you may hear rumbling through the town. If Cob has not already introduced you to the strange mix of people in Sombrero, here is something to think on. The Americans and the Mexs mix freely up to a point. Working together and seemingly liking one another. But there is a line where trust sometimes has a problem adjusting. There is underlying suspicion that the Mexs are not altogether honest. That they are always working on their own agenda. This suspicion has impacted Dr. Esteban's acceptance in the community."

Chapter Five

GWYNETH HAD WALKED BARELY ONE TOWN BLOCK from Gabriel Shultz's office when the peace of the town was broken by the thunder of running horses. Everything and everybody close by stopped what they were doing, turning to watch the spectacle. Idly, Gwyneth counted fourteen horses and riders. She wasn't surprised to see the sheriff riding at the front, taking the lead position with the bunch, but she was certainly surprised to see Cob riding stirrup to stirrup with the sheriff.

Either she stood out in her city-purchased clothing and her off-white Stetson, or Cob was being particularly astute. In any case, he noticed her and pulled away, riding directly to her. Before he could say anything, Gwyneth raised her voice above the noise of the street.

"Cob, what on earth is going on?"

"Sheriff's posse, Gwyneth. Those rustlers we brought in somehow escaped the sheriff's custody. They've been gone a few hours now. Sheriff sent for me, knowing I'd want to be a part of their capture. Took a bit to find me and then to ride to town. Brought four Sombrero riders with me.

"We'll have to talk later. Lost too much time already. Someone reported that the rustlers headed west, a bit south.

Rough country up there. Man could lose himself in the folds of those hills and never be found. But some of these fellas know that country well. We'll get them. I'll be back soon."

"Why go? Why bother, Cob? They did the ranch no harm."

"A man lets one rustling go, next thing you know, your ranch has become a target. It's not like the old days. We don't hang them where we find them anymore, but we don't let them off free and easy either."

"Actually, I understand all of that, Cob. I just wonder if it isn't time to count the cost. Let them run. The country's better off without them. I've also doctored long enough to know that it isn't always the ones that stand on the right side of the law that win. When guns are drawn, there's no telling the outcome. As you have reason to remember, even a good rider can be thrown from a horse. But go. I know you feel you must. Just don't play the hero."

"I have reason enough to return, Gwyneth."

With that, Cob whirled his horse and set off after the others, leaving her to think of the meaning of his last comment.

Gwyneth continued her walk toward Dr. Esteban's office with a heavy heart. From their very first meeting, back in that little trail town in Kansas, Gwyneth had cared for Cob. And even from that time, she had always been aware of Cob's feelings toward her. That he hid those feeling well wasn't to deny them. But now, after the years of widowhood and the reuniting with Cob, was there room in her life for new feelings? Different feelings? Expanded feelings? Feelings that might take on another name, another meaning?

She prayed as she walked, picturing a successful and nonviolent recovery of the rustlers.

The steeple was not within sight as she walked, hidden behind a long row of small adobes along with a few cut-lumber structures. Glancing eastward at the next corner, she glimpsed the church itself. The brick structure appeared to be no more than a few years old. But then, why would it be older? The town itself didn't exist before Cob and a few others decided they needed a trading center. The idea developed quickly, with Abe and Helen being among the first to establish a business.

As Gwyneth neared the church, she saw a small cluster of adobe structures. Her mind caught on the fact that most small adobes seemed to resemble one another, and she wondered at the lack of creativity.

She smiled to see the doctor's office jammed between a cantina and what appeared to be a restaurant, although the white, frilly, folded-back curtains in the window caused her to question her own first judgment. She hesitated at the clinic's door, not sure if knocking was in order or if she should just turn the knob and walk in, as she had done earlier with Dr. Shultz. Her thoughts were broken when the door opened and a mom, leading a weeping little girl by the hand, stepped out. She took that as permission and moved into the small waiting room. The door to the second space was slightly ajar, and she could hear noises coming from inside. With a one-knuckle tap to gain attention, she said, "Dr. Esteban, may I talk with you for a short while, please?"

The door swung fully open, exposing a slim, attractive man of perhaps forty years. He held his six-foot height, tall for a Mexican, with ease and confidence, but the graying hair spoke of struggle and long days of work. He didn't speak. Only his eyes asked the question.

"Dr. Esteban. I am Gwyneth Wycome. Dr. Wycome. I would speak with you for a short while if your schedule could make room for a visit."

With virtually no accent, Dr. Esteban smiled and replied, "Well, Doctor, since my humble rooms hold only you and I at this time and no one is anxiously pacing the floor in some home, waiting for a visit from the doctor, I can hardly use the excuse of being busy. Please allow me to clean up in here. We will then move to the Cafecito, just one building away. Lupita, who may one day become my wife if only she were wise to see, offers coffee and what I believe you would know as sweet rolls, baked fresh."

"Thank you, Doctor. I am anxious to taste the sweet roll and to meet your future, perhaps, wife. And, of course, to talk of crying children and medical wonders."

"Aw, yes. The crying child took a rather unfortunate tumble from the tree the children play on. She lost some skin on her shin and created a rather nasty split on her kneecap. The mother could have cleaned and bandaged it at home, but I ask very little for my help with children, so some find it convenient to visit the doctor. And just to speed the healing and to allow me to think I have helped in some small way, I secured the cut on her knee with three tiny stitches. She was very brave as she watched the needlework being done.

"It is good to sometimes help. Do you not agree, Doctor?"

Gwyneth allowed only her smile to pass as her answer.

More than an hour went by as the two doctors visited at the Cafecito. Lupita was a lovely young lady who smiled generously. Gwyneth could easily see why the doctor was taken with her.

The questions and answers flooded Gwyneth's mind as she walked back to the cottage she and Summer would be sharing. Dr. Diego Esteban was a well-trained physician, more at ease with medical work than surgical. He had worked out a comfortable arrangement with Dr. Shultz when scalpel and anesthetic were called for.

Being raised near the Mexican/Texas border, he was fluent in both languages as well as both cultures. Several northern medical schools had turned him away, mostly for racial reasons, but he finally found acceptance in a small school in the South. He was still facing racial issues but was surprisingly accepting of the matter. *"I cannot change what will not be changed,"* was his answer to Gwyneth's remark.

His practice held little promise for riches and none at all for fame. The Mexican men, being proudly independent, were reluctant, at any time, to seek medical help. And the women seldom sought medical assistance except for birthing, with centuries of tradition behind them, and being reluctant to expose themselves to a male doctor, they sought only the Comadrona, or midwife.

With the non-Mexican population deeply suspicious of the abilities of the Mexican doctor, Diego Esteban was left with only a small population to draw his patients from. He nevertheless welcomed Gwyneth to town, suggesting she drop by his clinic from time to time to partake of the coffee and sweet treats the lovely Lupita had on offer.

Chapter Six

It was late in the evening three days later when the posse returned. Their entry into town held none of the pomp and confidence their leaving had displayed. There was a muted stillness among the trail-worn riders. Weariness and perhaps regret, or more likely, a sense of failure or at the least, partial failure emanated from their midst. There was mercy in the fact that there were few citizens who had yet to go to their beds. The streets were not quite empty of life but what little life there was had drawn into the saloons and the one cantina.

Gwyneth and Summer were readying themselves for bed when there was a frantic knocking on their door. When Summer opened the door just a crack, peering around the edge to see who was there, a sheriff's deputy almost shouted. "Hurry. The doctor is needed. At Doc Shultz's office. Come quickly!"

He shouted his message, turned, and headed back to the sheriff's office. There was no questioning or doubting the urgency of the communication. It took only moments for the two women to shuck their sleeping garb, climb back into their day clothing and grab up their black medical bags. Running faster than she had run in years, Gwyneth still was unable to keep up with the younger and much more nimble Summer. They pushed through the crowd outside the doctor's office with no apology and entered the room. Gwyneth didn't stop until she was in the examination room. Summer took a stand at the inner door, noting first the happenings inside, then, after pulling the door closed behind herself, turning toward the gathering of men. These men had come from the saloon, judging by the breath of the two closest to Summer. Not asking for directions, but feeling her thinking was clear and correct, she raised her voice to be heard above the talk.

"You men. Quiet. Quiet, you hear? Unless you have a medical problem yourself, I'm going to ask you to leave. Go anywhere you wish but clear this space. The doctors and the patients all need quiet. Now go. When there's news, I'll find a way to get it to you. Go, and close the door behind you."

In a matter of seconds, the space was empty. A welcome quietness descended upon the little clinic. Only then did she check the oil in the table lamp, feed a bit of wood into the stove and put three pots of water on to heat. On the one remaining space on the stovetop, she placed the newly filled coffeepot. She then stepped into the yard, searching through the darkness for the well and pump. With the bucket refilled she again washed her hands and joined the doctors.

There were three men needing attention in the examination room. The sheriff was lying on the wheeled stretcher Dr. Shultz did most of his work on. The doctor was bent over, trying to gain a more detailed look at the wound, struggling against the dim light the lamp offered. Summer took a quick look, left the room in search of another lamp, found one and returned with it lit. She placed it close to the lamp Dr. Shultz was already depending on and stepped back.

"Thank you," mumbled the doctor, without looking away from his work.

A man Summer recognized as a Sombrero rider was lying

on a built-up padding of blankets, on the floor. The third was Cob, who was sprawled across the two-seater couch with his knees resting on the arm and his head propped up with a pillow at the other end.

In the corner closest to the rear door was a small pile of bloody and filthy clothing: shirts, two pairs of trousers, a rolled-up wad of long johns that would never again be worn. And thrown carelessly on top of the other clothing was a bloody cowhide vest. Her memory said this was Cobs.

The man on the floor was naked from the waist down, save for a towel dropped across his midsection. This she saw in a flash as she scanned the room. Before doing anything else she searched the little clinic until she found a cabinet with a small supply of towels, cotton swabs, and on the bottom shelf, three blankets. She unfolded one blanket and draped it doubled over the Sombrero rider. The injured rider thanked her with a cross between a grimace and a smile.

She identified Cob, lying on the half-couch, only from the partial view of his head and face. Gwyneth, bent over the man, studying something intently, obscured the wounded area.

Summer announced her entry by saying, "What can I do, Gwyneth? I've topped up the lantern, wooded the stove and put water on to heat. Made a pot of coffee. What's next?"

"You can run over to the sheriff's office. I'm told one of the rustlers is badly hurt. They have him in a cell up there. Check him out. See what he needs and make your own best judgment. I have no time for him right now."

Before Summer followed up on those directions she asked simply, "Cob?"

"Cob needs all the help I can give him, and after that he needs a healing touch from the Lord. If I believed in such things, and I don't, I would say he needs a double dose of the luck of the Irish."

Such was the concentration of Dr. Shultz that he might as

well have been in another space altogether. Summer knew from experience that Gwyneth was the same. Once focused on a situation she seemed not to even hear what went on around her.

Summer took up her medical bag and ran toward the one-cell jailhouse. As she had done at the clinic, she instructed the men hanging around outside to get themselves gone. One belligerent posse member said, "Don't you be telling us anything, girly. Ain't none of us even know who you are and we surely ain't about to listen to what some girl kids got to say. That man in there shot our sheriff and Cob. One other from the ranch. Good men all. I was there. I saw it all. Should one of them up and die, why we'll just naturally take this fell outta the jail and hang him."

Taking hold of authority no one had burdened her with, Summer stood her ground. "My name is Summer Wilmore. Nurse Wilmore, come to town with Dr. Gwyneth, who's down at the clinic trying to keep the men alive. She doesn't need any nonsense from the likes of you. Now you men get yourselves gone, as I've already said. The doctors and me, we've got work to do. And while you're on your way to wherever, get rid of that rope. You're talking and acting like a fool. Now make room."

Slowly, grudgingly, the men moved off first, two standing at the back of the bunch. Then two more, and then the rest, moving in a group. Summer stepped into the sheriff's office to see a man holding down a swivel chair behind a desk with a shotgun resting over his knee, pointed at the door. He swung the gun aside as Summer appeared.

"Heard ya, girly. Good on ya. They wouldn't no way listen to me. I'm just the jailer. Got no more authority than noth'n. It's a caution what a pretty girl can get a man to do. The man you're looking for is bedded down in the cell."

"Where are the other two rustlers?"

"Wherever it is dead men go girly. Wherever dead men go."

With a shudder, Summer moved past the shotgun that again was pointed at the door and stepped into the cell. All she could see through the darkness was the bare shadow of a man on the bunk. She stepped back out and went to the door, dropping the bar across it. She then picked up the lit lantern from the desk and said, "On your feet, man. I need your help."

Reluctantly, the deputy stood and followed, leaving his shotgun on the desk. Summer settled the lamp on the chair beside the bunk. "We've got to get his coat and shirt off. And those bloody pants. I can't see anything before that's done. You get started on that. Strip him to his skin. Top and bottom. Gently, if you please. Lay a blanket over him. I'll get a fire going. We'll heat some water."

The doctors and Summer, putting the knowledge she had gained from months working with Gwyneth to good use, all put in a long night.

When Summer had first lifted the blanket, the jailer had laid over the rustler, she had wavered, feeling a slight faintness at the sight of the torn, blood-soaked flesh. She had seen such as that before but never while working on her own. Her instinct was to step back to allow Gwyneth room to work. But Gwyneth wasn't there. Getting that feeling under control she took a closer look at the prisoner and then ran back to Dr. Shultz's office. Breathlessly she reported, "Gwyneth, the prisoner has been shot twice. Once in the upper arm, cutting through the bicep. The second time just above his knee. That shot tore away a strip of skin and flesh along his thigh before eventually digging in deeper. Came out just below his belt, in back. Had to have been sitting the saddle to get in the way of a bullet taking that path. He's lost a lot of blood. Still losing some. Both wounds have exit points so there's no need looking for the lead. Grubby, like the rest of his body, and there's bits of cloth and such visible in the wound."

Gwyneth glanced away from Cob for just long enough to look at her protégé. "Good work, Summer. Good assessment. Is the man awake?"

"He is. Awake and hurting and complaining. Demanding to have a doctor come. Says he never shot anyone."

"You go back and pad up that blood leak as best you can. Tell him to demand all he wants. We're trying to save lives here. His needs simply don't matter right now. Pour some disinfectant on the exposed wounds, wrap it with gauze and get back down there. Tell him if either Cob or the sheriff dies, I'll come shoot him again myself. And if he keeps whining and complaining I may shoot him anyway, just on general principles."

Cob was the worst hit, having taken lead twice, once in his shoulder, the second in his upper chest, glancing off the collar bone before nicking the lung, but somehow missing the critical veins and arteries in the area. Immediate medical assistance would have kept serious risk to a minimum but the ride of several hours, returning to town, greatly reduced his possibilities of survival.

Glancing to the floor beside her Gwyneth saw that the Sombrero rider was awake, suffering in silence. Speaking to him she said, "I know you're hurting but there's nothing happened to you that you're likely to die from. We'll get to you just as soon as possible. But I'd like if you would tell me about the shooting and the ride back to town."

Speaking barely above a whisper the rider replied, "Fella named Collis, nothing else, just Collis, built himself a cabin up in the way-back and beyond country. Drove in maybe a hundred head. Turned them loose and came down to work on the Sombrero. Them rustlers, they somehow stumbled onto that cabin. There's no doubt they heard us coming. As many as we were there was no way to keep silent. Two rustlers forted up in the cabin. Third one waited in the brush. Wasn't none of us knew where that cabin was. We came into the clearing all bunched up on account of we had just rode through a break in a jumble of boulders. That there third fella, he come a charg'n out from behind the cabin, firing and shouting like one of them heroes you read about in kids story books. Well, he didn't last no time at all. Blown from his horse and we rode right past him, into the firing coming from the cabin. Sheriff and Cob, leading the way, they were hit right off.

"Those two in the cabin had just no chance at all, although they was firing as if they did. Never heard such a rash of lead from just the two shooters. Sounded like as if they were one of them there Gatlin guns, although it was just their Colts and carbines.

One of them made a lucky shot, took my animal out from under me. Afoot, I was then and another lucky shot, lucky for the shooter that is, not so lucky for me, gave me this here little gift I'm hoping you can fix up soon as you're done with Cob. Might could be I'll get to laze about the ranch for a few days till it heals up.

"Anyway, we rained enough lead down on that there cabin, to where you'd of thought we was fighting a whole regiment stead of just the two rustlers. Finally, Cob, although he'd already been hit at least once, took the matter to hand. He spurred his horse right up to the cabin and through the open door. There was an almighty flurry of shots and then silence. Cob, now dripping blood and leaning a bit sideways off the saddle, rode out and hit the trail to home, saying nothing at all.

"A couple of our boys dragged the dead men from the cabin, leaving them lying in the yard. We loaded up the wounded and headed for home. Near enough a long half day to get here, the last of it in the dark. Me, I rode in on a rustler's animal a sett'n sideways on the saddle on account of this here scratch on my leg. The sheriff, we had to stop and tie him onto his saddle, lying his head onto the horse's neck. Cob, hurting as he was, he sat up the whole way. In the lead too, he was. That there is a man to follow, and we followed."

Although the Sombrero rider had gone on longer with his story than what Gwyneth had asked for, the details were helpful.

Gwyneth and Dr. Shultz listened without interruption. When the telling ended the two doctors locked eyes with a knowing look and went back to their work.

There was no good way to be shot in the upper chest. And bouncing on a horse over rough terrain didn't improve chances of survival even a little bit. Cob, having sat upright, had given himself a better handle on survival than he would have, lying as the sheriff had done, in a prone position.

In Dr. Shultz's clinic, as soon as Gwyneth saw the wound high on Cob's chest she had propped up the semi-conscious man against the arm of the chair, with the help of a couple of small cushions. Lying prone could risk complications with the nicked or punctured lung.

When he was settled on the couch, Cob had been conscious enough to lock eyes with Gwyneth, grin and whisper, "Welcome to Texas, Doctor."

Gwyneth didn't answer. She couldn't have gotten any words past the lump in her throat, even if she knew what words to use. Several times in the next minute she wiped tears from her eyes onto the sleeve of her dress, before reverting to her professional doctor mode. Gwyneth moved the lamp away from the vicinity of the couch and reached into the cabinet for a small bottle of ether and a cotton square to administer it with. Relying on Dr. Shultz's understanding she said, "I'm opening the door for a moment Gabriel, just to clear the air. I'm going to put my man to sleep now."

In a flash of unsought inquiry, she asked herself why she had called him *my man*. It was true that a big part of Cob's effort to entice her to follow him to Texas was to win her in marriage, he made no secret of that, but she had made no commitment. She pushed the thought aside continuing her words to Dr. Shultz. "I'll use only as much ether as necessary. I'll be moving the lamp back to where I can see something, but I'll wait a bit with the door open."

A distracted *hmm*, was Gabriel's response.

Wishing Summer were there to aid in the surgery, slowly, attentively and cautiously Gwyneth readied herself to open the path to where Cob's injury would need attention. First the lung and only after that, the damaged shoulder. Idly, she thought *Cob, you're going to lose some use of this arm, but you won't die from the wound. First, the lung.*

Chapter Seven

The Sombrero rider seemed to know he would be some time getting back on a horse. He had what was barely a flesh wound, but it was on the inside of his upper thigh. To treat him properly, he was going to need considerable stitching and, if possible, a skin graft to close the gouge left by the passing of the lead. There was no getting around the fact that it was going to be sore in the extreme for some time to come.

As if telling the story took up the last of his strength, he appeared to have fallen asleep.

Dr. Shultz had been the one to pull the man's pants and long johns off and do the original assessment of the wound. He had pressed a thick bandage to hold back the bleeding, giving the rider instructions to hold that tightly.

Now, having fallen into rest after too long without care, Gabriel said, "That one feels as if he's about to die, but he's not. He came awful close to losing more than just a bit of skin, but he may not realize that until he stops hurting. But he has lost some blood. The sooner he can get some attention, the better."

Summer returned just moments later. Gwyneth said, "Summer, see if you can find out where Dr. Diego Esteban lives. Go wake him up and get him down here, or find someone to do that for you. Then go to the hotel. We're going to need three rooms. No, four. Also, find the other Sombrero riders. Get them down here."

Summer went first to the hotel where she found a Mexican on night duty at the front desk. She booked the rooms side by side for easier access for the doctors. Asking if the clerk knew where Dr. Diego Esteban lived, the clerk answered with a smile "Sí, señorita, he is my very good friend."

"Please, sir, he is needed. Could you run quickly and get him here? To Dr. Shultz's clinic."

"Sí, señorita, I go. You will watch here? The desk?"

"Yes. Just go."

~

As Gwyneth worked on Cob, she spoke to the man on the floor who was again awake.

"What is your name, please?"

"Grad Wilsey."

"Well, Grad Wilsey. We need someone to ride to the ranch. Cob said there were four of you who rode with him. Who are the others?"

"Colt Brown, Beau Davis, Chuck Moore."

Gwyneth was still talking with Grad Wilsey when Summer and Dr. Diego Esteban entered the room. Never turning her eyes from Cob, Gwyneth said, "Good work, Summer. Now there is one more thing I need you to do. Then, I promise you can take a rest from running here and there. Go to the saloon. Don't go inside, but send someone else in if there's anyone around. We need the Sombrero riders down here, sober or not."

Speaking to Grad Wilsey, she said, "Spill those names out again, Grad."

Summer listened carefully as the names were slowly leaked from the hurting man's mouth.

"Get the three of them down here if you can, Summer."

As if a word from Gwyneth was her charge to act, Summer whirled around and was gone. Within ten minutes, the three men shuffled into the clinic, led by Summer.

While they were waiting for the riders to appear, Gwyneth spoke to Dr. Esteban, who was kneeling beside Grad Wilsey, examining the wound.

"Diego. Thanks for coming. If you could patch that fella up, it would be much appreciated. There's water on the stove for scrubbing your hands. Summer will help you with the stitching. She's very good at nursing. You tell her what you want from her, and it will all go just fine. You will find what you need in that cupboard behind you."

Summer reveled in the praise from this woman and doctor that she so idealized.

Hoping she hadn't pushed familiarity too far, realizing she had been treating Dr. Shultz's clinic as her own, she sought words to say in explanation or apology. A clearer second consideration left her confident that none of it would matter. The care of the patients was what mattered.

With a simple *Si,* Diego set to work, first going to the stove for hot water.

Gwyneth said, loud enough for the men in the outer room to hear, "You Sombrero riders. Cob isn't going to be with you this night, nor for some nights to come. I believe he would want you to ride back to the ranch and carry the news. Tell Trinity that he will be in charge until better news is available. Also, tell Juanita to pack up some things she might need and come to town. She will be living at the hotel, caring for these men. It is up to you men how she gets here. Go now, there is nothing here for you. Tell the ranch we will send out news as soon as it becomes available."

Summer knelt beside Grad Wilsey, with a pan of hot water and a couple of clean towels. The first thing she did, as the blanket covering him was removed, was use a towel to preserve Grad's dignity, and to save herself from as much stress as possible. Thinking back to the first time she was confronted with a similar situation, when the man up in Pueblo had fallen on his own knife, and grinning at her naivety and at how little she really knew about men and life, she had gently folded the towel to protect what little privacy remained in the situation.

She then raised a screaming howl from Grad as she laid a hot towel over the wound and softly began washing off the evidence of dried blood and trail dust. Surprising everyone in the room, Summer said, "Hush that noise up now. If you're going to insist on getting yourself shot up, you're going to have to pay the price like a"—she nearly said man, before she thought better of it— "like a hero of the hunt."

The words sounded silly even in her own ears, but it was too late to take them back. She proceeded to clean the area, glancing once at the patient's face, to find his eyes tightly closed and his lips pursed to where even a whisper would not escape. It was a good position to hold, as Summer applied the next treatment, that of running a liberal amount of disinfectant, the same one that had caused her brother to scream, along the opening in the flesh. She warned him of what was to come and didn't apply the disinfectant until he nodded his head in permission. Still, his body literally shook for the few seconds the spiking pain lasted.

Dr. Esteban dropped back onto his knees, not the best position for laying a row of stitches in a man's leg, but there was no choice. With a cheerful expression that surprised the others, he said, "Now, *Eres un guerrero. ¡Ánimo*! We work, yes? As this delightful and very beautiful young señorita has already advised, it is best that you lie still and quiet. And that you hold your leg in the position, like so. We would not wish to make a mistake and have to start all over again, so? You are going to have a lovely scar. A scar to talk about, but probably not to see. A scar such as this, on your cheek, would be a thing for the señoritas to lightly touch as they marveled at your bravery. But here?" He allowed the rest of the thought to remain silent.

Gabriel Shultz turned his mind away from the sheriff's

needs long enough to say, "I'll have to remember that, Diego. I have often wished I had a better bedside manner."

Chapter Eight

Dr. Shultz spoke over his shoulder to Gwyneth. "Dr. Wycome, if your patient could do without you for just a minute or so, I could use some help."

Gwyneth responded, "I can't leave Cob just now. How about you, Diego? Are you about done there?"

"To have but half a scar would not be a happy thing for this man. I need two more minutes."

"Summer? As soon as you can be spared, will you please see what you can do for Dr. Shultz while Diego is finishing up?"

Summer leaned back from the stitching Diego was completing, and stood, saying, "Once more, I will wash my hands, Dr. Shultz. Then I will be right with you."

When Summer stepped to the side of the stretcher opposite Dr. Shultz, she was told, "Summer, you can see, I'm sure, that the bullet entered the shoulder area from the front. You will also see where some muscles were separated, torn apart. These must be repaired for the sheriff to retain his arm movements and control. If you could place your fingers on either side of this grouping of muscles, just about where they're torn, holding them clear, and isolating the damaged ones, I intend to suture them to restore their integrity. I simply need you to prevent anything from getting in my way."

"I'll do my best, Doctor. Just tell me if I'm doing it wrong."

"That I will, my dear. That I will."

Dr. Shultz was still busy repairing the bicep muscles when Dr. Esteban stood to his feet, the suturing of Grad Wilsey now complete. With the repair and bandaging of the wound completed, the cowboy was able to slowly, grimly, rise to his feet. Gwyneth didn't like to appear as if she was interfering with Dr. Esteban's patient, but weariness took the place of caution.

"Grad, you get yourself onto a chair. You act the hero now you're on your own. No one's going to redo that repair this night. Summer mentioned something about coffee. If you're very careful, perhaps you can find a cup for yourself. Then sit. And stay seated."

Chapter Nine

Dr. Diego Esteban cleaned up the area where Grad Wilsey had been lying, returning the cleaned and scalded tools and the remainder of the suture thread and unused swabs. He then moved to the window not far from where Gwyneth was hovering over Cob. Her work was completed and the incision sewn up, but still she stood. Moments before, she found herself enjoying the touch of his skin as she wiped some fallen hair from his brow. She immediately disciplined herself and moved her hand away. Diego had seen the action. He smiled at her, saying, "It is good to care, no?"

Without expecting an answer, he turned to the window. Grasping the bottom of the roller blind, he tugged once, twice, and again to release the spring catch and then allowed the mechanism to pull the cloth to the top. The room was suddenly ablaze with morning sunlight. Summer entered the room at almost the instant the blind rose. She carried a tray holding three cups of coffee and a small pitcher of separated cream.

"For when you can take a break, Doctors."

Gwyneth responded, "I've had this wrapped up for a while. I'm only concerned about Cob's reaction as he comes out of the ether. I think it's all right. He's shown no reaction yet."

Dr. Shultz set her mind at ease with, "If he's shown no adverse reaction yet, he'll be all right. I believe you can join us for coffee with some ease."

Dr. Shultz said, "There's nothing more I can do for those muscles. And nothing at all I can do for that bullet gouge alongside the sheriff's head. I've cleaned and disinfected it. Now we'll see what time will bring. He may wake up feeling young and spry, and he may not wake up at all."

To continue that conversation would add an unnecessary dreariness. It was as if they collectively decided it was time to think of other things.

Gwyneth pulled a chair to a position where she could see the others, all the while keeping an eye on Cob. Hoping to lighten the heaviness of the night somewhat, she smiled at Diego and said, "If we were closer, Diego, we could enjoy one of Lupita's sweets."

"Ah, the lovely Lupita, she who is sunshine to my heart. She who is sweetness itself. My heart is light just to think of her."

"Have you told her these things, Diego?" asked Gabriel Shultz.

"She knows, *Señor*. The true heart needs no words. Her heart tells her what my heart feels."

"That may be so in the storybooks people write, but if it were me, I would speak my own words. Words for her ears, not just for the heart."

"Ah, sir, but you are not of the *Enamoradizo/a*. The heart requires someone to love, so? And if that love is not returned, what is sweeter than a broken heart, when there are so many other beautiful ladies to see to its healing."

"You've got me there, Diego. I'm afraid my European thinking takes me in another direction. It would suit me better to not have a broken heart that needs fixing."

Gwyneth spoke into the conversation for the first time. "We have not talked about personal matters, Gabriel. Are you married?"

"I am, I'm pleased to say. Married and content to be so. That same sun that shines into our window shines on every one of us this morning. And everyone responds with their own way of thinking. I wish you well in the pursuit of the lovely Lupita, Diego, but I go home each evening to a home-cooked dinner and a relaxing time of ease. There is no pursuit of happiness that some find so elusive. Once found, I never thought of another."

Laughing now, Gwyneth asked, "Are you learning anything here, Summer?"

"If I am learning anything, it probably has more to do with washing those cups than anything else."

BY MID-MORNING, Juanita arrived with the rear compartment of a ranch buggy laden with boxes of materials and spare clothing she had packed and brought along. She went first to the hotel, requesting to be shown to her room.

"The ranch booked four of them. You're the first here. I'm guessing you can take whichever one you want."

From the hotel, she had the driver take her to Dr. Shultz's office.

Working together, they managed to get the blanket-wrapped Grad Wilsey seated in the buggy and then into the hotel. To Gabriel's question about his well-being, he answered, "I'm fine now. And thank you all. But I'm so tired. I believe I'll have me a nap."

Cob and the sheriff were toted to the hotel on the flat of a door, with four strong men volunteering to do the toting. They were soon bedded down, with Juanita letting everyone know that she was now in charge. Everyone but the doctors were ushered out of the rooms. She then stationed herself between Cob and Gwyneth. Gwyneth took the hint, smiled, and turned for the door.

With all of that dealt with and behind them, Gwyneth and Summer attended to the prisoner. The jailer watched every moment of the treatment as if the doctor was about to turn the prisoner loose again. Never taking his eyes from either Gwyneth or Summer, he locked the cell door when their work was done and ushered them to the outer door, glad to see them gone.

Thankfully, there were no other calls for medical help that morning. Dr. Shultz left for home and breakfast with his Ursula. Gwyneth and Summer took breakfast at the café, and Dr. Diego Esteban smilingly said, "I too need some rest, but first a coffee and one of Lupita's sweet rolls. Perhaps also a smile, a treasure to keep and hold. A smile to greet the doctor and the morning."

Chapter Ten

"No, you ain't going to be see'n my stiches. You jest get along with yerselves and leave me be."

Grad's welcome back to the ranch was, typically, a bit on the rough side with ribald remarks and teasing about riding side-saddle. The fact that every man on the place was happy to see him return was well hidden. And for Grad, to be home again felt better than he could have ever imagined.

Summer, who had driven the ranch buggy out to the Sombrero with Grad sitting wide-legged on the seat beside her, listened to some of the nonsense before turning the rig toward the barn, thankful that her name had not come up in the conversation.

Grad had said little on the short buggy trip, but following a few false starts, he finally managed to say, "Y'all wouldn't no way say anything, would you?"

Not being clear of his meaning at first, Summer finally had a stroke of understanding. Even in the freewheeling, rough and ready environment of ranch life, the understood proprieties were well safeguarded. To suggest that a man couldn't do his job or that he was somehow not man enough to ride the river with or stand up to the long haul was to invite a fight. That didn't mean they were protected from teasing so long as there were no serious undercurrents in the bunkhouse talk.

To be wounded in such a delicate area was trouble enough. To have it known that a pretty young nurse had been closely involved in his treatment might make life unbearable.

"No, Grad. I would never have said anything in any case, but one of the first things Gwyneth taught me when she called me off the ranch was that we never, under any circumstances, talk about a patient. You have nothing to worry about from me."

Grad heaved out a sigh of relief, leaned back against the seat, and appeared to enjoy the remainder of the ride.

At the barn, Summer backed the rig under the lean-to roof before stepping to the ground and unhitching the horse. She led the animal, with trace chains dragging, into the barn. She was about to slip the harness into her arms when the voice of Clive Gentry, the Sombrero wrangler, called her off.

"Hold on there, young miss. That be my job ye're a doin' there. And you so all dressed up and young and pert, too. Like to hurt yerself carry'n on like such. You allow Ol' Clive ta handle the leathers. You can go back ta yer tea party up to the big house."

With a bite to her voice, Summer said, "Is that so? Tea party, is it? Well then, here's an invitation to my tea party."

As she spoke, she finished slipping the harness into her arms. She turned toward the voice just in time to see that the wrangler was about three feet away. As he was beginning his reach for the leather, Summer let it drop. Clive made a quick grab for it but missed, nearly losing his balance at the same time. As the harness crumbled to the floor, Summer said, "I thought you were the wrangler. Perhaps the ranch should hire me on to do things right. I could help you until you catch on to the job."

Clive was so angry that he missed the trailing reins when he straightened after picking up the harness. As he stepped away, his foot came down on one of the reins, causing the harness to pull sideways in his arms.

"Here, I'll help you," Summer said as she picked up the loose leathers.

A glare to rival the sun shone from the man's eyes. But he turned and carried the lopsided load to the harness room. In the few minutes he was gone, Summer led the animal to a box stall and closed the door.

Clive muttered something that might have been, *You still here?* when he came from the harness room.

Summer smiled and said, "I'm here, Clive, and we had best get acquainted. My name is Summer. I came here with Cob and Dr. Wycome. I've been nursing with the doctor up to Colorado. I was with her and the other town doctors when the posse men returned. But the thing is, Clive, I'm ranch-raised. Gwyneth, that's Dr. Wycome, who's also horse- and cattle-wise, she pulled me from the ranch just less than one year ago. My father was not one to spare his daughters from work. I've about handled it all, saddle horses to two-up Clyde teams. I'll ride anything you can rope and saddle. I'll drive a team as well as anyone on the ranch.

"But let's forget all this and be friends. I'm not living on the ranch, so I won't often see you. But I could show up from time to time. It might be best if we were to be friends.

"Okay, Summer. I'll hold back my tongue while you get a grip on that smart mouth of yours. It's pretty enough, but too smart by half."

"I'm not usually that way, Clive. Just setting the record straight, the way I had to with my brothers. But that's past us now. Now, what we have to do is pick out two good horses and saddles."

"You need to explain that."

"Well, I need some way to get back to town. And Gwyneth,

she and I like to ride in the evening, after the work is done. I mentioned that to Cob earlier this morning, suggesting I might buy a couple of animals from the town livery. He said there was no need, that there were lots of horses on the Sombrero. I know the one I want, but I have to confess, Cob didn't offer that black yearling. So, it's up to you. What can you spare?"

"Noticed the black, did you? Well, at least you have an eye for horses."

~

After Grad, who was hurt less than the others, the prisoner was the first to heal, although that brought little happiness to him as he considered his likely future. The town deputy sheriff had sent for a Ranger and a judge. Holding a quickly arranged trial in the saloon, the deputy, who was standing in for the still waylaid sheriff, explained to the judge that it was after the sheriff sent the rustlers' names off to the Ranger office that the men became desperate to escape.

"Turns out, sir, that those fellas had a long history. Stage holdups. At least one train robbery. Several banks robbed, and a series of dead and wounded littering their back trail."

With the evidence placed before the accused, the man had simply hung his head, saying nothing. The trial was short and concise. The prisoner would be escorted by the Ranger to the state prison, where he would be hung.

With Cob and the sheriff still hovering between life and death, no one was happy, but at least that part of the episode could be put behind them.

Chapter Eleven

Cob was kept almost in a sitting position to ease his breathing and to encourage the healing of his lung. To keep him from forcing the use of his shoulder, Gwyneth tied it in a sling and wrapped the sling to his chest. Speaking to both Juanita and Cob, as if they were a pair of miscreants, where one could be guilty of assisting the other in finding a way around doctor's orders, she warned of future problems with the shoulder if thc healing were interrupted in any way.

With his writing hand tied to his side, Cob managed to put a short telegram together, addressed to his brother at the southern, original Hat Ranch. It was short and concise.

Louis

After a bit of a dust-up with some rustlers, I'm forced to stay in town, close to the doctor. Suggest one of you ride up here and take over until I'm up and around.

Cob

The next time Gwyneth came to examine Cob's wound, he passed her the letter.

"I'd like if you'd give this to Trinity. Have him pull someone from the crew. Send him to deliver this note to my brother down at Laredo. It's about a ten-day ride. Tell Trinity to outfit the rider well and get him going on the jump."

Summer, standing beside Gwyneth, said, "I'd ride out there myself, but that broken-down paint gelding Clive picked out for me won't hardly make another trip this week, him needing rest and all. Now, that black. With him, I could make the ride as often as you wish."

With a sign of resignation, Cob said, "Go get the black. I'm tired of your talk. Tell Clive I said so. Bought a new saddle for the youngster. You might just as well take that and have the whole of it. Then, will you leave me alone for a while?"

"If you're a good patient and do everything Gwyneth tells you to do, I promise to be good. I'll see if I can kick a bit of life out of that paint and get this message on its way."

Gwyneth and Cob watched as Summer walked out, closing the door behind herself.

"You need to send that girl back to her own ranch, Gwyneth. She's going to have cowboys crawling on their knees trying to gain her attention. She'll end up owning the whole country before you know it. That's the future if she stays here. Already controls my ranch, as much as the boys would deny it."

Gwyneth had been secretly smiling as Summer twisted Cob into knots, finally winning her battle and leaving before Cob could change his mind. "Cob. You're loving every minute of your little battles with Summer. Anyway, you've got to admit she has an eye for horseflesh. The first time I laid eyes on the black I near lost my breath. But he'll rot away in that stall. Needs to be ridden."

"I know that. But it was supposed to be me who rode and trained him."

"And you will be. Just not yet, a while. In the meantime, Summer will care for him well, you needn't worry."

DR. SHULTZ WAS anxious about the sheriff. He had come every day to check on him but saw no response and no improvement. He worked regularly with Juanita, stretching his arm, folding it at the elbow, and gently working the shoulder joint. All of that showed good progress on the muscle surgery. The doctor even showed Juanita how to keep his legs flexible, lifting them to work the hips and the knees by folding the leg back onto the sheriff's body. These exercises were repeated regularly, all to the good in the doctor's mind. But there was no mental response at all eyes never opened, he never attempted to talk, he had trouble swallowing the light gruel Juanita prepared for him. The sheriff would forever have a small trough down the side of his head, above the ear, but the wound was healing slowly, the hair growing back where it had been shaved off.

THE DAY after Cob had sent Summer off with his message, she arrived at his room all bright and chipper, smiling and ready to report on her ride to the ranch.

"Good morning, Cob. It's a bright and beautiful day out there. If you keep doing what the doctor says, I expect you'll have many such days in the future to enjoy."

Cob cut out her next thought before she could get started.

"Who did Trinity choose for that ride south?"

Pretending she didn't hear the question, she said, "Clive was relieved to have that black away from the ranch. Said the animal wasn't much more than a nuisance. But he acted pretty good on the ride home and again this morning when we were out for our exercise run. There might be some hope for him if I can keep him long enough to train him. But I must say, that's a nice saddle. Might be the best I've ever ridden on."

"Summer. Pay attention. Who took my message south?"

"Oh, that. No one went. There was no need."

"Wha—"

"Oh, don't get all flustered. The message went all right. Already got a reply for you. You never did seal the envelope. Trinity opened it, want'n to see exactly what your instructions were. He passed it to me. I rewrote it into a telegram, and off it went. Oh, and you owe me sixty cents. Reply came in this morning."

Reaching into her pocket, she lifted out a handwritten telegram form and passed it to Cob. He unfolded it and read, "*Sorry to hear. Be there in two weeks. Gathering bunch for Ft. Worth too.*"

Summer gave him time to read the few words before she asked, "What does that mean? That about Fort Worth?"

"Fort Worth is where the stockyards are. It means there's stock on the Hat that need culling out. They're putting together a drive. Won't be anything like the old drives, but it will give the young bucks something to cut their teeth on. Some from the south are loading their stock onto rail cars, but Louis, he'll have none of that. Figures God gave them animals four good feet for a purpose. And he ain't one to thwart the Lord's purposes. And there's no freight bill to pay at the end of the drive."

"So, it's all good news. You're healing up. I can hear it in your breathing. Your shoulder is pretty much back to being usable. I caught you doing exercises the other day. Oh, you stopped as soon as I rounded the doorway, but I saw. And now I have a thought for you to put your thinker to. I'll ride out to the ranch this afternoon and bring the buggy back in. I'll bring the black along on a lead. Tomorrow, you can tug some street clothing on, at least enough to be decent, and we'll get you down to the street. I'll help Gwyneth make a picnic basket, and you can show her around the area.

"She'll have to do the driving, but she won't mind that. She might even pass you the reins for a minute so's you can show off a bit, show her what a big, strong man you've come to be, a-ly'n in this hotel bed. I know she'll be eager to go. We were talking about it just last evening—the new farmland being worked out of the scrub brush, the irrigation projects, all the new folks arriving, building, and planning. Unless I miss my guess, Sombrero is about to grow and keep on growing. It's going to need a new name, that's plain enough, but Sombrero will do for now. So that's a plan and a date. You get Juanita to help you ready yourself for the day, and I'll sort the rest out. And if you were to have a bath and a shave, kind of set yourself up for fit company, I expect the world would keep right on turning as it should. You be ready by ten in the morning."

"You have it all planned out, do you?"

"Are you going to pretend you don't like the plan?"

"No. No. Probably not. I'll have to talk to Gwyneth though."

"You leave Gwyneth to me. You just get yourself ready."

JUANITA WAS TAKING particular care of the sheriff. Cob was able to handle most of his own needs, including walking slowly up and down the hotel corridor. Although Cob was her first concern, between them, either Gwyneth or Summer seemed to have taken over most of the few things he couldn't do for himself. That left her free for the sheriff. It troubled her greatly that this man, whom she had only met casually before, but who she remembered as a strong, determined, peace-loving man, should be lying inert, day after day, because of some murderer's bullet.

She knew absolutely nothing about head wounds, and by

Dr. Shultz's own admission, the medical world didn't really know much more. But by her simple reasoning, she concluded that continuing as they were wasn't to anyone's benefit, least of all, the sheriff's.

She would have been mortified at her thoughts only days before. Venturing into actions not of the doctor's direction was unheard of in her world. But, giving in to the frustrations that waiting—while nothing improved—brought upon her, she closed the hotel room door for privacy and studied, once again, the face of the unconscious man.

Hesitating at first and then acting on her thoughts, she laid her hand on the sheriff's cheeks. If he was awake inside his mind and knew what was happening around him, she wished him to know that someone was there. That someone cared. She held her hands gently quiet for a half minute before pressing harder and firmer. Almost rhythmically, she began massaging his face. Watching his eyes the whole time.

Her bravery built as her fingers moved. From his cheeks to the area around his ears, then quite firmly behind, and all around his ears. All actions done with no thought other than to hope the sheriff would feel something. And perhaps allow an eyelid to flutter open. Determined now, she moved her hands to the back of his neck, her fingers digging in with some force in the soft areas, with less force where the skin was close to the bone of the skull. She continued with the forceful massage down his neck and onto the soft areas between his shoulders.

She had allowed ten minutes to pass while her fingers worked, and her mind prayed. Somewhat humorously, she wondered if it was all right to pray in Spanish while praying for someone who spoke only a few words of her mother tongue. Perhaps God speaks all languages. How was a simple house servant to know such things? Did the God of the Americanos see or hear when a servant is wishing for His help, even when she is praying only in her mind and with her hands, not with her voice?

She had suffered in her mind the first time she bathed the sheriff and washed his hair, sensing the improprieties of the task. Dr. Gwyneth had smiled when the two women talked about it, explaining that she had done the same many times, closing her mind to all but serving the patient. So, Juanita repeated the washing each morning. But this wasn't quite the same as massaging. She wasn't sure of the right word or description, but it felt more of what she thought of as *íntimo*, intimate. She blushed at the thought.

Working her hands back up his neck, she continued until her fingers were tangled in his hair. Being gentle around the nicely healing wound, she covered his head with her working fingers, back and forth, repeating the motions. She faithfully held her eyes on his eyes, but there was no sign of awareness. She couldn't have seen it with the sheriff's hands under the bedcovers, but as she massaged, one finger twitched.

Chapter Twelve

WITH SUMMER NEEDLESSLY GRIPPING COB'S UPPER arm, he took the hotel stairs one step at a time until he reached the foyer. Summer removed her arm to preserve Cob's dignity while he slowly, carefully, made his way to the door and onto the boardwalk. With just a little more exercise, he would be up and walking again just fine. The buggy was there, all polished up and ready. Waiting. Gwyneth was seated, with the reins in her hands, welcoming him with a smile. Cob's carbine was resting in the saddle scabbard he had fixed to the side of the box long ago. He wouldn't feel comfortable without it. A few well-wishers had paused in their day's business to watch and wonder at the goings-on. Cob had regained most of his strength, although the arm was still in a sling. But with the use of his other arm, he was able to mount to the seat without help.

Gwyneth smiled him a welcome and lifted the reins from her lap. Cob looked down at the boardwalk and spoke, in a not altogether friendly manner, to Summer. "You including yourself in this little outing?"

Grinning, she answered, "Sorry. I know you'll miss me, but I'm working with Dr. Shultz this morning. If you have questions when you return, I'll do all I can to help."

"I'm sure you will."

To Gwyneth, he said, "Let's get out of here before she changes her mind."

Gwyneth laughed and slapped the horse into action. "I'll drive. You point out the way."

"Stay to this road about one mile. Turn either to the east or west. Makes no difference. Lots going on both ways. I haven't been up this way for some time, so a lot will be new to me."

The conversation on the buggy was slow starting. Gwyneth finally broke the ice, saying, "I'm hoping we're able to stay clear of dust. I've brought along a face mask just in case there're folks clearing land up here, inviting the wind to turn the good soil into an airborne flurry. You're healing up well, but we need to keep you breathing clean air."

Cob's response was, "Looks more like rain than dust, but this is Texas. Could change twice before noon."

After another interval of silence, Cob asked, "What have you been up to since I've been lazing up at the hotel?"

"Between a few opportunities to work with the other doctors, I've been talking to people, Cob. Businesspeople. Cattle people. Citizens. A few miners. Or at least some who hope to be miners, if they ever find something to mine. I've ridden around a bit, but only in the ranching country close to town. Pretty country up in those hills to the west of the Sombrero. Rough in places, but pretty."

"It's rough enough all right, Gwyneth. And you shouldn't be up there alone. Men familiar with the area have found themselves lost and wandering. One canyon, one treed hillside, looks much like another, and what you took as a landmark appears totally different on your return."

"I appreciate the warning, but I'm aware of that problem. I'm constantly looking down my backtrail. Ran across three small outfits settled down in the outback. Good folks I'm prepared to say after just our brief time together. One shack was home to two brothers. It was almost embarrassing, they couldn't do enough for me, when really, I didn't need anything from them. I finally convinced them it would be enough if they just told me about the country around. I told them about being a doctor, how I was just sizing up the need for another doctor around about."

"That's the Hillson brothers. I don't know how they survive. They have a couple hundred head up there, but most of them haven't been seen since they turned them out. They've certainly had nothing to drive to market. They're not rustlers, I'm satisfied to say that. Live mostly on venison is my guess. I don't know why they do it. They could at least round up their animals and see to their growth in numbers. We'd lend them a couple of men if they'd ask.

"Anyway, what's all the questioning about?"

"My questioning is about the future of the Sombrero area. You already know that Abe and Helen couldn't be more enthusiastic than they already are. I've spent some time with them too. And I met one of their daughters and her family. Abe believes the future of farming outshines that of ranching. A lot of wells are being dug or drilled. Windmills almost blanket the area."

"And what does all that mean to you and what you're planning?"

"Cob. You know what I'm planning. I've never hidden that from you. I studied and worked hard to become a doctor. I've gotten over most of my desire to service the tiny settlements on the frontier. They're simply too small and too far apart for a doctor to make any kind of a living. Or to be in the right location when a need arises. I can see a doctor spending most of his time riding a buggy, driving from one need to another. There's other reasons for that, but we don't have to discuss them. What I'm now doing is trying to decide how many doctors Sombrero needs, along with Dr. Shultz and Dr. Esteban.

"Both are good men. Dr. Shultz is the better trained, but Diego Esteban is very good at what he does. He prefers to avoid surgeries, but the two men have worked out a compromise that seems to be satisfactory for them. On sheer population numbers, there's room for another two or three doctors. That's without much growth in population. If farming proves up like everyone thinks it will, you'll soon enough have a city on your hands. But what is needed most is a hospital. You've seen yourself how much follow-up work there is in dealing with surgeries or serious illnesses. Not everyone can stay at the hotel, and even if they could, the doctors don't have the time to be seeing to them there. The town needs a hospital. Or at the least, a large clinic."

Cob had no response, although the faraway look on his face told Gwyneth that he was deep in thought.

Gwyneth halted the buggy from time to time to either stare out over the thousands of acres of relatively flat land waiting for the plow or to chat with workers to ask what they were doing or what they hoped to grow. There was a bewildering variety of crops suggested. Even Cob was impressed.

"If they do even less than half of that, they'll still be doing more than most would give them a chance of accomplishing."

"Take a guess, Cob. From what we've seen today, what will the population of Sombrero and the farming area around it be in five years?"

"It scares me to say it, Gwyneth, but it will certainly be in the thousands. How far into the thousands will depend mostly on the success of the early planters."

"And the prospects for a hospital?"

Cob had no reply. He daren't speak of it, but he was wondering if the hospital focus was driving him and Gwyneth further apart. When his every desire was to find something that would draw them closer. To break off the conversation, he said, "I thought Summer was going to get a lunch put together."

"And she did. I helped a bit. But let's drive over to that group of trees and find some shade before we stop."

Chapter Thirteen

Juanita, with Cob needing less care each day and Grad Wilsey back at the ranch, focused her attention on the sheriff. Ever mindful of her position in life, a house matron, nothing higher, she knew to be cautious when around the *Señor*. He was dependent on her efforts, but that changed nothing. He would forever be of the *clase alta*, a wide step above her birthing. But somehow, without her willing it, with all she had done in caring for the wounded and unconscious man, feeding him, bathing him, making him comfortable, an unfamiliar, one-way closeness was developing. She even started wondering if she dared ask someone what his name was. He might respond to his name being spoken into his ear. Perhaps more than simply hearing her whisper *Señor* as she called on him to wake up. But she must be very careful. There were, after all, the proprieties to keep in mind.

So, back to the massaging. But first, the exercises Dr. Shultz had shown her. Arms up, down, sideways, and then the legs, side to side one at a time, and then to bend at the knees and fold the knee up to his body. Repeat, repeat, repeat. Juanita rested for a moment before approaching the massage.

The sheriff's neck was the first to receive a massage, then the head and, as foolish as it would sound to tell someone, the feet. She thought of it in an awake moment during the night. She thought of her own feet that, since coming to the ranch, were seldom without shoes, and she nodded in certainty.

There are few parts of the body more sensitive to touch than the sole of the foot. Especially with these men, who wear boots and spend most of their lives either holding down a chair or sitting a-saddle. They never walked barefoot, as did the peons she was raised among. Even as she had the thought, she decided it was true. She only had to prove it, no one else needed to know.

She entered the hotel room with a breakfast tray from the café, a tray of gruel, like every morning. But this day it was different. On this day, Helen had walked down from her store with a small basket holding three pawpaws. Meeting in the dining room kitchen, she suggested the sheriff might enjoy a sweeter taste than the grain gruel he had been living on. Overjoyed to receive the fruit, and somehow feeling the two women might have something in common, she whispered, hoping no one near them would hear. "*Señora* Helen. I do not know the name the sheriff is called by. Perhaps could you—"

Helen spoke before the question was fully asked, saving Juanita embarrassment. "Of course. Someone should have told you. His full name is Olaf Bergstrom. Often, the men just call him Swede, but he doesn't like that. Call him Olaf if he ever wakes up."

The two women parted with a small smile. They now held a secret between them that had drawn them a tiny bit closer together. Even with so little—a name for the *señor*, and a simple smile from Helen—Juanita felt like she was more than she had always seen herself as: only a house matron who sometimes came to town for supplies at the store of Abe and Helen.

All her life, she had been taken for granted. She had accepted that, as being from her class, although there were times she longed for more. There had been a time. A time long ago. A time with a man. The only man who wasn't one she wasn't hired to serve. A good man, her husband. Her Ricardo. A brave man, but not wise. He had believed a rider who came to their village. A rider who wore a fancy coat with bright trim and brass buttons. A man who was going to win a victory in one of Mexico's endless wars. A man who was in truth *El General Sin Ejército*, a general without an army. Later, when it all came to nothing, with many paying a solid price to win the nothing, the man in the fancy coat had sent her a message. A sad and life-changing message, but a message she welcomed. She had to know. Many had gone off and were never heard from again, leaving wives and sweethearts forever wondering.

The sheriff, *Olaf*, she whispered to herself as she put the spoon to his mouth, feeling the excitement and the danger in her new knowledge of the man's name. He showed just a bit of reaction, almost enthusiasm, just the tightening of his lips against the spoon at the taste of the fruit-laden gruel. It was the first time she had seen any response since the shooting. She completed the feeding, cleaned up around, returned the tray and bowl to the kitchen, bathed him as she did every morning, and straightened the bedding under and around him.

She went to the chair beside the open window and sat. What she planned must work. *¡Por favor, Dios! Only You can make this man, this Olaf, come awake. By your mercy, Dios, allow me to serve You. You and this man.*

Almost trembling, she moved the single, covering blanket aside. It was warm in the room. By noon, it would be stifling. She must act now. She pushed up the legs of the white cotton peón pants she had dressed him in. To lead up to what she was planning she lightly massaged the feet as high as the ankles. When she felt the sheriff was relaxed enough, although she wasn't sure if that was the correct feeling she sensed in her touch, she slowly moved downward, finally rubbing the bottoms of the feet with the palms of her hands.

Almost holding her breath, she extended her fingers. She

always kept her nails neatly trimmed for working in the kitchen, but there was enough nail left to leave an impression. First, the left leg—a light touch and then slowly dragging the nail of her index finger from heel to toe. No reaction. But next, the right leg. The same finger action, but this time with a bit more nail scraping. Nothing until the third repeat. Then a slight movement of the fingers on his right hand. This time, she saw the movement. This time, his hands were lying in the open, and they had moved. She had seen it.

¡Gracias, Dios! Thank you, God. This man, he is alive inside. Only he must now come awake.

She repeated her efforts, seeing soon after the finger twitch, a movement in his face, as if he was trying to open his eyes but was only able to arch his brow, just a bit. She kept on but finally decided, when there was no more movement, that he'd had enough on the feet. She would massage his head like always, and then both would rest, Olaf in his bed and she outside, on a chair in the shade by the hotel door.

Gwyneth and Cob ate their lunches in almost total silence. But in that silence, each believed they could hear the thoughts racing through the other's mind. What they had seen was an eye-opener for Cob. He knew there was talk of farms and development, but keeping busy on the ranch, he hadn't bothered following those developments. Not that any of it really troubled him. Why would it? The farms took nothing from the ranch, and the added prosperity would add to the overall well-being of the town and territory. No, it was nothing to do with what they had seen that was holding him silent.

Gwyneth was also mulling the morning's discoveries. She came away completely convinced that someone was going to build a hospital. And someone was going to manage that hospital. And someone else was going to fill the need for a physician and surgeon in that hospital. Why not her? She was prepared to believe she had equal or better training than other doctors within riding distance. On top of that was her years in Chicago, where she saw, and was involved firsthand, in offering top-class medical care to all who came.

She also knew what Cob's wish was. A wish she had been finding more acceptable as the days went by since that rainy night on the veranda in Pueblo. As she thought earlier, it wasn't romance. Or at least not the romance of her earlier, younger time. Her time with Trent. She was now older, more stable, more settled down. She couldn't think of another word, so she settled on romance. Did she dare speak of love? Cob hadn't said the word, and she wished he had. Or would. Still, she understood, in part, at least. Dr. Cliff Rickhart, a man she worked side by side with at Chicago General, and who clearly wished to pursue her romantically, couldn't bring himself to even ask her to join him for dinner. When he finally got around to inviting her out, the evening had included his parents. What a disaster that evening turned out to be. To think of that same man using the word love was beyond her imagination.

She was convinced that Cob would spend the remainder of his days demonstrating his love, knowing no other way, and believing that was adequate. And perhaps it was.

In silence, they loaded up the picnic basket and folded the ground sheet. Gwyneth stood by in case Cob needed a steadying hand before she walked around to the other side of the buggy and mounted. With extreme tension building between them, Gwyneth slapped the horse's rump with the reins and pointed the rig toward town. Only once did Gwyneth speak. That was to say, "It's a beautiful country, whether we're speaking of these flat lands or your rolling hills."

Cob offered no reply. Not till they entered the town did Cob speak, and that was only to say, "Keep going, unless you have something else needing doing. Take me home. It's time I was back on the ranch. I'd like Juanita back home too, as soon as she can be spared from nursing the sheriff. You can be the judge of that."

Following another moment's silence, Cob suggested, "Perhaps the sheriff should be moved out to the ranch too. Juanita can care for him there as well as in town."

With that, while Gwyneth considered the suggestion from the medical point of view, they lapsed back into silence. The strain on both was visceral. It remained that way during the short ride to the Sombrero Ranch. When the headquarters buildings came into view from a slight rise in the trail, Cob softly said, "Stop here."

With a quiet whoa, the horse came to rest. Cob used his left hand to lift his still bandaged right arm into a more comfortable position while he turned a bit sideways on the seat. Looking directly at Gwyneth, he said, "See all that, Gwyneth? That and all the lands for miles around? And all the cattle? That's all yours. Yours and mine. That's your home. I would never ask you to give up on your doctoring. But I'd like if you would first be Mrs. Cob Fleming and then Dr. Gwyneth after that. You've had a long time to think and consider, Gwyneth. I'm here this final time to tell you that I love you and I want you to be my wife. I say final time because I don't think I could survive going through this again. What is your answer, Gwyneth? Will you marry me?"

For the first time since they sat down on the grass for their picnic, Gwyneth allowed her lips to form a small smile. "Why yes, Cob. Yes, I will. And feel it a privilege in the doing. I will admit that it was no easy matter working out the change, from knowing and liking you as such a very good friend, and then having to admit to myself that I love you. I suspect I was always a little bit in love with you. But now I love you in full. Yes, I will marry you. Could we leave the rest for some day soon? Some day when I am not so totally exhausted. I wish to be at my very best when we plan out our lives.

"I'll drive you to the ranch and then go back to town. You

have one of your men drive you back in one day soon. We'll go on another picnic. And will you promise me that you won't climb on a horse this afternoon, pretending there is nothing to fear? You're not totally healed yet, and if I am to have you, I want all of you, not a man who spends the rest of his life laboring to breathe."

"I'll agree to all of that, Gwyneth. Drive on down. I'll have one of the men take you home."

Chapter Fourteen

THE THOUGHT OF MOVING BACK HOME DELIGHTED Juanita. At the first mention of moving the sheriff to the big house on the ranch, she hesitated, her eyes studying Gwyneth as if to ask, *Are you sure?*

"Cob promises that you will have lots of time to care for both the house and for the sheriff. He will take his meals at the cookhouse, and the house laundry will be brought to town. No one but you has been able to get a move from the sheriff. It is important work that you do. Everyone is very grateful for your efforts, and we all want them to continue."

"Pardon, *Señora* Doctor, what is this word grateful. That is bad, *Señora*?"

"No, that is good, very good. I do not do so well with your language, Juanita. I think it is like, *agradecida.* Grateful means like, *Mil gracias*. Grateful—*agradecida*."

"Ah, that is good. I not make trouble?"

"No, Juanita, you are not making any trouble. You keep doing what you have been doing. The wagon is coming in today to move the sheriff to the ranch. Cob would like if you would gather up everything and clear out the hotel rooms. This afternoon you will be back home. You and Cob, and the sheriff. And

I wish to thank you for all your work too. You saved me from many hours of caring for these men. So, thank you."

Juanita flashed a bright smile at Gwyneth, nodded, as if it was a slight bow, and rushed into the hotel.

Unsure of her next move in the matter of becoming Mrs. Cob Fleming, Gwyneth pushed it to the back of her mind and went to see Dr. Shultz. She had a strong desire to talk of hospitals and of providing medical assistance to the expected hundreds of new residents that were, or at least might, in the near future, pour into the Sombrero area.

Finding a somewhat discouraging satisfaction with the current situation in Dr. Shultz's plans for his future, she moved on for a visit with Dr. Diego Esteban. The always bright and contented Diego spoke of the future in terms much more in keeping with Gwyneth's than Dr. Shultz had.

"Aw, but to build a hospital, my dear lady. That would be something. Something perhaps too *grandioso* for a poor, *humilde* doctor such as Diego Esteban."

"It is all right to dream big though, Diego. You dream of the lovely Lupita, who seems so very far away. Can you not dream of one day having a hospital to serve all people?"

"You are unfair, Doctor. The lovely Lupita will one day choose a man. And why not Diego Esteban, who loves her with all his heart? This I can hope for. But a hospital!"

"It is all the same, my friend. Only one is sought with the heart. The other with the hands."

"And maybe with a bit of *dinero. Mucho dinero*. Who is to have this *dinero*?"

"The people. Diego. The people have the money, and they need a hospital. They will give the money."

"You trust in the people more than Diego does, my good doctor."

"Well, we will talk again of this."

"Yes. And one day we will talk of a nurse. A nurse who knows the, what you say in English, midwife, I think, the

Curandera-partera. One day, Diego would like to have such a nurse. Your nurse, Summer, I believe her name is, and a beautiful name it is, a name fit for such a beautiful young *señorita.* I saw that she was much help to you and to Dr. Shultz when the men were needing to have their lives saved. Such a nurse I would like to have one day."

"I will think on that, my friend. I will come for a visit again. Soon."

GWYNETH WENT NEXT to a land agent. Her inquiry for only a piece of town land was a bit of a disappointment to the man, since he made his living arranging the sales of farmland. But patiently, he asked the appropriate questions. Gwyneth and the agent huddled over a map of the town and area until Gwyneth finally laid her finger on a square bordering the south limits. All to the further south from there was marked as ranch land, showing no division marks, indicating that it was probably Sombrero Ranch land. She would check that out with Cob. As she left the office, she thought, *Why not now*? Continuing the silent conversation, she said to herself, *Why not, indeed.*

She was soon sitting the saddle, pointing for the ranch.

Chapter Fifteen

Moving the sheriff to the ranch went off simply, if slowly. The single concern arose when the men carrying him into the ranch house accidentally bumped his head against a door frame. Cob and the cowboys doing the carrying were appalled, fearing they may have hurt the man. Juanita saw the matter differently, as did Gwyneth. What turned the tide for the ministering women was the tight-lipped groan that escaped from the sheriff's mouth. It was the first audible sound the man had made since the shooting. And the first hope that all their work and concern might be close to returning dividends.

Juanita had told no one, not even Gwyneth, about the massages and the slight movement of fingers and facial muscles, plus, occasionally, a leg attempted to pull away from the finger scraping over the tender sole of a foot. But there had been no response to the whispering of his name into his ear.

After settling the patient comfortably in one of the spare bedrooms, Juanita went from room to room, finally arriving in the kitchen, seeing what misdeeds might have been done in her domain while she was away. She would tolerate no interference. The Sombrero Ranch big house was her house. Even Cob cleaned his feet before venturing further than the doorway. When she was satisfied with her inspection, she lit the big stove and filled the stove's reservoir with fresh water. Coffee would soon be ready and a decent meal for Cob and for Gwyneth, if she happened to stay until mealtime.

GWYNETH MANAGED to drag Cob away from the barn and get him seated at the table in the house. She laid out the map she and the land agent had studied, leaving a few markings for later discussion.

After confirming that the ranch property line was the same as the south border of the town, Gwyneth pointed at one of the markings and said, "I wish to purchase one-quarter section, one hundred sixty acres, from the ranch. Right where it's marked out. I will pay the going price."

Cob burst into rare laughter.

"My dear doctor, you have no need to purchase anything. Let me know what you want, and we'll set up a sale agreement. We can make it legal with a single dollar. We'll send the agreement down to our lawyer in Austin and make it all legal and done.

"I know your heart is settled on a hospital, but what in the world do you want with a whole quarter section? I doubt any hospital will ever need all that much land."

"It won't be just the hospital. It will one day be a residence for nurses. It will be a recovery residence for patients. It might even be a retirement home for the elderly or for those who have been injured and will never again be able to work. It may even be a space where I can keep some horses and perhaps a milk cow or two. Once we start, there's no real telling where the effort might lead us."

"All right. Consider it done. I may be a few days getting

time enough to measure and mark it all out, but I'll get it done."

"Cob Fleming. Now you listen to me. You have nothing to do. Absolutely nothing but take care of yourself. Do you remember that we had a deal? No work for you. No sitting a horse. No anything that will get in the way of your healing."

"I'll have to get down to that piece of land to measure it out and to make sure you're choosing the best we have on the Sombrero."

"You can go down in the buggy. Take a working man with you. Drive a better stake in where I just pushed a small tree branch into the sod. You'll find it easily enough. I tied a red rag to the top. To measure out the side of the claim, you can tie a rag on the buggy wheel. Have your man drive the buggy along the perimeter while you count the turns of the wheel. Measure the wheel and multiply by the turns. When you count out the correct distance, drive another stake in. You can do all the rest just on the paper. It will all be good enough until a surveyor can be brought over from where they're laying out all those farms. Simple. Even a cowboy can do that much."

That last bit she said as kind of a dig. She knew Cob was capable of many things, but sometimes he had to be reminded of that.

WHILE THEY WAITED for the surveyor, Gwyneth spent the time writing letters and talking with people. With no rail service to carry the mail, she wouldn't expect answers for a few weeks. There was talk of a rail branch line, but so far, no work crew had been seen.

Cob was beginning to show some interest in the hospital. When Gwyneth informed him that she intended to build an office and clinic with her own money to get the project started, he objected, insisting that he would be responsible for her costs if she was his wife. So, believing that time was soon, he would begin caring for her with the clinic construction.

The argument failed to bear fruit for him. It was her clinic, and her money would be used. When he finally lifted his Stetson and ran his fingers through his hair, she knew she had won. Not that she was interested in winning, she told herself. But her silent argument with herself was beginning to sound hollow, even in her own mind.

Cob had proven useful in that he knew a builder who could be depended on. The builder was American, but much of his work was in adobe, for which he had a crew of Mexicans, skilled at their trade. The only near dispute with the builder came when Gwyneth insisted on a poured concrete floor, rather than the packed earth dressed with decorated clay tiles. When the need for sanitation was explained and that blood running between the tiles would be unacceptable, the way was cleared for a start.

Gwyneth and Summer hosted a dinner for Dr. Shultz and Dr. Esteban. With large sheets of paper purchased at Abe and Helen's trading post, the four medical people became clinic designers. At the end of the second evening of placing sketches over and beside other sketches, and finally putting it all together, complete with room labels and an easy extension to the future hospital, they all sat back in their chairs and heaved a sigh of relief, satisfied that no one could have done better.

With only a slight nudge from Gwyneth, Dr. Shultz thought he might consider joining her in the venture. Diego Esteban thought it best if he would stay where he was, until, perhaps, another time. Gwyneth was sure his decision had more to do with the lovely Lupita than it had with medical services.

Chapter Sixteen

THE ARRIVAL OF THE HAT RIDERS, PUSHING TWELVE hundred rangy, trail-worn animals, came a few days later than the promised two weeks. A Sombrero rider sent out to meet them directed them to the untouched grass to the north of the ranch headquarters and almost to the town limits. Gwyneth and Summer, on horseback, exploring the particulars of their quarter section—the few gullies, and the rolling hills, a portion of the larger rise that separated the Sombrero Ranch from the town of Sombrero, plus all the semi-desert scrub and brush, the mesquite, some sugarberry and persimmon and more, that neither woman could name, as well as the upland live oak and cedar elm.

The first sign that their aloneness was about to end was the bawling of cattle. Both women raised their eyes from the land they were studying, holding their horses steady while the animals approached. Cob had dug a water hole some years before, not too far from where the hospital was to be located, taking advantage of a small stream feeding out of a cluster of rocks that edged the highest point of the sloping land. They could see the riders, directing the herd as any trail herd is directed, with a point man holding the course while riders held each side tight and controlled the wanderers. As the herd broke into plain view on the downside of the slight grade, they smelled the water. The disciplined drive broke into a free run for the water hole, leaving the riders with little to do but try to prevent an all-out stampede.

When the run began, a bunch of perhaps fifty head turned to the side, heading directly to where Gwyneth and Summer sat their mounts, half hidden in a copse of mesquite that shaded the shorter growth. With no need for discussion, they did what they had always done on their home ranches. Summer, the most adventurous, pushed her black alongside the lead steer, her black gelding matching the steer step for step, pulled her hat from her head, and whopped the thirst-driven animal across the face, all the time pushing him back into the big bunch.

Gwyneth followed along behind, swinging a quirt she carried, hanging from the saddle horn, but seldom used. Within seconds, the breakaway bunch turned, following the steer Summer had pushed. Neither woman paid the slightest attention to the frantic male voices they heard over the tumult, warning them to get away. The mini crises were soon brought under control, with the animals now focused on the source of the water.

A few animals waded right into the dugout. Most stopped at the edge and dropped their heads. Those that were crowded out went in search of a second source of water, bawling the whole time. Some lined up along the trickle of water that fed the dugout. They wouldn't get enough, but it would hold them until the others moved away.

It had been the first time Summer, to her delight, was able to work the black gelding, even if only for less than one minute. The horse had all the instincts. Cob may have begun the training process, but those instincts hadn't come from training. Once directed toward the lead animal, the gelding had needed no direction. Smiling from ear to ear and perhaps taking an unnecessary chance, Summer dropped the reins across his neck and took her hands off. The gelding stayed tight to the steer until Summer called him off.

As Gwyneth and Summer pulled away from the herd, Gwyneth jerked her head away from the cattle at the sound of a man's voice shouting, "Git yerselves away from there. Yer like ta git yerselves killt. Them there ain't no yard animals. Now git away. Consard, foolish women. Git yerselves back ta yer nitt'n an stay away from where men 'r working."

The women eased back on their mounts, smiled at each other, and ignored the shouting man. When the rider pushed himself between the driven cows and the women, they pulled up and waited. A second, younger man, was riding their way.

The first man, whapping his knee with his hat for emphasis, hollered, "Of all the consarned foolish things I ever did see. You fool women, git yerselves back ta town and away from men's work. Now git before ya git yerselves kilt."

Summer smiled at Gwyneth and said, "I believe he said that before already. Do you suppose those are the only words he knows?"

"I wouldn't know about that, Summer, perhaps if he'd settle down, we'd be able to find out. Perhaps even talk to him."

"Here comes a younger one. Looks much the same as this one but younger. Might be he's learned more words, although he's young yet. Probably needs more time to mature some."

The young rider pulled his running horse to a stop beside the older man and stared at the women. He started to smile before saying, "Father, I don't see as any harm's been done. There's probably no more need for harshness. I'm sure the girls have learned their lesson and won't butt into men's work again, will you girls?"

Summer said, "I don't know, Gwyneth. The younger one seems a bit more human, although the older one recognized us as women. Of course, the young one, calling us girls, may just have dust in his eyes. Anyway, I suppose we might just as well saunter back. If they need more help, we could come back out."

They started their mounts, but Summer stopped and turned in the saddle, looking at the younger of the two men. "You fellas do understand you're on private property, do you? The land under your horse's feet belongs to a private holder. The rest of the hillside is part of a larger ranch. I'm sure no one will care, just so's you don't plan to settle here. Just the same, you might want to ride up to the Sombrero and kind of ask permission. Just a suggestion."

The younger of the two men eased his horse closer before looking again at Summer, asking, "And what do you two have to do with the Sombrero Ranch?"

"Oh, we just kind of became friends, and then when there was some shooting, we kind of helped where we could. Nothing special, you might say."

"Shooting? What's that all about?"

"Oh, I don't have the right to speak for others. But you ride over to the ranch and ask for Cob. Nice enough fella. A bit slow on the uptake. But once he gets the drift of what's happening, he more or less understands."

"And who will I tell them sent me?"

"As far as names go, I haven't heard yours or the older man's. That's all the time assuming you go by names like most of us do. But since you asked, I'm named as Summer. My friend here is Gwyneth. The names may mean something to Cob, or they may not. You'll have to find that out for yourselves. But we have to get back to our nitt'n now, following the advice so freely given by your angry friend."

"He's not my friend. He's my father. And he's not angry. He was scared. Scared for you two. His name is Louis. Louis Fleming. I go by Tab Fleming. And I kind of think Cob will know who we are, and you as well, I'd say. We'll get along now, but I'm looking forward to meeting you both again. That's assuming you're not risking your lives doing men's work."

Summer smiled her most beautiful, teasing smile, saying, "Why, I can't imagine why we would ever wish to meet again."

With that, she whirled her mount back toward town with Gwyneth following.

Tab noticed the Sombrero brand on the black gelding and wondered.

~

LOUIS AND TAB FLEMING, father and son and part owners of the family's Hat Ranch in southern Texas, left the herd with the cowboys and spurred toward where Summer had pointed. Neither had ever been to the Sombrero Ranch, and to avoid asking anything more of Summer, they decided to follow the well-worn two-track trail leading south from town. The ranch came into view within minutes. They rode up to the cookhouse and dismounted, tying off and entering the eating place in search of coffee.

They introduced themselves to the cook and, at his invite, helped themselves to a cup and a slice of pie each that was left over from the midday meal. The cook rang the iron triangle just once, a signal to the big house that someone had come.

Cob was resting, reading a book in his own room, but Juanita knocked on the door and gave him the news.

In less than a full minute, the Fleming brothers were wrapped up in a resounding, back-slapping reunion. Cob's firm handshake was his welcome to Tab. "Didn't know you were planning on coming along, Tab. It's good to see you though. Where are the cattle?"

Before his father could get a word out, Tab said, "They're over the hill, down toward town, right where your rider told us to put them. He didn't tell us there would be a welcoming party waiting for us though. Caught us a bit by surprise and got Father a bit worked up."

Cob turned to Louis with a question on his lips. Before he could get it asked, Louis said, "Jest a couple a medl'n town women. Out pretending they're cowboys. Suppose they had their fun and all, but that's no place for them. Sent them off packing to town."

"Two women? On horseback? Did they give you any names?"

"The older of the two said she'd answer ta someth'n like Gwy or the like. I didn't rightly get it all. The young smart-mouthed one called herself Summer. Got that plain enough. You know them?"

"Yes, you might say I know them. And I'm kind of doubting that you sent them off packing. They're not the type that take kindly or willingly to being run off from anywhere. Gwy will be Gwyneth Wycome. Dr. Gwyneth Wycome. She's the woman I'm going to marry just as soon as I'm sure I ain't going to die.

"Summer is a nurse. And a good one. Smart. Good at pretty much anything she takes on to do. Ranch-raised. Rides like the wind and knows cattle and horses. Talked me out of my best yearling gelding. Gave him to her just to get shut of her. Get her away from the ranch. Afraid she'd end up controlling the whole of the Sombrero if I let her hang around too long. Already has the entire crew having fits over her, the older men wanting to protect her, and the younger ones living in hopes that one day she'll smile at them. Goodlooking woman, but dangerous. Knows how to have her way around the ranch. I wish, Tab, that you'd marry up with her and take her back south with you. Or take her, whether you marry her or not."

"Don't know as how I'm hon'n to marry up just at this time. But what's this about you marrying as soon as you know you're going to live? You need to spell that out."

"It's just a small thing. Got into a bit of a kerfuffle with some rustlers. Took a sheriff's posse after them. Got them, but the sheriff, he's over there in the house, there right now, in bed. Took a bullet in the shoulder and another laced a groove down his skull. Still unconscious. May never wake up, but we keep trying.

"You'll remember my friend Trent. We rode together for some years. Started a ranch together out in Colorado. Got himself killed on a bad horse. I remember telling you about all that. Gwyneth is Trent's widow. After she sold the ranch, she took herself off east to study medicine. So, she's now Dr. Gwyneth Wycome. One day soon, she's going to be Dr. Gwyneth Fleming.

"Took a slug myself through the shoulder. Made a mess of my upper arm. It may never fully heal. Took a second slug through the top of my lung. Not sure I would have lived if Gwyneth hadn't been there to do her magic. I have a bit of trouble breathing, but it's getting better. Just waiting for that challenge to slide into memory."

"This doctor know she's going to marry you?"

Cob laughed and again slapped his brother on the shoulder.

"Yes, big brother. She's in agreement to the plans."

Chapter Seventeen

Out of growing boredom and with little to do after checking out the construction progress of the clinic building, Gwyneth and Summer saddled up and rode out to the Hat's market herd to say good morning to the riders holding the bunch near the now nearly depleted water hole. The grass that just one week before was abundant and still growing well, even as the season wore itself away, was now gone. The trickle of water that fed the dugout would be weeks refilling the now muddy, hoof trampled depression. Cob would be sending a crew down to reshape the dugout's edges, repairing the results of thousands of hooves trampling in, through, and over it.

With the water and grass gone, the herd would have to be moved. The logical move would be to pull out for Fort Worth. But that decision would be made between Cob and his brother. As much as neither lady at times hesitated to form an opinion, they understood that the move to market was not within their jurisdiction.

Neither of the Fleming men were with the herd, so after a few polite minutes had passed, visiting with the Hat riders, they turned toward the Sombrero. They found the men taking coffee in the cookhouse. As they entered the door, Tab jumped to his feet with a pleasant *good morning*. Remembering their manners, the rest of the men, more slowly, rose also.

Cob was the first to speak. "It's good to see you, ladies, but what brings you out this morning?"

Gwyneth answered, "It's time I checked on the sheriff again and Summer insisted that we inquire of your intentions. Since the water hole is close to dried out, she's afraid we'll be called on to carry water in buckets from the town well if you plan on staying much longer."

There was no real response except for a slight clearing of the throat by Cob, along with a glance at Louis.

As the men re-took their seats, Summer chose a chair across the table from Tab. She held her tongue from approaching Cob's nephew with any abuse but smiled radiantly as she said, "And then we have to keep our horses exercised and ready. Girl never knows when she's going to be called on to turn out and help a neighbor."

All further talk was interrupted by the frantic Juanita running down the porch stairs, leaving a slamming door behind her.

"*Señor* Cob. *Señor* Cob. You must come. Rápidamente. *Señor* Cob. *Señor* Cob!"

Cob jumped from his seat with Gwyneth only a few seconds behind him. He rushed to the door, hollering, "Here, Juanita. At the cookhouse. What's happened?"

"Oh, *Señor* Cob. The *Señor* Olaf. The sheriff. He is open his eyes. He is come awake. He tries to speak. He tries to, *sentarse.* How you say, *sit* ?" You must come, *Señor* Cob. And the lady, *señora*, the doctor."

Assuming her message had gotten through, she whirled and ran back up the stairs. Cob and Gwyneth were a full minute later, with Gwyneth holding Cob back, fearing more damage to his lung if he tried to run any distance at all. He was not yet ready to do any running.

When they arrived at the bedroom the sheriff was using, Juanita was attempting to lift the man to a sitting position. Gwyneth could see immediately that she was apt to hurt her back or even hurt the sheriff. Lifting a patient from their prone position required more than brute force. Gwyneth had taught Summer most of the tricks of their business, but Summer had remained in the cookhouse when the others ran out. The doctor would have to rely on Juanita for assistance.

First, laying her hand behind the sheriff's shoulder, she advised Juanita to allow him to lie back. Then, showing Juanita how to place her hands, and then advising that she squat just a bit with slightly folded knees, she was to lift with the strength of her legs. Juanita, proving to be a good learner herself, listened carefully, and between the two women, the sheriff was soon sitting, propped up with pillows. In that position, he was able to get enough breath to speak, although he had little strength for anything more.

Pulling his eyes away from Juanita, he glanced around the room and then focused back on the woman he somehow knew was the one who had been caring for him. He was slow bringing forth his first words, looking from one face to another and then examining the room again, sorting out the thought that he was not in his own home.

Cob, impatient to face the situation, said, "You're at the ranch, Olaf. You've had a bad time of it, but the doctors did everything they could. Then you were turned over to the care of Juanita. She can tell you later all that she did at the hotel when you were there, and continued once you were brought here. You've been here about two weeks. She's been giving you great care. You've given everyone a fright, man. I don't know as we'll want you for sheriff if you're going to sleep days and weeks at a time."

The last statement was said with a big smile, hiding Cob's relief to have his old friend showing life again. The sheriff's first words were said with the same feeling, if not with the same clarity of voice.

"Don't know if I'll want to be sheriff either if folks are going to keep shooting me."

When the slight humor was allowed to pass, Gwyneth said, "You stay here, Juanita. I'll get a fresh glass of water." She expected some objection. Juanita had always seen herself as a servant of others, taking pride in her accomplishments, and would never have allowed someone else to slide into her position, even for a moment. This time, she didn't even lift her eyes, looking only at the sheriff.

Cob caught the look but said nothing.

With the downing of two glasses of cold well water, Olaf was beginning to feel better. Better enough to talk, a bit, at least. The temptations to ask questions, such as *how are you feeling?* were pushed aside when Olaf said, "Any chance of a fella getting something to eat on this ranch?"

Juanita was all set to go to the kitchen, but Summer entered the room with a plate in one hand and a bit of cutlery in the other.

"I don't imagine you're hungry, Sheriff, after all the gruel you've taken in, and not doing any work and all, but just in case, the cook put a stick of wood in the stove and came up with this bit of a concoction that he's pretty sure you'll like. It's scrambled eggs with a liberal mixture of peppers and ground beef. I tried just a little bit off a spoon. Pretty hot with spices. No doubt Juanita could do it better, but this might pass for a start."

She passed the cloth-covered plate to Juanita and stepped back. The sheriff squirmed a bit, looking for comfort, and then reached for the plate. "I figure you've been feeding me right along, Juanita, but I think I can handle this one."

Turning his eyes away from the house matron for a moment, he looked at Gwyneth. "I only saw you once briefly before, but I'm guessing you're the doctor. You need to know I'm grateful. Grateful to all of you. You for the ranch taking me in, Cob, but more than anything, grateful to this gracious lady, Juanita. I don't know what all she did, but I'm guessing it was a lot. I could sense someone touching me, time to time, moving my arms and legs, pressing her hands to my face, but couldn't make out anything in detail.

"Heard noise but couldn't form no words out of the sounds. Then a voice was speaking my own name into my ear, close up, not loud, but I heard it all right. My name, and orders that it was time to open my eyes. Try as I might, I didn't think I could ever get 'er done, but then there was warm water washing my eyes, washing away all the gathering of overnight scum and whatnot. Loosened everything up. Next thing I know, I'm looking into the eyes of my guardian angel."

With a shaky hand, the sheriff pointed his fork at the pile of eggs and did his best to drag it to his mouth. He looked both discouraged and embarrassed when the whole scoop landed on the bedding. Determined to try again, his efforts came to the same result. It wasn't really in his nature, but he had to admit defeat. By that time, Summer was entering the bedroom again, this time with a tablespoon in her hand. She diplomatically passed the spoon to Juanita and relieved the sheriff of the plate and the fork.

Juanita accepted the plate, saying, "*Mañana*. Maybe tomorrow you eat. Today, Juanita help."

The first full scoop of the spicy dish caused the sheriff's eyes to open even wider, while he stifled a cough. His grin as he was coming out of the coughing spell suggested the spices were just fine and to his liking.

Summer grinned. "I'm thinking that dish will need a name. How about *Sheriff's Texas breakfast plate*? Or perhaps *Sheriff's Surprise*."

Into the following mumbles, she suggested, "Well, I've got things to do. I'm guessing this would be a good time to leave the sheriff to Juanita's mercies."

As the small group turned to leave, the sheriff surprised

them with a comment, "Thought I saw you take one back there in the hills, Cob. But here you are standing tall and all right, so maybe I just thought that up."

Cob replied, "We'll talk later, Olaf."

Chapter Eighteen

The Sombrero pushed several hundred head of mature market beef into the Hat's herd and, after one more night on the hillside grass, lifted the entire bunch off the bedgrounds as the sun was coming up on another pleasant Texas morning. They watered the herd on another nearby dugout and then set out in earnest. Four Sombrero riders joined the Hat's bunch along with a small remuda driven down from the hills for the run to Fort Worth.

Tab had been chosen to take the bunch on the last portion of the drive. Now he rode back and forth as the herd lifted off the bedgrounds, assuring himself that there were no stragglers forted down in the scrub brush. As he was about to join what Cob had called their *walking bank account,* he swung his horse to where Gwyneth and Summer were looking on, both looking beautiful, mounted on fine horse flesh, the gelding's pampered hides glistening in the morning sun.

Including Gwyneth, but speaking directly to Summer, he said, "We'll be coming back this way to pick up Father on our way south, home to the Hat. Will I see you then?"

"Unless I somehow manage to turn invisible, I see no reason why you couldn't."

He tipped his hat and grinned. "Don't turn invisible. I kind of like you the way you are."

Summer steadfastly held her eyes away from Gwyneth and locked on the retreating riders, but she hadn't escaped Gwyneth's notice.

"Another conquered rancher. You're going to have quite a collection the way you're going."

"It's nothing I'm doing. Just foolish men is all."

As Summer turned her horse back to town, Gwyneth whispered after her, "You don't have to do anything at all, girl. Just be there. Be seen. Be yourself. That's all you need to do."

Louis stayed behind on the Sombrero. The brothers hadn't seen each other for years, and the opportunity to reconnect was too good to pass up. Plus, there was ranch business to discuss. Tab, at twenty-three years of age, tall, slim, and handsome, tough and hardened to the ways of pioneer ranching, with his sun-browned face and hands, and thoroughly trained in all things involving cattle, was perfectly able to get the herd to market.

Chapter Nineteen

SUMMER HAD BARELY ARRIVED IN SOMBRERO WHEN she received a short telegram from her family advising that they were arranging for train transport for a visit. Summer figured the travel was also to re-acquaint themselves with a bit of Texas. Her father had mentioned many times how much they enjoyed their short time there before moving on to Colorado. But even when asked, they failed to come up with a credible reason for their move.

Sombrero was some distance from where the family had been, but as her father often said, *"Texas is Texas. They're ain't no other."* All of which made Summer wonder again why they had left. But her questions had never resulted in any explanation, so she finally learned to let it go.

The travelers would be following the same route she, Cob, and Gwyneth had followed. Figuring on train schedules and allowing for mishaps along the way, she and Cob, calculating together, guessed their arrival would now be within a few days. Together, they planned out how to meet the train and how many would be arriving and needing horses to carry them the last few miles to their destination. Summer's best guess was that only her parents and, perhaps, her brother Charles would be spared from the home ranch.

"We'll send three horses and the buggy. Grad Wilsey will drive the buggy. He's still recovering from the shooting, but he can ride a buggy seat. He'll trail the horses off the back of the buggy. I'm sure he'll be able to sort your folks out from the others in town and lead them back here."

Summer was not inquiring or suggesting, she was stating a fact. "I'll ride the black."

"Surely you're not figuring on making that ride with just the one man to protect you!"

"Cob. I can't believe I heard you say that. Of course I'm going. And if there's anything Grad can't manage, I'll be sure to lend a hand."

Cob expelled a great sigh, signaling that he understood the conversation was completed. He would appeal to Gwyneth but only to make a show of his reluctance, knowing it would all be in vain. He thought of his nephew, the very competent Tab. *Tab, you've fallen head over heels, but you'd best think deeply. Life with Summer would be full of adventure and good things, but it wouldn't any way be easy.*

BEFORE FULL SUNRISE the next morning, the small entourage put the Sombrero Ranch behind them and headed south on the well-beaten two-track. Between Juanita and Wally Tibbs, the camp cook, they saw to it that there was food enough for the return trip, and more. There was also a small stash of blankets and rain gear. Leaning on her training, Summer gathered up a supply of medical items to cover anything from a cactus thorn removal to a cut or break, all the time hoping none of it would be needed or used.

Grad Wilsey, normally one of the toughest and most adventurous cowboys on the Sombrero, was fighting embarrassment at holding down the buggy seat while Summer rode the beautiful black gelding.

With one stop, when Grad figured the sun was about at its zenith from their perspective, he hauled up at a small dugout on a neighboring ranch. With care not to lose his footing or risk re-injuring himself, he led the horses down the muddy grade to the water. Summer broke out a metal, reused cookie container and a glass jar of lemonade that Juanita had prepared and wrapped in wetted paper and then in a heavy towel, hoping it would hold some of its cool until the travelers wanted it. Lunch took less than one half hour, the horses were again watered, and the southward trip continued.

Intimidated by this very attractive nurse who had been on hand all through his embarrassing medical treatment, as well as taking a hand in the procedure, Grad held to his silence until Summer, smiling, said, "Grad, I'm getting pretty tired of your constant talking. I'm hoping for a bit of quiet this afternoon."

The normally good-natured cowboy took the comment in the way it was meant, responding, "Just nothing much to say, I guess. Kind of wondering too what excuse I'm going to give your folks for me riding this here wagon seat while you set the saddle on that black."

"You leave that to me, Grad. I'll not embarrass you."

The relief on Grad's face showed on his lips and with the releasing of the furrows in his brow.

WITH ANOTHER FOUR-HOUR RUN, they turned into the whistle-stop village, heading directly to Ramone's livery barn. To her surprise, the first person she saw was Charles, her older brother.

"Charles. You're here. I'm late coming for you. Sorry about that, but I had no real way to know when you'd arrive. Where are the folks?"

"Welcome, little sister. Ramone was just laying out horseflesh for us. Father got tired of waiting. Folks are over at the café drinking coffee and telling lies. Father has them half convinced over there that the B4 is the biggest, best, most prosperous ranch in this whole grand country. Danged if he hasn't."

"Well, let's go find them."

Turning to the hostler, Charles said, "Sorry, Ramone. We'll have to do business another time."

"En otra occasion."

The greetings and the introduction of Grad took only minutes. Billy was anxious to get underway, but Summer held him back.

"It's a comfortable one-day run, Father. But if we leave now with evening coming on and tired horses in the stable, we'll end up sleeping on the ground and still taking most of tomorrow to complete the journey. We'll lay up here in the hotel for the night and get a clean start in the morning."

THE TRIP WENT as Summer had planned. The family was introduced around the Sombrero Ranch before they continued on to the town of Sombrero. With hotel rooms confirmed, they settled in for a week's stay. They set that first evening aside for visiting and renewing Summer's knowledge of things on the B4. The next few days would see the family, especially Summer's father, Billy, and Charles, riding the countryside from the uphill ranches to the flats that were being turned into farms.

Billy had a special interest in learning all he could about the irrigation projects, how to build them, and how to put them into use. Gwyneth had asked to be excused from most of those activities. She wished to concentrate on the clinic construction as well as having long private visits with Cob. They still had much to talk about.

The first morning following their arrival, Summer walked to town from the cabin she and Gwyneth were sharing. She was to meet her parents and brother and proceed toward the café for breakfast. She was walking alone, nearing the small café, when there was a loud, grating, "Well, looky here. If it ain't that pretty nurse all fitted up and rar'n to go."

Paying no attention to the people steadying in on the outburst from walkways on both sides of the road, and glancing back with a knowing grin at the two men riding with him, he continued, "Ain't she jest the pretty one though. Come ta town jest as we're back from our adventure. Jest in time fer me ta take 'er under my wing. Teach her about life, sort of. What do you say there, pretty one? Climb up here behind me here and we'll git started on yer learn'n process."

His loudmouth jabbering and staring at Summer had distracted him just enough for Charles to step off the boardwalk on the opposite side of the road unnoticed, taking a few steps and placing himself within a few feet of the man's horse. Out of the corner of his eye, the talker finally caught a glimpse of Charles and tried to spur his horse into the road and away. He was too late by a wide margin.

With a single step and a small leap, Charles had him with one hand by the leather gun belt. His other hand rose to grab the man's shirt front. With a single heave, accompanied by a shout of fear, the rider was lifted from the saddle, his feet dangling helplessly, and his arms waving frantically for something solid to grab onto. The next second, he landed on his back in the filth of the road, with a thud that knocked the air from his lungs. Even only half-conscious, he was reaching for his gun. But Charles already had it in his hand.

With a simple flip of his wrist, Charles tossed the weapon to the low roof of the ladies' wear store in front of which the incident took place. The beginnings of a crowd were gathering in front of the store. Charles brushed the man's still grasping hands aside, lifted him to his feet, and proceeded to give him a beating no man could endure for long.

Billy, somewhat larger and nearly as strong as his son, but slower moving and with much less mercy, had forced the two companions to dismount at gunpoint. Facing them, he resettled his weapon into its holster, half hoping one of the two cowering strangers would reach for their Colts. Disappointed when they didn't, he settled for grasping a handful of hair on each head. He used the grip to smash their heads together, knocking both into a sound sleep.

He was preparing to walk away, continuing toward breakfast, when a voice from behind him said, "You're pretty casual with what you leave cluttering up our streets there, mister."

Billy and Charles turned together to see the sheriff's deputy, his shiny badge offering a target for the morning sun.

"Just some trash, Deputy. Figured maybe you had someone who takes care of such as that."

"Well, mister. I figure we'll leave them for a spell. If such should happen that they fail to wake up, the blacksmith, who's strong enough to lift most things, or people, makes a few extra dollars helping out time to time. And to set your minds at ease, I'll say I saw and heard it all. Don't give the matter another thought."

Turning his eyes to Summer, he said, "Summer, seems as if you're known to these folks?"

"These are my parents and my brother. Just come down from Colorado for a visit."

"All right. Welcome, folks. And just as a suggestion, I'd advise you to keep an eye open. These boys are going to be on the prod when their hurts heal up. They'll come with guns the next time."

Summer, never having seen the bunch before, although clearly, she herself had been seen, asked, "Who are they, Deputy? They live here? I've never seen them before."

"That one your brother explained the facts of life to has a

mother here in town. Sad situation. Came to town among the first. Old man was a lunger. They were heading further west, but he gave it all up here. Knew he was dying. Built a cabin for the family, using up most of what little they had. Boy was about sixteen, seventeen then. They no sooner got the old man under the sod when Carl, that's this one's name, Carl Macon, grabbed up their only horse and most of what little his mother had in the sugar bowl and taken out for who knows where. Shows up time to time. Always has a bit of money to leave with the widow. Then takes off again. Up to no good, I'm thinking. Wild. Always talking guns. Seems to be riding with someone different each visit. Bares watching is my guess."

Turning to Billy, he asked, "You folks planning on taking up land around here?"

"Just looking around. Come to check up on our wandering little girl."

As the deputy said, "Good to meet you folks," he was thinking, *that's some little girl you got there.*

DURING BREAKFAST and extending into the morning's visit, Summer kept looking at her father and wondering, wondering if the deputy had accidentally stumbled on a truth she had been excluded from. And that put her thinking about Abe and Helen, a couple she had only met briefly, but whose past, wandering, quick decisions, trying new things, had been explained by Gwyneth. Was there a pattern here that somehow explained her father's many questions about farming and irrigation?

Perhaps it was the way with some travelers, or movers, as some called them—move and then move on again, never quite settled.

Chapter Twenty

Gwyneth and Dr. Shultz were sitting out the evening under the shade of an ocotillo shelter beside the doctor's house. Ursula Shultz sat with them, refilling the coffee cups and bringing another plate of muffins. She had a solid interest in the conversation, although she avoided making comments when the talk dipped into medical matters.

Gabriel Shultz said, "I like your ideas, Gwyneth. And your explanation of the beginnings of the two hospitals you worked with in Chicago is a common story across the land, and further, if we were to take in the old countries.

"Churches and religious institutions have been the thrust behind many schools and hospitals. Perhaps most schools and hospitals, for that matter. Beyond that are the hospitals that have begun just as you're beginning. A clinic and then a bigger clinic, leading to growth upon growth as the community grew. It's not that far to jump, moving from a simple doctor's office to a two- or three-doctor clinic, or even larger, growing piece by piece. And there is no doubt that this area is going to grow. I haven't been out into the flatlands to take a look for ages past, but from what I hear, there's no stopping it now. With that and the new services opening stores in town to support the farmers, the town will grow too."

Ursula spoke for the first time. "And the money for making this clinic will come from where? Schatzi."

Gwyneth answered the question before Gabriel had the chance.

"That is always the question, isn't it, Ursula. What I am proposing is that I will build the clinic and furnish my portion of it. I have the money I will need from selling my clinic up in Colorado. In fact, the building is nearing completion. Two or three more weeks should be enough. And I hope the furniture I ordered from Chicago will be here by that time. Gabriel would only have to move his furniture from the rooms he's renting now and set up his operation in the new facility. Gabriel will have no expenses that he doesn't already have. We will have two rooms each. There will also be a recovery room with space for six beds. We designed the building so it will be easy to add onto when there's need."

The evening wound down with more coffee and many questions, ending with the promise from Gabriel Shultz that he and Ursula would go to the building site for a good look the next day.

The entire, available Wilmore family, Billy, the father, Gladys, the mother, Charles, and Summer, who her father had lovingly renamed Sissy since her girlhood, together rode out to examine, for the third time, the vast, virtually untouched semi-arid land available for purchase and ready for the plow. The ride included another, more careful and detailed explanation of the irrigation processes being built and used.

Summer said nothing until they were seated in the café over dinner that evening. Hoping she had chosen just the right time, she hesitated once and then proceeded with, "Father, what's this all about? Are you seriously considering giving up on the B4?"

"You may have to humor an old man for a bit my dear Sissy. Whatever we do won't be just my decision. We're a family enterprise, and a family enterprise we will remain. At least for those who haven't gone off in search of their own honey pot at the end of the rainbow.

"Your sister is married and settled onto the B/C ranch, and a good match she seems to have made for herself. And then my very ambitious Sissy has pulled away from the tribe and gone her own direction. And good on you for doing it. There's a couple of other girls moping around like birds with a beak full of dry grass, wondering where to build a nest in a land with no trees. And another, yet too young to notice.

"The boys are great cattlemen with coin in their pockets and nowhere to spend it. They have their eyes out for likely mates with none in sight. I'm expecting one of them to build a tower one of these days, like a pirate climbing the ship's rigging, looking from horizon to horizon and seeing the promise of land nowhere.

"Aw, 'tis a lovely land we took as our own, my Sissy, but 'tis a lonely land as well. And to admit to it fully, a little on the frigid side, time to time. But no, we've made no decision, nor will we until we know the whole of it. You've naught to wonder about till the time comes. And be sure, we'll not interfere with your medical path. I'm hearing good reports from Dr. Shultz as well as from Dr. Wycome, whom we are delighted to see doing so well for herself."

"You've been snooping again, have you, Father? Well then, in that case, I'll do a bit of it myself, starting with hearing your explanation for why you left Texas in the first place."

Billy hummed and hawed and fiddled with his knife and fork until Gladys said, "There's no reason for her not knowing, my dear. And as far as that goes, here sits Charles, our eldest, who never has asked the reason, but who I'm sure remembers the event, in part, at least."

"Right ye are, me love. Well, here's the whole truth of it. Spoken from adult to adult. We were enjoying a good life on a lovely piece of land a short bit to the south from here. But a couple of neighbors weren't so content. On the surveyed edge of our claim, which was legally registered, as well as bought and paid for, with no debts to strangle us, there existed a lovely bubbling spring, fed from a crack in the stone hillside and running clear in a winding three-foot-wide channel across our claim. The water was ours by right and possession, but we had no intention or need to hold it for ourselves, nor could we if we had wanted to. There was a good and sufficient flow of water after it left our land, water that was free for the using by the next man.

"Unfortunately, 'tis in the nature of mankind to be, at times, fools. And such did two neighboring cattlemen prove to be. They somehow found a way to justify getting themselves into a great, foolish brawl over what was already ours. Denying the law of the land and claiming water was open to all, and our holdings as well, and with me having considerable skill with weapons but no desire to prove it against another of God's creatures, we made the two of them an offer, to be made fast by the first to speak up and drop the coin into my hand. Figuring 'tis a big land, with opportunity on every hand, we thought it better to not enter into what was surely to prove to be a bitter and forlorn squabble over water, with no winner at the end.

"With just a bit of persuasion, meaning I was forced to demonstrate the foolishness of the careless use of that wonderful tool Mr. Colt put into our hands, both neighbors had an epiphany of sorts, you might say."

"Oh, cut the foolish wandering in your talk, my dear. Summer, Charles, what your father is trying to not have to say is that within a very contracted period of time, mere seconds I'd say, the cattlemen and a few from the town, were shown that an

Irishman can do more than fill the air with verbiage. When challenged, is what I mean to say."

Charles looked at his father with new eyes. "Father, are you a fast draw artist in disguise?"

"No. No, nothing like that. But when challenged, a man with responsibilities must care for what is his. Nothing more."

Summer shook her head, saying, "You are the most exasperating pair, you and mother. You're trying to say you survived a gunfight in the town's street and then decided to sell out and leave. Did you leave dead men behind you?"

"No. No. Nothing like that either. Oh, would be the truth to admit they may have been laid up for some time, but dead, no. And by then we had already decided to pull stakes."

Charles stood, placing his cloth napkin on the table. "Summer, you try to figure all of that. I'm weary of imprecise talk, doubting we will ever be able to follow the tale to the bottom of it. For me, I'm going to take a walk around, hoping not to hear another Irish fable this day."

WITH CONSIDERABLE ENTHUSIASM, Dr. Shultz informed Gwyneth that he and his Ursula had decided her invitation to build a clinical business together was too good an opportunity to pass by. And with the services of nurses such as Summer being included in the deal, his enthusiasm increased even more.

Gwyneth smiled and shook his hand, promising to talk early and often as the building was being completed.

Privately, Gwyneth speculated that the good German doctor, as credible as he was in the profession, would be unable to think as big or creatively as it would take to see an actual hospital in their future. That didn't bother her, as moving from a multi-personnel clinic to a hospital required considerable population growth that, although currently promising, was still not a sure thing.

Chapter Twenty-One

Riding in orderly fashion, like soldiers out of uniform, sitting their saddles, but more relaxed and somewhat slouched than true military men would be, the returning Hat and Sombrero riders were led along the town's main street.

Gwyneth and Summer happened to be stepping out of the café after dining with Summer's family as the men drew into view. Tab immediately spotted Summer. Pulling to the side and turning to his men, he said, "You fellas know the way from here. You'll remember that we all agreed, one drink. No more. Then make your way out to the ranch. I'll be along."

Some jokester in the group hollered, "You sure you're safe enough, boss. Looks kind of like dangerous ground to me. Fella could find himself tangled up in a situation he can't get out of. Could be I should lie aside within hollering distance just in case of need."

"Get on with you and no more talk."

"If you say so, boss. But remember, I offered."

A wave of Tab's arm ended the guffaws and brought the road back to its former silence.

~

At the news that the two women were intending on riding out to the ranch that evening, Tab suggested that they should ride along with him. For companionship as well as for safety.

Summer put on her brightest smile before saying, "For whose safety, yours or mine and Gwyneth's?"

Tab had met and known more than just a few girls before his trip to Sombrero, but perhaps none quite so free with the quip. The first few times he was the target of Summer's wit, he had been a little shocked. But the more time he spent in her presence, the more relaxed he was about it.

They agreed to ride together and were about to step off the boardwalk to retrieve their horses from the livery when Dr. Diego Esteban rounded the corner with a serious look on his face. He brightened immediately at the sight of Gwyneth. He had to pause before speaking to catch his breath.

"Ah, my most dear Dr. Gwyneth. How good it is to see you. I have hurried this way, hoping to find you. I would talk with you if you could find the time to be free."

Gwyneth turned to Summer. "You go ahead. Be careful what you step into. And tell Cob I can't make it this evening but I'll see him tomorrow for sure."

"We'll miss your company," grinned Tab.

"Yes, I'm sure you will."

Gwyneth turned back to Diego. "Diego, my friend. You have been running. Is it coffee and talk you wish, or is it something back at the office?"

"Por favor, Doctor. I would have you come to the office if you have time. The lovely Lupita, she is, how you say, hurt? She no want me to look. She say, '*Me da mucha pena.*' Embarrassed. But she is suffer much pain."

"Let us walk quickly then, Diego."

~

AT THE LITTLE CLINIC, Gwyneth hurried past Diego, indicating that he should remain in the front room. She entered the little clinic's examination room and closed the door. Lupita was lying on the wheeled stretcher with another woman standing over her.

"Hello, Lupita. My name is Gwyneth. I am a doctor friend of Diego's."

The other woman, evidently fluent in both languages, rattled off Gwyneth's statement in Spanish. Lupita answered in a weak voice, "I see you in *cafecito*. Diego, he says you are a good doctor."

Again, this time, going the other direction, the words were repeated through Lupita's friend.

"Tell me what happened, Lupita, and where are you hurt."

Lupita understood enough to ignore her friend's verbal interruption. With pain-filled eyes locked firmly on Gwyneth's, she held her hand near the top of her right leg without actually touching it, then dragged in through the air to near her waist.

"Is here. Much grease from stove. It come on me. Much burn."

Gwyneth drew back the blanket that covered Lupita and reached for the hem of her greased, stained dress. She lifted the garment and a simple layer beneath, which acted as a petticoat. She then lifted the chemise, which lay next to her skin, covering the pantalettes. All of these layers were badly stained by the yellowish grease. The grease-stained pantalettes were sticking to the skin, as if they were pasted onto the burn. Removing them would be a delicate and pain-inducing operation.

Even with her doctor being a woman, Lupita cringed in modesty at every step as her skin was being bared to view. When Gwyneth took a pair of scissors and began cutting the pantalettes so the final layer of underwear could be removed, Lupita grabbed the cloth, attempting to hold the last barrier to her nakedness in place. Gwyneth tried not to show her frustration at the wasted time, with medical treatment and modesty being in opposition to each other.

Where the grease had soaked onto the skin, there was terrible evidence of scalding. She could hardly imagine what it would look like if the first heat of the grease hadn't been absorbed by the layers of clothing. Gwyneth, anxious to assess the extent of the damage so she could begin treatment, gently pushed Lupita's hand aside.

"Lupita. I understand, but these must come off. You are badly burned. We must do something quickly, and I can't work without the pantalettes coming off. No one else will be here. I have told Diego to stay in the other room."

This time, a two-way exchange of rapidly spoken Spanish ended with Lupita lifting her hands to her face. Gwyneth realized she had begun crying, but she ignored the patient's humility in favor of the required treatment.

Gwyneth finished cutting away the stained cloth and studied the burned area. The surface of the entire area had taken on an intense redness along with fluid-filled blisters. The surrounding area was shiny, with wet-appearing skin as if it were weeping fluid. Although Lupita had been stoic throughout the situation, Gwyneth knew she was suffering considerable pain with periodic sharp intensity.

Speaking to Lupita's friend, she asked, "How did this happen?"

"Lupita, she tell me when she turned from her stove, the handle of a hot pan caught on the strings of her apron. She turned back to catch the pan before it fall. Too late, she reached for the handle, but the grease, it pour on her."

Gwyneth leaned back, studying the wound. Knowing Lupita would not be healing quickly, nor would she be caring for her little *Cafecito,* she decided all the clothing must be removed. She explained to the other woman, who she had found out was called Anna. Lupita had about given up on the protection of her modesty. The overwhelming pain was pushing all else aside. Removing the clothing was a struggle, but Lupita finally lay naked on the stretcher, covered with a warm bed sheet and a blanket, with only the burned area exposed.

Gwyneth mixed some cold well water into a small pot of hot water from the stove's reservoir until it was just slightly above skin temperature. She had instructed Anna to have a good wash and, with the warmed water, to clean all the area around the burn, readying it for treatment. With that done, Gwyneth soaked a cloth in a mixture of warm water and mild carbolic acid, gently laying the warm, wet cloth over the wound.

When all was in readiness, the doctor mixed a few items Diego had on hand—all the time wishing she had access to her own supply of medications—making a mild, light poultice. She left the poultice in place for a few minutes before removing it and making a new one on another clean cloth. Between poultices, she cleaned the area again with a disinfectant, being careful not to burst any of the blisters that had formed, before very gently wiping it with an olive oil mixture and reapplying the poultice. Except for some pain relief, she had done what could be done. She would leave it that way until morning.

Anna removed Lupita's clothing from the room while Gwyneth smiled and said, "You are a very brave young lady, Lupita. You are going to have to lie down for a few days. No work in the *cafecito*. There is a bed in the back room. Anna and I will help you walk there. I will leave you with Anna. If she needs me, she can come to my cabin. I will return in the morning. You are going to be fine. Everything will heal and be just like before. Maybe just a bit different in color. But no one is going to see that, yes?" Smiling at the doubting woman, she said, "You lie still and relax, but don't scratch the wound or rub your other leg against it."

Anna was gone with the clothing for only seconds. She had heard Gwyneth's instructions and repeated them for Lupita.

For the first time since arriving, the injured lady returned a small smile.

"I am going to give you a very small amount of painkiller. I will leave a bit more for Anna to give you later. But after that, there will be no more until morning."

Chapter Twenty-Two

The following morning, when Summer emerged from her sleeping quarters in the rented cabin, Gwyneth was sorting out items from one of the medical supply trunks.

"What's happening, Gwyneth?"

"What's happening is I have a job for you today. Probably at least tomorrow too. Could be three or four days. A young Mexican lady managed to splash a pan of hot cooking grease on herself. I treated it last evening as best I could. These items I brought along from Pueblo will help. I want you to sit with the lady today and manage the wound. Do you think you can spare the time from Tab to do that?"

"If you promise not to tell him where I am."

"Do you think he'll come to town looking for you?"

"Actually, no. They're talking fall roundup out at the ranch. I expect they're all pretty busy. Cob has turned it all over to Tab so he can sit aside and 'boss from a distance,' is the way he put it. He's expecting you out there today too."

"All right, let's get some breakfast and I'll walk you over to Diego's clinic."

~

Gwyneth found the Sombrero Ranch in a turmoil of activity. Louis and Tab had decided to stay for the roundup, throwing the Hat riders in with the Sombrero crew. Louis had ridden to the telegraph office, sending a wire to the Hat. *All okay here. Stop. Good market. Stop. Staying for roundup. Stop. Start Hat roundup.*

At the ranch, the loose remuda had been brought down from their fenced horse trap and run into the big corral, where one by one, the animals would be checked for health and injuries and have their feet trimmed and re-shod. Two of the best riders would work their way through the herd, taking each animal out for a run to work out the bad habits gained during their months of freedom. On occasion, these rides turned into a spectator sport as the animal only reluctantly submitted to the rider's demands.

The cook and Juanita, working together, built a long list of supplies needed for the weeks in the hills, chasing cattle. Abe had stocked his store to the limit, knowing the ranches would all be in for similar orders. He would fill the orders, load his wagon, and deliver the purchases to each ranch, enjoying that short time away from the demands of the store.

Cob and Gwyneth were sitting in the shade, watching the activity. "Bring back memories, Gwyneth?"

"Yes, of course. But you will surely remember that we had no hills such as these you live in. Our roundups weren't truly roundups. The cattle never got far from home."

"Any regrets?"

"Setting memories of Trent aside, not really. I have come to believe that all of life is made of choices. Where possible, we choose by our priorities. What do we want most? Sometimes what we want most is within reach, but often it's not. As much as I loved Colorado and the ranch, I never for a single day forgot my wish to study medicine. Of course, I realized that wish, finally, but oh, my, at what a price."

Knowing exactly what this woman he loved was referring to,

but also knowing there were no words that would do anything but clutter the beautiful morning with sadness, he held his thoughts to himself, kicking himself for mentioning regrets.

Allowing the emotions in the air to settle out, Cob said, "I agreed to not push you unnecessarily, Gwyneth, but help me understand what's now standing in the way of our marriage. Your clinic is nearing completion. The other town doctors are seeing you as a friend, not a competitive foe. I have had a close call with eternity, but thanks to your skills and the blessings of God, I'm doing fine. I have reconciled to the truth that I will never again have robust good health, and that's all right. The ranch is established enough that it doesn't need me on the long rides or at the branding fire. Why, I could almost call myself a gentleman rancher." He smiled at the thought.

"I have been giving the matter a lot of thought, Cob, and you're correct. The last piece of the puzzle I was waiting to put into place was having Dr. Shultz join me. And of course there's Summer. When we left Pueblo, I had no idea she was going to follow. But I'm happy she's here. While the clinic remains small, she's the key to my and Gabriel Shultz's success.

"Now tell me the truth, Cob. Do you still feel as strongly on the matter as you thought you would earlier on?"

"Gwyneth, my love and longing for you has only grown stronger. And while I was prepared to give you time, like you asked when I came to you in Pueblo, I'm starting to feel like we're wasting time. Some days, my mind is so cluttered with longing I can hardly hold my end up here at the ranch. I'm afraid I've been of little value the past while. If you're concerned about me having regrets over the loss of a bachelor's freedoms or some such, you can set that aside. I will have no regrets. Only hopes for the future. It may take me a day or two to get through my thick noggin that I can no longer wander off without informing another person, but I'm actually looking forward to that. To being a couple. Available for, and responsible to, each other. No, there is nothing from my end preventing our marriage."

"Perhaps I've been overthinking it, Cob. It now shocks me to hear of kids simply getting married, believing the future will work itself out. I guess that's what Trent and I did in that little Kansas town. We had little enough to start out with and no positive idea of even where we were heading when we set out. West is a direction. If it's applied to the land, it's a mighty big target. And yet. Yes, and yet.

"So here we are. Please give me a day or two. I'll come back with a date for your approval. I'll be wanting to talk with Summer's family. They'd be disappointed if they weren't here for the occasion. I'll include the end of roundup in my calculations too. And of course, there's Abe and Helen. It wouldn't do to forget them."

"If Tab and Summer had their way—"

"It might be best if we were to let that one go. I know they could throw a wrench into our timing, but I'm trusting that one or the other of them will keep a level head."

As they were resting, easing away from the topics of marriage and the past, Juanita came from the front door of the big house carrying a package. She stepped into the buggy that had been sitting behind a harnessed horse while the two were talking. Gwyneth had somehow missed seeing it. With the skill of an experienced driver, the house matron turned the rig in the narrow space available and drove from the yard. She passed under the big log gate with *Sombrero Ranch* chiseled into it and headed north on the two-track leading to town.

Gwyneth watched, uncaring, and then casually asked, "Is Juanita doing some of her own shopping now?"

"What Juanita is doing, my dear, is feeding the sheriff and managing his house. She only reluctantly allowed him to return to town and has been fussing ever since."

"Is there more to it, do you think?"

"What I think don't really matter. I'm supposing we'll somehow figure it out or someone will tell us."

"I had best get back to town. Diego Esteban's lady friend took a very bad grease burn last evening. I did what I could. Summer is watching over her today, but I'm feeling that I should check on her. She won't let Diego anywhere near her. I almost had to tie her up before she finally allowed me to remove her multiple layers of grease-stained clothing. And you can bet no male doctor is going to treat her. I understand modesty, but in matters of, perhaps, life and death, depending on blood loss, infection, and a host of other possible troubles, I'd let modesty fly away if I could get the help I need."

"Many of the Mexican women would too, depending on class and teaching. But the middle-and upper-class women hold to virtue with a death grip. Until they're married, that is. From then on, they seem quite eager to follow the Lord's advice to multiply and fill the earth."

Thinking that no more needed saying on that subject, Gwyneth stood and walked to her horse. "I'll see you tomorrow. At the risk of being a nagging wife that isn't a wife yet, I'll remind you again..."

Grinning, Cob broke into her unneeded warning. "Yes, dear. I'll remember."

She smiled over the saddle of her horse before she swung aboard. A slight wave sealed the parting.

GWYNETH RODE DIRECTLY to Diego's medical clinic. She heard voices coming from the treatment room. Gently pushing the door open just enough to peek in, she saw Diego wrapping a bandage on a Mexican man's left arm. Thinking there would be no harm to her intrusion, she knocked on the door and waited. It was only a moment before Diego opened the door. At the sight of her, he expounded, with some flair, "Welcome, my dear doctor friend. If you have come for the Lupita, she is in the other room, as you advised her to stay."

Gwyneth was always amused by the twisting of tenses and scrambled word usage when people were using their second language. She was well aware that she did the same herself.

"Thank you, Diego. I'll go in. Have you seen her?"

"Oh, no. Lupita, she would think that a great shame. I suggested to her that if we were to marry, the shame would go away."

"And what was the result of that suggestion, Diego?"

"A wave of the hand is difficult to tell about, my dear doctor. But that was the answer."

"Perhaps it wasn't a good time to make that suggestion."

"Ah, again, Doctor, you are correct. Still, when the heart is in love, what is one to do?"

Gwyneth smiled and pushed past the lovelorn doctor. In the small anteroom, she was pleased to see Lupita sitting on a stuffed chair, in a somewhat slouched fashion, favoring her scalded side, and with her leg stretched before her. She appeared to be relaxed and pain-free. Summer sat beside her on a cheap wooden ladder-back chair. Their greetings were with smiles, rather than words. Without taking a break in their actions, Summer reached into a paper bag and lifted out another colorful garment. Lupita placed the one she had been holding on top of a third garment she had obviously looked at before. Lupita stared at the dress with wonder, as if she had never thought of owning such an item. Summer gave her a few moments to enjoy the piece, then held up the bag and bid Lupita to glance inside.

"That's the last of it, Lupita."

Lupita didn't understand at first, but suddenly, along with her face blossoming beautifully in a faint red, she quickly closed the bag and held it to her breast. That she was both pleased and mortally embarrassed was obvious, but the source of the embarrassment was to stay hidden in the bag.

"What's this all about, Summer?"

"Just a bit of girl shopping. Nothing more."

"And how did that come about?"

"Well, her other clothes were ruined between the grease and your scissors. A girl has to have something to wear. I found a bit of change lying on the table here, and I happened to know where the dress shop was, and Anna was here to stand in, so..."

Thinking that in Lupita's culture, to be middle or upper class may not necessarily mean wealth, Gwyneth said, "It looks as if your taste in clothing suits her. Am I to assume the remainder of what's in the bag are what you call unmentionables?"

"Perhaps."

"Changing to the purpose of our being here, how is the burned area?"

Summer reached for the clothing and started replacing it in the bag. "The doctor wants to see your burn, Lupita. Perhaps you should return to the bed."

When Lupita struggled to stand, Gwyneth reached for her hand, just to steady her, not to lift. Back on the bed, Gwyneth lifted the covering garment that Anna had probably brought from Lupita's home. She gently lifted the covering cloth and bent close. With a nod and a private *hmm*, she moistened a swab of cotton and very gently wiped the area. She covered it again and pulled the garment into place.

"If you will promise to be good, Lupita, and stay lying down, and don't get the injury dirty, there is no reason you can't go home. Either Summer or I will come to see you tomorrow."

"Okay, I go."

"You get dressed. Summer and I will walk you home."

As they were leaving, walking very slowly and carefully, with Lupita glancing down every few seconds as if to sneak another peek at the dress Summer had chosen for her, Diego was standing in the back door watching every move.

Chapter Twenty-Three

GWYNETH FELT SOMEWHAT GUILTY FOR MAKING IT appear as if she was delaying the marriage. And she was. But it was for reasons she fully understood, and hoped Cob was able to understand also. She had somehow found a way to justify her impetuous marriage to Trent. They were young. They were hopelessly in love. She was alone on a wild frontier. Marriage to a good man would add a much-needed sense of security to her life. Everyone else seemed to be married by her age.

But now, after years of widowhood, she was no longer fascinated by the mysteries of marriage. And above all, she had worked very hard to become a qualified doctor. She wasn't about to throw that away. So, there were things to do and matters to think about. Serious matters.

Gwyneth had worked through her list of concerns, reducing it to one major issue. The smaller things were either already dealt with or could be dealt with simply, as time went along. That one major issue facing her and Cob this day was where they would live. It was important that she be within easy range of the clinic. The ranch wasn't a long ride from town, but it might be too long when life-and-death medical services were required.

Three days had gone by since she last saw Cob. It was time to make a decision or two. Saddling her horse, she rode once more to the clinic project and then on to the ranch. On her way, she was startled to see three horsemen sitting a short way off the trail, staring at her every move. She held her animal to a steady pace but also kept an eye on the strangers. Remembering what Summer had said about the men who had abused her in town, she was sure these were the same ones.

She was too far away to see more than their general appearance, but she was nervous of them. She was also thankful that it wasn't Summer who was riding alone. The men may have lost whatever self-control they still possessed if it was the beautiful young nurse who had so tempted them before. Touching the outline of her handgun through the cloth of her skirt, she continued on, hoping the men would stay where they were.

Feeling a bit of the joy of wedding planning escape her mind, Gwyneth told herself it was too beautiful a day to let it be spoiled by such as three unlawful men. She would continue to enjoy the morning, the many birds that fluttered around the scrub brush, the few cattle she could see on a distant hill, and life itself.

Gwyneth's first question for Cob was, "Did you hire some new riders for the roundup? I saw three men sitting idle on the way here. Off to the west a quarter mile or so, where that sheltering rock marks the dip in the trail. Two were riding paints. The third a sorrel. Rough dressed fellas, as if they'd been sleeping in their clothes."

"That doesn't sound like any of our men. But it does sound a bit like the ones that confronted Summer in town."

"I had the same thought."

Cob hollered for the wrangler, who was the only man within sight. "Few strange men down by that dip in the trail. Round up those Wilmore fellas, Billy and Charles. Suggest they might want to check it out."

Gwyneth was surprised at the mention of the Wilmores.

"They've offered to work the roundup with us. Said they were going to hang around a while anyway. Might just as well be working. Get them away from the women's nattering in town. Those were their words, not mine. With them and the Hat crew, they'll get near as much work done as I ever did myself."

Gwyneth laughed at his oversimplification of the situation and the exaggeration of his own abilities. Cob joined her laughter, knowing they had not eased up on their seriousness near enough, and hardly ever laughed together. They would have to work on that.

Together, Cob and Gwyneth walked to the cookhouse. Gwyneth took a seat on the roof-sheltered porch while Cob went in for coffee for the two of them. When they were settled comfortably with the cups balanced on their knees, Cob asked, "So what have you got for me?"

"I have a serious suggestion, but it somewhat depends on what's happening here on the ranch. I really don't think Summer has much interest in following Tab south to the Hat, but there is no doubting their interest in one another. What are Tab's intentions?"

"We've been talking, Tab, Louis, and myself. There's more family down on the Hat. Tab isn't needed so far as ranch management goes. His mother might have something to say about his remaining here, but he doesn't seem to be concerned about that. We've been talking about him staying to manage the Sombrero under my guidance. Might solve a couple of problems and maybe create one of its own. My interest is the ranch, and I'd be happy to have Tab step in. He's a good man and a good cowman. What he and Summer do is entirely up to them."

"Then here's my suggestion, assuming that's how it works out in the end. You turn the ranch management and the big house over to Tab. We build a new house for the two of us on the clinic property. You would be close to the ranch trail with only a half-hour ride any time you decided to come up here, and

I have only a few minutes walk to the clinic. How does that sound to you?"

"Sounds like a situation that would put Tab's mind at ease about me being underfoot all the time. Yes, I'm happy with that suggestion."

"All right. I have to get back to town. You settle with Tab. I'm agreeable to almost any marriage date that suits activities on the ranch, so I'll leave that with you."

"You hold up just a bit. I'll find someone to ride down with you. Until we know who those riders are, we'll be very careful."

Chapter Twenty-Four

Two days later, after Gwyneth had cared for the matters in town, including looking in on Lupita. With nothing more calling her name, she rode again to the Sombrero. Filling two coffee mugs under the spout of the large, cookhouse, never-empty pot, Cob again joined his soon-to-be wife on the veranda. Gwyneth had left the naming of dates in Cob's hands. Now he had sorted out all the possibilities with Tab and made a decision.

"One week from tomorrow, Gwyneth. Tab and I came to an agreement. He'll stay on and run the roundup. I'll not work the roundup at all, just watch from the sidelines. And there's a very good chance he'll stay on for the long haul. We still have things to talk about on that.

"We'll marry one week from tomorrow. We'll stay in the big house until our new home is ready. We'll get married here on the ranch. One week from tomorrow, on a Sunday. That frees up Abe and Helen and anyone else who wishes to join in. Being on a Sunday, the wedding won't cost them any business income.

"The horses for the roundup should be worked out, and the chuck wagon readied by that time. Monday morning, after the wedding, all being well, the crew will set out. The place will be pretty empty for a couple of weeks, but that suits the situation. How does all that sound to you?"

"It sounds just fine. The guests will have to be fed. I'll talk with Juanita about that."

Chuckling through his smile, Cob said, "You leave Juanita alone. She already has it all worked out. She's been thinking on it since you first got here, and perhaps even before. She's a force when she locks her mind on something. She'll have more Mexican women out here than you could ever believe. No one will go hungry, I can assure you of that. And there will be nothing at all for you to do. Just look your normal, beautiful self and smile at everyone."

Gwyneth grinned at Cob's enthusiasm, trusting that it was not misplaced. Looking for a bit more clarification, she said, "My guess is that leaving the food to Juanita means the Mexican flavor will be prevalent. And the gathering, or celebration, if you choose to call it that, will have a Mexican slant as well. I've heard of their fiestas, but I've never seen one or been involved. But my understanding is that a fiesta is more or less open to all. Will that be the situation here?"

"Yes. And there's no avoiding it. You are, after all, my dear, marrying the don of what the district knows simply as *The Ranch*. Half our crew is Mexican. We speak almost as much Spanish out here as we do English. We won't quite have a fandango. Simply a fiesta. It will be loud, happy, and fun. With food that never runs out. Music and dancing until folks come near to dropping where they stand. Even if you're just watching from the sidelines, you'll love it."

Cob, in his enthusiasm, came very near to saying the fiesta would be something to tell their grandchildren about, but he shut the thought off before it escaped his mouth. The fact that Trent and Gwyneth had failed to produce a child was a deep hurt for Gwyneth. And now that neither Gwyneth nor he himself were young anymore meant the possibilities of children were greatly reduced. It was a good subject to avoid.

Gwyneth sorted out everything in her mind before saying, “Then it sounds as if I’m not needed. So, how would it be if I go to town and arrange for the pickup of the clinic fixings? I ordered it all from Chicago and I got a wire yesterday saying it was at the depot waiting pickup.”

“You ask at the livery in town. Tell them you have a job for Antonio. He goes by Tony when he’s dealing with us Whites. Runs a one-man freight outfit. Honest and reliable. Put him on the job. He’ll treat you right.”

Gwyneth kept her eyes open all the way to town. The trio of riders hadn’t been seen again. But there was no telling when they might pop out of the brush. Billy and Charles had searched the area, finding tracks enough but nothing more.

Chapter Twenty-Five

Between the upcoming wedding and the roundup, the ranch yard was abuzz with activity. Mexican carpenters had been brought in to put down a floor for dancing. A large ocotillo structure was put up to provide shade and shelter. The tables and the few chairs available would be sheltered in its shadow. When the chairs ran out, the women, Mexican and American both, would stand, something they were used to, not considering it an imposition. The men, as would cowboys everywhere, would simply take their plate, find a spot beside their mates, and settle comfortably to the ground, or squat on their heels.

Abe arrived with an overloaded wagon of fixings for the meal. A beef and two goats were slaughtered and hung in the springhouse, where they could be kept cool while they aged. A neighbor would supply several dozen chickens from the large flock he raised for sale. It would be his eggs on the table as well. Where Juanita managed to find some of the other items would remain a mystery.

A large selection of clay pots would ring the dance floor. The dance would go on well after the sun had shone its last for the day. As darkness fell, fires would be lit in the pots to supply enough light for dancing. Hanging lanterns would grace the ocotillo shelter. As long as the dance lasted, so long would the food keep rolling out of the kitchen.

And all the while, the blacksmiths were nailing shoes onto trimmed hooves, and cowboys were competing to see how many horses they could settle out of the rough string brought in from the grass. Wagon wheels were being greased, the chuck wagon and the hoodlum wagon were both readied for the loads the men would throw in after their last night in the bunkhouse.

Trinity Castillo, ranch foreman, along with Tab and Cob, had their heads together for hours, it seemed, planning the pattern of the roundup, naming off the most trusted men as leaders for the various groups of men that would take on a specific area. When Moses Boone, the only black rider on the Sombrero, was named as leader, Tab raised his eyebrows. Cob took in the meaning and said, "Tab, you've seen Moses around here, but you haven't ridden with him. There isn't a man on this ranch, White or Mex that wouldn't follow Moses. Hardly ever hear a word out of him, but what he says bears listening to."

Wally Tibbs, ranch cook, would be taking out the chuck wagon with Tiny Capstan, a sixteen-year-old from town driving the hoodlum wagon and foraging for firewood, and doing whatever else Tibbs told him to do. Wally insisted on having Sofia Gonzalez ride along as cook's helper. She was a great cook in her own right, and a strong and determined widow of three grown boys, and no one to trifle with. Any rider who misunderstood that would suffer the consequences. She had struck a rider so hard with a piece of firewood a couple of years before that he missed the remainder of the roundup. Cob had fired him as soon as they were back at the ranch.

~

In town, the clinic now had the roof on. A telegraph wire had confirmed that the doors and windows had been shipped and would be at the depot at the flag stop station in a few days. Antonio had gone for the clinic fixings. All in all, the clinic opening was something Gwyneth could almost taste. And as she waited and fussed, she was sketching out a house for Cob and herself. The one decision she had made without discussion with Cob was her name. Legally, she would change her name to Fleming, but she would retain her present name and continue being known as Dr. Wycome, as she always had.

Chapter Twenty-Six

Summer had stayed later with Lupita than either had intended. The two young women had found they enjoyed each other and their time together, beyond the medical necessities, which were growing less troubling each day. In truth, Lupita, now that she understood the dangers of infection, could manage for herself.

A simple inquiry about the meaning of a Spanish word Summer had not heard before set the girls to learning each other's language, laughing as they teased each other about accents and inflections. Summer was a long way from fluent, but she could grab a word here and there in the rapid fire of the spoken conversations.

On this evening, with summer gone and fall's earlier darkness descending on the streets of Sombrero, she was nearing the cabin where Gwyneth would be waiting and wondering, hurrying her steps, not really in fear, just anxious to be indoors.

At the sound of horse hooves striking the road's hard, dry caliche base, Summer cringed slightly, easing toward the adobe structure of a small, closed, and darkened café. She hoped not to be seen, but the sneering voice put that hope to rest.

"Well now, looky who's here. Oh, you cain't no way hide

yourself in that little bit of shadow, Missy. Might just as well face the truth. You're mine, and I've come fer ya. I've been watching an' wait'n my chance. Ain't no way around it. You're mine now. All alone and with just me and these here fellas to protect you. Now come on over here and climb up behind me. It's that or I come fer ya and thet won't be no picnic fer ya at all."

Summer recognized the voice as belonging to Carl Macon, the same one who had foolishly confronted her on the main street of town. The same two silent riders were backing the man's play. That time on the main street, her father and brother took care of the threat. This time, she was alone. But, really, not quite alone. Even as the man was talking, she was building up her fortitude, fearing she was about to be forced into something she didn't want and had never done before. But first, she would try words.

"Mister, if you had the brains of a flea, you'd ride on and leave me alone. There's no way you can get away with what you have planned. Now turn your animal and ride away."

"Or what, Missy? You going to call your big brother again? He's nowhere near here. I've checked it all out. Those others, they're working the roundup out at the ranch. You ain't got no help coming, Missy. Best you jest come along with me."

When Summer didn't move, Macon stepped to the ground and tossed his reins to one of the others. He had taken a bare two steps toward Summer when the lead of the .32 shot struck his belt buckle and glanced upward into his belly. With a startled gasp, he fell to the road. The other two riders were shocked into inactivity for a second, making no movement, but both uttering surprised exclamations. Not knowing what the men's intentions were, Summer, to be on the safe side, pointed her weapon at the closest one and squeezed the trigger. She had shot close but hadn't intended to hit the man.

The buzzing lead was too close for the rider's comfort. With a cruel kick of his spurs, he whirled his horse around, heading out of town and toward the open rangeland. The second rider followed.

Several doors slammed and a man's voice hollered out, "What's going on out there?"

Summer stood in shocked silence at what she had done. There was little doubt her attacker was dead. After he had fallen, his only movements were to wrap his arms around his belly and groan. Thirty seconds later, he shuddered, straightened out one leg, and released what was his last breath.

Summer was without lucid thought or action. She simply stood, the .32 still hanging, forgotten, from her fingers.

Cautious, slow footsteps were drawing the inquisitive man close. Reasoning that he was merely curious and not a threat, Summer hesitated and then returned the little gun to its hidden, sewn-in pouch. The man wouldn't have been able to see Summer to identify her, but he could see the outline of her dress against the white of the adobe, identifying her as a woman.

"What's happening? That you doing the shooting, miss?"

When his question met only silence, he took another few steps closer. Now he could see the body lying in the street.

"Whoa up there, girly. I'm guessing you're the one what done this since there's no one else around. Don't shoot me. Best you stand still while I get a lantern. See what this is all about."

This time, the man ran, guided by the slight bit of moonlight, his footsteps sounding loud on the boardwalk. He returned within a couple of minutes carrying a lit lantern. Summer hadn't moved. First, the man held the light over Carl Macon, who would never again threaten a woman.

Shaking his head at the idea of a woman carrying a pistol, he turned toward Summer.

"Relax, miss. I expect you had good enough reason for what you did. This here is Carl Macon. Known him for years. Always knew he'd end up this way. More likely up in the hills somewhere though, when he was caught rustling or whatever."

Lifting the lantern higher, he exclaimed, "Why, you're that nurse that came in with the doctor. The same one that's marrying into the ranch bunch. You'd best give me that gun miss, while I go for the sheriff."

As he held out his hand expectantly, Summer spoke for the first time. "I'll be dead on the ground beside that one before you get my weapon. And you come any closer, I'll give you a taste of the lead too."

Several more doors had opened and closed, and folks were gathering, some carrying lanterns. Recognizing a neighbor, the man standing beside Summer said, "Thornton, go for the sheriff. And the doctor. Although I don't suppose we really need the doctor no more."

Someone else said, "Sheriff's all tied up with that Mex caring for him. Best you go for the deputy. I'll call on the lady doctor. She's just around the corner."

Gwyneth came running to where Summer continued to stand. She took Summer by both hands, saying, "What in the world happened?"

Summer's response was, "That man's dead as he ever will be, but you probably need to make it official, word from the doctor and all. Someone's gone for the deputy. That's that Carl Macon. The one who approached me on the street last week. This time, he meant business. No fooling around with sweet talk. When he stepped to the ground and came close, I did what I had to do."

"All right. We'll just wait for the deputy and then we'll go home. No one is going to lay blame on you."

Another few silent minutes passed as they waited for the deputy. He finally arrived looking all official, but with his shirt tail still hanging out as if he had dressed too quickly. He bent and looked at the dead man before rising again to look directly at Summer.

"Looks like we got us a murder. Who did this?"

Summer spoke up, with resolve showing in her voice. "I shot that man, but it was nowhere near murder. He left me no choice. It was either defend myself or be forced onto his horse and taken away. I didn't much like the choice."

"And where did you get the gun?"

The voice of senior authority said out of the darkness, "Doesn't much matter where she got the gun, deputy. The fact is, she has the perfect right to defend herself. Now stand down. And you others, go on home. Someone get the smithy. Tell him to bring his wagon."

The startled deputy said, "Sheriff, you should be in bed resting till you're fit again. Leave this to me."

"Yes? And what would be your next move, Deputy?"

"Why, I'd put the shooter behind a locked door till morning when we can find the truth of the matter."

"Put a lady who only protected herself in jail. That's just fine, Hammond. You see to the clearing of the trash from the street. I'll see to talking with Macon's mother. The rest of you go home. You too, Summer."

As the bystanders began moving away, Gwyneth stepped over to the sheriff.

"Olaf. Do you feel all right? That crease in your skull is still in need of some healing."

"I'm feeling just fine. Got me the mother of all headaches, but feeling fine."

~

THE NEXT MORNING, Summer and her actions were the talk of the town. No one knew where the weapon had come from. The speculation was wide and varied, but by noon the story had settled out. Macon was no loss to the town, although they all felt sorry for his mother. What the sheriff had said in private to his deputy was never repeated, but the deputy lost his strutting walk and spoke more carefully.

The town left Summer to herself to sort out her feelings. But Lupita, Gwyneth, and Juanita, especially, expressed firm opinions about women protecting themselves. When Sofia Gonzalez heard the story, she beamed with delight. Struggling with her English, she said, "You tell Missy Summer...just tell her..."

Gwyneth smiled at her. "I know what you mean, Sofia. I'll tell her."

Chapter Twenty-Seven

It was becoming a race between the wedding preparations toward that magical day and the completion of the clinic, which, to Gwyneth, would be another magical day. Gwyneth and Summer were working steadily in preparation for their first medical patient. They had all they needed in the structure, but there were, as yet, no cupboards. The builder put up some rough shelving for them. They'd make do until the ordered cabinets arrived.

To the delight of both women, the well digger rose to the top of his ladder with a smile on his face and mud on his boots. The mud could only mean he had struck water.

Smiling, Gwyneth pointed at his boots, asking, "How much water. Is it a good well?"

In good, but slightly broken English, the answer was, "Aw. Miss Doctor. I must dig one more layer, then you will have a good well. The blue clay, it is make good for well. Then we build the casings and put up the rope pulley. You will be very happy with this well."

Gwyneth thanked the man who bowed in gratitude for her thoughtfulness.

Walking away, Gwyneth imagined the sheet of paper lying

on the table inside and saw herself ticking off the line that mentioned the need for a well. *One more thing done.*

The next day, Dr. Shultz hired Antonio and his team and wagon to move him to the new clinic. Everyone was all smiles at the prospects for the future and the fact that they were underway. Cob arrived in the buggy, with Tab driving to congratulate the girls. Perhaps overexpressing himself, Tab, for the first time, reached out and touched Summer, giving her a big hug and a smile. She didn't object or seem to mind.

Dr. Shultz was the first to bring a patient to the new clinic, a fact that suited Gwyneth just fine. She was to be married the following day, and her mind was totally on that matter and all it involved. She had been up to the ranch that morning. The place was abuzz with activity, partly for the roundup but mostly for the wedding. The cowboys had been assigned the barn and its immediate yard for their final preparations. The rest of the ranch yard was out of bounds. The place was spotless. Even the bare ground around the house, bunkhouse, and cookhouse had been raked of all debris and swept till it looked almost like reddish-colored poured concrete.

Gwyneth approached the house only once, finding out she was not really welcome.

Somewhat embarrassed, although she had not felt embarrassment since her college days when she was first assigned a male cadaver to learn her surgery lessons from, she, struggling for the right words, tried to tell Juanita that she only wished to check the bedroom she and Cob would be using.

Juanita smiled as widely as had ever seen her smile.

"You go home. Is all good. You trust Juanita."

As if they were conspiring between themselves, the two widows shared a smile and a knowing look. Gwyneth nodded her head in understanding and rode back to town.

The next day, around noon. Cob would drive the washed and shined buggy to town for his bride. Gwyneth had laid out the beautiful dress she had purchased in Pueblo, along with her new shoes, a small lady's hat, and the unmentionables she would have never dreamed of owning until she came under Bea's influence way back in Chicago. Now it was all just the waiting.

Chapter Twenty-Eight

GWYNETH AND SUMMER SPREAD THEIR WEDDING clothes on the bed in what Juanita had termed *the dressing room*. Both ladies had given up on the idea of the many undergarments so commonly worn on high occasions, the chemise, corset, bustle, petticoats. They were all ignored in favor of simplicity. Years of wearing split skirts or work pants had conditioned them to trust their own bodies for how the clothing fit, draped, and enhanced itself. At Cob's insistence, Gwyneth set her fancy lady's hat aside in favor of her Stetson.

"It will look better and more authentic in the photographs."

Gwyneth raised her head with a wondering look.

"Photographs?"

"Of course, my dear. You wouldn't allow such an occasion as this to pass by without a permanent record, surely."

Giving way to the heat of the day, the ladies wouldn't dress until just before the event was to begin. Juanita had provided water, basins, and towels for the last-minute washing away of the morning's perspiration. Ladies didn't talk of such things, but everyone acknowledged the need in silence.

Being ready and only requiring a few minutes to dress, they

sauntered out to the yard. The Mariachi band that would set the tone for the dancing to come later was playing a series of nameless tunes, playing them quietly and slowly, as if to set the tone for the more thoughtful and graver, and holy part of the festivities.

The food was piled high in the big house kitchen and the cookhouse, but none would be made available until after the vows were exchanged.

Even the cowboys were dressed in their finest, clothing most had closeted away in wait for community dances and such.

The minister from the small church in town that Gwyneth and Summer had been attending, Pastor Ronald McVeigh, arrived, looking solemn. A genial, good-natured man, Gwyneth knew his solemn look would hold only for as long as the ceremony lasted. His wife, simply but pleasantly dressed in a pale-blue gown, smiled and wished Gwyneth many years of happiness.

There was no sign of Cob or his brother Louis, who would be standing with Cob during the wedding. Gwyneth had begun teasing Summer about her standing up with Louis when everything in her was wishing it was Tab. Summer's silence was signal enough to drop that line of talk.

THIRTY MINUTES before the slated time, Summer suggested it might be time to get dressed. Gwyneth's agreement was interrupted by a shout of warning, a scream of fear, and another scream of pain, the clattering of iron wheels on stone, and the breaking of wood. Finally came the terror and pain-filled scream of a horse.

The music stopped and every head turned to the east, just beyond the big barn. There, the two-track trail joining neighboring ranches to the Sombrero wound around a small but steep hill, disappearing into the brush and continuing east. The trail was only used for interactions between ranches and was not seriously maintained. Most travel was by horseback, where stepping around a washout or a boulder left in place was no problem. Wagon travel, on the other hand, with the steepness of that portion of the trail and the roughness of the clearing, required a deft hand on the leathers, and a close watching of the trail ahead.

The Colin Bradshaw family held ownership of a small outfit about ten miles to the east. Cob would say later that Bradshaw was well known for either being late to an appointment or not showing up at all.

On the wedding day, as usual, the Bradshaw family was the last to arrive, with Bradshaw himself making excuses and his wife casting blame on anyone near. The Bradshaws, rising early, as always, and working hard, along with their four growing children, the oldest being a boy of fourteen, had lost track of the time. Throwing caution to the wind and depending on the team and his driving skills, Bradshaw was attempting to make up some lost time in fast travel. The lively team harnessed to the buckboard had no objection to running. It almost seemed as if it was their preferred gait.

Colin Bradshaw, being a casual sort of man, even when pushed for time, was leaning back on the seat, enjoying the day and the travel, sure everything would work out fine, when they broke over the ridge of the small hill behind the Sombrero's barn and then faced the hundred yards of steep grade. Even with Colin Bradshaw pulling back on the reins, the team surged forward. The first scream heard at the Sombrero yard was that of a twelve-year-old Bradshaw girl, a pretty but somewhat simple thing. Her terror spread through the family.

Bradshaw tried all he knew to haul the team down, all to no avail. Overshooting a small curve in the trail, the team dragged the wagon to the side, a back wheel struck a rock, and the dried-out oak of the rear axle gave way. The wagon almost leaped into the air as it bounded over the rock with an awful, crashing, breaking sound. Falling to the side, the wagon tipped enough to drag the wagon tongue out of line and into the rear leg of the offside horse. The frightened animal fell, and the wagon trip became a train wreck. The horse's scream heard in the yard was from the animal's shock when its leg broke.

Bradshaw was still working the reins long after all hope was gone. Mrs. Bradshaw was on her knees, gripping the seat with all her strength while holding her youngest with one arm. It wasn't enough. She and the children were dumped to the side like someone might tip over a box, shaking it to remove the last of its contents. Crying and wailing rose from the scene.

Without really thinking, both Gwyneth and Summer were running. Tab, who had watched in horror, as had almost everyone in the yard, hollered to the crew to get another wagon down there and to come and help. Gwyneth was the first on the scene, somehow outrunning the younger Summer. She moved quickly from person to person to check for life, and then for serious bleeding. Summer was lifting a child out of the brush, a child whose arms flopped uselessly, as if he were unconscious.

The arrival of a few men helped to straighten out the chaos as they unhitched the team, leading one horse away. The second animal, with the broken leg, would be shot, but not with everyone looking on.

A flat-bed wagon driven by a cowboy was directed to where the family members could be lifted aboard. Gwyneth and Summer confirmed that, although there were injuries, no one had died. Bradshaw himself appeared to carry the worst of the injuries. He was also the only one showing blood. Gwyneth bent to see what she could do, instructing Summer to get the rest of the injured on the wagon.

Bradshaw had apparently landed headfirst in the scrub brush. He was unconscious, and he had a stiff stub of a dead plant of some kind protruding from one cheek. She had no idea what plant the stub came from, and it didn't matter. What mattered was that whatever had caused the branch to break originally had left a jagged, sharp end, an end that had penetrated Bradshaw's cheek and torn a chunk out of his tongue before exiting out the other cheek. He was bleeding freely.

Gwyneth hollered to a cowboy to get help lifting the man onto the wagon. She watched as this was done, instructing that he should be laid with his back against the side rail, propped up so the blood could drain from his mouth. He had already swallowed more than enough blood. When the entire family was aboard the wagon, Cob, who had come from the house in answer to the shouts of the wedding guests, said to the teamster, "You get this load down to the clinic. Carefully. No foolish rush for time that might cause more injuries. Now go."

Turning to another couple of crewmen, he said, "Boys, bring Big Ed down here. Throw a collar on him and bring some rope. Drag this poor fella with the broken leg out into the hills a ways and put him down. Don't make any show of it."

He was about to see what Gwyneth wanted to do, but as he turned, he was just in time to see her riding out of the yard on the trail to town. Louis stepped up beside him and said, "It was your idea to marry a doctor, brother."

"Pretty poor timing if you were to ask me. Bradshaw seems to be able to mess up everything someone else would do with no trouble at all. I guess I'd best tell the guests what's going on."

"You go, Cob. I'll stay here and clean up some of this mess. Tell them there will still be a wedding. And perhaps suggest to Juanita that a bit of food and a couple bottles of wine might be just the thing."

Gwyneth tied her horse at the clinic and hurried for the door. Dr. Shultz looked up from the document he was reading with an unasked question in his eyes. When Gwyneth rushed right past him, he got up and followed, with another question, this time spoken out loud, “I thought you were getting married today.”

“Good memory, Gabriel. And so, I am. But there was a wagon mishap up at the ranch. Couple of broken bones, I’m thinking, and one man injured and bleeding. The rest, I don’t know yet. They’re on their way with Summer riding shotgun. I need to prep my room. Wouldn’t hurt if you were to take a look at one or two. Two adults. Four kids. A family.

“I’d appreciate if you would take a look at the two younger kids. I don’t know exactly all that happened to the father. I expect he conked his head pretty hard. He’s bleeding from a gash on his tongue, but he won’t die from that. There. I hear a wagon now.”

The teamster and Moses, the Black cowboy, eased the wagon close to the clinic door and each took a child in their arms, laying them down inside at Gwyneth’s direction. When they returned with the two older children, Moses was carrying the fourteen-year-old with the broken arm. She had him laid on the wheeled stretcher, ready for treatment. Summer quickly grabbed an apron from the hook on the wall and covered her riding clothes with it. Speaking over her shoulder, she asked, “Do you want me to take this one?”

“Please. If you need help, call me.”

Now taking charge, Summer said, “Moses, roll up your sleeves and pour yourself a basin of water. Take it out back. There’s a shelf there with soap and a towel. Give yourself a good scrubbing, then come back in here ready to do as I ask you to.”

Grabbing another basin, Summer prepared to do as she had directed Moses. She then scrubbed the boy.

Feeling for the break to determine how shattered the arm was, she spoke to Gwyneth without looking her way.

“It feels like a clean break just below the elbow. Just a bit out of line, but I can fix that. It would still be best if you could take a quick look.”

With Gwyneth’s approval, Summer called Moses, saying,

"Now hold above the elbow and on the wrist. I'm going to feel for the bone's movement while you pull very easily on the arm. I'll tell you when to stop. Then you hold that position until I'm done."

~

LESS THAN HALF AN HOUR LATER, the boy was beginning to wake up. The first thing he did was feel his arm, finding a rough plaster cast in the place of his bare skin. His eyes flashed up to Summer, whom he had never seen before. Not waiting for him to speak, Summer smiled and said, "You had quite a ride. Flew like a bird. Not very far, mind you, but it was flying just the same. Landed kind of hard though. Broke your arm. Moses and I, we've just fixed it for you. You'll carry this plaster for a couple of weeks. It will hurt a bit, but a big tough ranch hand like you won't have any trouble with that.

"Now I need the stretcher you're lying on. I need it for your mother. I'll help you to stand, and you can sit on the chair for a while. Or lie on the floor if you feel sleepy."

Still without speaking, the boy swung his legs sideways, holding his arm the entire time, and was soon resting on the chair.

Moses gently picked up the mother and, with Summer tugging the lady's dress into place, laid her on the stretcher. With the release from Moses's grip, the woman's eyes popped open, closed for a breath or two, and then opened again. She stared at Summer as her son had. Glancing around the room as best she could from her prone position, she stopped at her boy with the cast and then continued on to where Gwyneth was kneeling over her husband.

Summer anticipated the questions to come, explaining, "The boy has a broken arm. Not too serious. He's carrying a cast now. He'll soon be up and raring to go again. The other children are with Dr. Shultz in the other room. They've got some bruises and a few small cuts from the brush y'all landed on, but there's nothing serious. Gwyneth is caring for your husband. We'll put him up here on the stretcher a soon as we find out if you're hurt. Now, how do you feel, except banged up and bruised? I can't feel anything broken. You've got a nice egg on the back of your head, and I can't do a thing about it. Do you have a headache or do you have a more serious hurt anywhere, more than simple bruising?"

"I've got a headache and I'm feeling dizzy."

"Okay, let's wait just a moment for Gwyneth to have a look at you."

AT MRS. BRADSHAW'S SUGGESTION, Moses took two chairs outside into the shade. One for Mrs. Bradshaw, and one for the boy with the broken arm. "Bit of fresh air might cause this dizziness to settle down." The ranch wife cringed a bit when Moses took her shoulder to aid in her rising to a sitting position. The black man pursed his lips in his silent way and ignored the insult. He continued holding her while she stood to her feet, and until she was safely seated outside. Gwyneth had assured her that there was no obvious injury. Still fighting dizziness, she settled in for a rest. As her children, one by one, arrived at her side, showing cleansed and taped cuts, she hugged each one but didn't ask either doctor or nurse about her husband. Gwyneth wondered if the slight odor of alcohol on Bradshaw's breath pointed to the reason for the wife's coolness.

Moses performed the last of his services, lifting Colin Bradshaw off the floor and placing him on the stretcher. Gwyneth said, "Thank you, Moses. I don't know that there's another man on the Sombrero who could lift that man. And do it so gently. You're a good man, Moses. We're about done here. Thanks for your help. You men can return to the ranch now if you like."

Summer said, "Go rent me a horse first, Moses, please. I came in on the wagon, and I'm not going to miss this wedding for the lack of a ride. You get me a ride and then go back and tell them we'll be along, by and by. They'll be happy to hear that no one died."

Gwyneth called Gabriel Shultz into her treatment room and showed him the holes in Colin Bradshaw's cheeks. She had carefully removed the dead branch and the bits and pieces dragged in with it. She had propped Bradshaw's mouth open with a small fold of paper. Dr. Shultz immediately noticed the gash across the patient's tongue. The bleeding had slowed but not stopped completely. The edges of the gash were a bit ragged, but she could trim those off to make a clean mend.

"This one is new to me, Gabriel. And I don't remember dealing with it in college. Have you ever had reason to sew up a tongue?"

"I've been tempted a few times, but no. I've never done that."

Summer grinned at the doctor. "Do I dare guess whose tongue you would like to sew up?"

"No, young lady, and if you did, you would almost certainly be wrong."

Returning to the discussion with Gwyneth, he said, "It's all just flesh after all. The tongue gets a good deal of work, and it's made of a different consistency, but at the end of it all, it's still flesh. If you have circular needles and can reach in there, I'd just go ahead and do it. Leaving it open is not the answer."

Seeing no need for further discussion, Gwyneth said, "Summer, you prepare just the smallest bit of ether. I don't need this man waking up while I'm sewing up his mouth.

~

GWYNETH FIRST SEWED THE CHEEKS. There would be matching scars and indentations where there was lost flesh, looking almost like bullet holes, but there was no preventing that. Only then did she reach for the small tray of thin catgut soaking in disinfectant, with the small circular needle already threaded. She had trimmed the torn and ragged pieces until the edges were as smooth as they would ever be. Then, with Summer watching the patient's breathing and eye movements, Gwyneth reached in as far as her fingers would go, but before she made a suture, she realized, logically, that the tongue was not going to simply lie there and allow her to do her work.

Gabriel Shultz had been watching the procedure. Quietly and simply, he said, "Wait a moment until I get a bit of gauze. I'll use it to grip the tongue and hold it tight for you."

"Smart man," was Gwyneth's response.

The procedure was completed in a matter of minutes. There was no further need for doctors or nurse. The only concern Gwyneth would leave behind as she returned to the ranch was the fact that Bradshaw had shown no signs of waking. But watching him, like watching for a kettle to boil, wouldn't bring him around any sooner.

Dr. Shultz offered to stay, allowing Gwyneth and Summer to return to the ranch. When Gwyneth stepped outside to say farewell to Mrs. Bradshaw, she was welcomed as if she were the return of Florence Nightingale herself. The thanks and the apologies for disrupting the wedding were almost overwhelming. A short explanation of her husband's treatment sufficed. The woman didn't seem to be worried very much one way or the other.

Gwyneth's last word to her was about Dr. Shultz staying on to see to their care and the fact that the catgut stitches would dissolve in a short while, warning against the patient picking at them, simply to leave them alone.

Chapter Twenty-Nine

DOCTOR AND NURSE, SOMEWHAT FRAZZLED AND JUST a bit thrown off balance from the happenings of the day, emerged from the clinic's door to a welcome sight. Instead of a rental horse standing next to Gwyneth's trusted animal, Tab stood there, waiting beside the ranch buggy.

Tab was smiling from ear to ear. "Ah, here you are, the two most beautiful and wonderful ladies in the entire hill country, released from your civil duties to return to the festivities. I have had a shortened recounting of your tender care for the Bradshaw family from Moses. I have concluded that if I ever fall out of a wagon, I'll want no other than y'all to see to my care, wiping my feverish brow with the hem of your garments, and weeping all the while."

Gwyneth was beyond listening to lovers' nonsense. Summer may be able to absorb more of the blarney, but she had already had enough.

"The two of you take the buggy. I'll still ride my horse."

There didn't appear to be any room in her declaration for discussion, so Tab took Summer by the elbow, carefully assisting her into the buggy before mounting himself. By the time he had the rig moving, Gwyneth was well on her way.

A cheer arose when the girls rode under the big log arch and into the ranch yard. Cob was there immediately to take Gwyneth's hand as she stepped to the ground. Trinity Castillo took Gwyneth's horse, leading him toward the comforts of a stall in the barn. Another ranch rider cared for the buggy. Cob escorted his long-awaited bride-to-be and her attendant to the house. Stepping inside, he said, "Juanita, I'm sure these ladies would benefit from a plate of your delicious cooking and then a bucket or two of hot water in their changing room."

With only a few words to her helpers, Juanita had the bathing matter cared for. The food she looked to herself. Summer took only a single bite before saying, "I had no idea I was so hungry."

Cob replied, "It's well past lunchtime, ladies, of course you're ready for sustenance. And now, if you will excuse me, I'll see what I can do about gathering up the pieces of this celebration. A bit of music should do the trick."

NEITHER GWYNETH nor Summer had anything to say as they washed away the sweat and dust of the day's activities. Silently, Gwyneth was wishing there was a way to wash away memories as easily as she washed her body, not just of the morning, but of Trent, their lives together, their unrealized hopes. She simply could not drag those memories into marriage with Cob. It wouldn't be helpful or fair to either of them.

Summer completed her preparations and said, "I'll be downstairs. Don't take too long."

Gwyneth dawdled as she put memories to rest-memories and their emotions. She was being married in just a few minutes —married to a good, kind, and stable man. She had to go to him, offering the same. It was the emotional stability part that concerned her most.

A bare half hour later, with a single clang on the house

triangle, the door opened, allowing a charming and resplendent Gwyneth to step onto the veranda. Her modest but beautiful, off-white gown, topped by the carefully brushed Stetson, caused a low murmur of approval to run through the gathering. She stepped toward Abe and linked her arm through Abe's arm. He would escort her to the altar and stand in for the father she had lost so many years before.

Summer, less modest, but ravishingly beautiful in a colorful gown few others could have worn with such natural ease, stopped just a short step behind the bride. She, too, held her head high with her Stetson crowning her glory.

The quietly played music continued as Abe and the ladies descended the stairs to the well-trod path joining the house and ranch yards. The guests, cowboys, local businessmen, and neighboring ranchers, Mexican and American, stood silently as Abe stopped while Gwyneth and Summer approached the altar where the minister waited. Beside him stood Cob, anxious to finally claim this woman he had loved and waited for over so many years. Louis waited to take Summer to the side, standing together in support of the bride and groom.

There was no pulpit or other furniture standing between the couple to be married and the minister who stood patiently, his open Bible held in the palm of one hand.

On either side, generously loaned from the Mexican church in town, was a pair of beautifully carved wooden candelabra, lit but showing little light under the mid-afternoon Texas sun.

As the crowd stood silently by, Pastor McVeigh pointed a serious look at Gwyneth and held it. There was a question attached to the look. Gwyneth easily saw the question and, with a slight smile and a nod only the pastor would see, she gave her answer. The same look was pointed at Cob, who answered immediately, almost anxiously.

With the couple's silent affirmation, the pastor smiled, turning his eyes to each portion of the crowd, and said, "We are gathered here before God and a crowd of witnesses. This is a solemn but a happy occasion. It brings God delight to see the marriage of two of His children who come in genuine love and the promise to continue that love."

He then, from memory, repeated the note he had been working on for the past week. He had wanted it short but meaningful. He had come to believe that, with the help and guidance of his wife, as well as the searching of God's Word, the words he spoke were proper and encouraging. He concluded by saying, "With that as God's guidance to you, let us continue."

The entire formal program took less than ten minutes. Ten minutes under the Texas sun, where the couple would live out their lives.

At the end, when Cob was invited to kiss his bride, he hesitated, then reached for Gwyneth's Stetson, leaving his own in place, and very gently, almost shyly kissed this woman, now his wife, for the very first time.

With the ending of the formal service, Gwyneth stepped back, took Cob's hand, and led him to where Abe, now joined by Helen, were standing. They had been a thousand miles away the day Gwyneth had married Trent, their son. The loss of that son had left feelings and emotions that none of them had ever truly gotten over. Gwyneth knew it was the fear of those emotions rising up at inappropriate times that had cautioned her and caused her to refuse Cob's earlier proposal. What Abe and Helen had done with the emotions, she didn't know. It had never been discussed and probably would never be discussed.

She reached for Helen's hands and pulled her into a hug. The women whispered into each other's ears, words meant only for them. When they broke the hug, both were weeping. Without wiping her eyes, Gwyneth looked to Abe. He and Cob had just broken off their handshake. Now it was Gwyneth's turn. Abe was not an expressive man, and under other circumstances, Gwyneth would not have dreamed of hugging him. But on this occasion, it seemed right. Abe put his hand on Gwyneth's shoulder, and from there it all came together. Naturally. Perhaps even overdue. The messages of love and caring were spoken wordlessly, and the meeting was not prolonged.

Understanding that the entire crowd was watching, Gwyneth gently broke away, turned, and smiled at the onlookers.

As if guided by an unseen, knowledgeable hand, the Mariachi band chose that moment to break out in a celebratory piece, whose tune and title, if it had one, was known only to themselves.

The kitchen doors opened, and a line of women and younger girls stepped out, each carrying a plate or tray. Juanita was at the serving table, ready to give instructions on where to set the dishes. The rate the dishes arrived, overloading the table, and the assortment of foods was a delight to Gwyneth, who had never before attended a fiesta.

At the end of the ocotillo shelter, two chairs had been placed alongside a small table. Paper lanterns and other colorful decorations surrounded the chairs. Gwyneth and Cob would be served their food first, along with a small glass of wine

Mateo Aguilar, the padrino assigned to see to all the details of the wedding, escorted the newly married couple to their special table. A part of the role of the padrino was to be seen, or in the way, as little as possible. His movement in leading Gwyneth and Cob was so discreet as to be almost unnoticeable. When they were seated, he melted back into the crowd.

Juanita chose two lovely girls just coming into their adulthood to serve the married couple. Juanita carefully filled two plates, laying them on small silver trays and passing them to the girls. So excited to be honored this way, the girls were almost shaking. They took a tray each and carefully, slowly, walked to the shelter. With a slight bow, they placed the trays before the recipients and silently moved away.

The remainder of the guests would make their way to the serving table at their own pace. Some were more interested in visiting than eating. Some were huddled around a clay jug, talking and laughing. What was in the jug was never asked.

The dancing and singing lay before them. As the evening encroached on the festivities, lanterns would be lit. Sweet goods would be laid out. A cautious amount of wine would be made available. Little ones would be tucked away for sleep anywhere the mothers could find space. Some guests, from close by, would pack up and head home. Those with further to travel would find a place to sleep, anywhere but the big house. Even Juanita would not dare enter after the kitchen was cleaned.

With the completion of the eating, dancing, and well-wishing, Cob would lead his bride to the house, enter, and lock the door that was never locked.

Chapter Thirty

One week later, with Cob and Gwyneth taking their rest on the veranda, the bawling of cattle caused Cob to rise to his feet. He turned to Gwyneth, saying, "That's the first of them, just about on our estimated time. Sounds like a big bunch."

With that, he hurried down the stairs and across the yard. Clive Gentry, working in the barn, also heard. He rushed out to open the gate to the big corral. He then ran back into the barn and mounted a tough-looking gray he kept saddled during the working day. Cob held the pasture gate open for him. He would hold his riding animal aside, only helping if it appeared that the driving crew could use the help.

Cob took a position on a raised platform he had built at the yard side of the corral so he could see over the high fence. With arms crossed, leaning on the top rail, he waited for the first of the white faces to appear out of the semi-desert brush. He had referred to their herd as their *walking bank account*, and so it was. These, just arriving, along with the hundreds more yet to be brought in, would be counted and carefully sorted. The culls would go directly to market to keep the herd free of nonproductive animals. The heavy steers and the heifers not being held back for replacement animals would join the culls in the drive to Fort Worth. Their sale would finance the ongoing needs of the big ranch and support the families who were dependent on it.

The calves would be branded, and the bulls cut. Young bulls were a major nuisance on the range, and the market was calling for fat steers.

Some ranchers with smaller herds were experimenting with vaccinating, but on the Sombrero, there was still considerable doubt about the practice. When Gwyneth questioned Cob about it, his response was guarded, knowing her knowledge far exceeded his.

Some years earlier, Cob had directed the building of a large dip tank for the control of tics. Ridding the herd of the blood sucking pests had proved worthwhile, in spite of the costs and trouble involved.

The whole of it was hard, hot, dirty work, and the cowboys loved it. They seemed to work the whole year through, waiting for the excitement of roundup. Riders working the branding fire would go through three or four mounts each day. A mountain of dried brush was cut and brought in for the branding fires. Some days and nights, it seemed as if it would require eternal patience to tolerate the bawling of both mothers and calves as the pairs were weaned.

As the gathering continued, the fields and corrals surrounding the Sombrero home ranch seemed to fill with white face animals, all requiring work. The earlier bunch of treated animals were driven back to their normal grazing grounds to make room for others. The last bunch came in from a higher range, further to the west, up in the highest, most rugged territory the ranch claimed as theirs.

Moses, who had the lead hand position of the six riders working that area, watched his gathering join and mingle with the earlier arrivals before passing his horse off to the wrangler. He then whapped his pants legs with both hands and hat and went looking for Trinity Castillo to report his findings. Those two huddled together for several minutes before turning to the big house. Reporting would generally be held until the day's end. When Cob saw the two men coming his way not much after noon, he moved down the stairs to meet them in the yard. He said nothing, knowing Moses had a report, and it probably wasn't good. Good news could wait. Trouble needed attention.

"Big bunch missing, Boss. I'm guessing at least three hundred. Maybe more, relying on the spring count to compare."

"Any sign of rustlers?"

"Looks as if they were living in that old tumble-down line cabin. In a hurry they were. No time for settling in. Both horse and cattle marks going over Top Up Pass. I followed for maybe two miles but couldn't spare no more time. Had to get back to this bunch. Trail showed plain, going west. Downhill all the way there for nigh onto ten miles, winding through those hills. Canyons and offshoots all over that country. Water most anywhere you need it. Grass too. Could be holding the bunch just about anywhere."

Cob scratched the caliche of the yard with the toe of his boot, thinking, picturing the location. When he raised his eyes to Trinity Castillo, the foreman knew what he wanted to hear.

"Moses's bunch was the last ones. We're down to a single branding crew. I've been able to give some of the boys a day off. If you're wanting to know how many we can spare for a search, I'll tell you, *as many as you want.* We could rig up and hit the trail in the morning."

Cob looked from Trinity to Moses, reading their thoughts. Finally, he said, "There's just nowhere at all to go from up there. There's grass in a few of the canyons and water enough if you know where to find it, although it's not like our side of the slope. They'll be holed up waiting, hoping we'll forget it. Except we're not going to forget it. But we can afford to set it aside until we get properly organized. Keep going on what you're doing, letting the boys and the animals have their rest. Let me plan this out and then we'll talk. Thanks for a good job done, Moses."

JUANITA CALLED Cob and Gwyneth for lunch. Wally Tibbs had pulled his chuckwagon back into the yard, backing it under the shelter that would protect it from winter rains and summer's blazing sun until next roundup. He put on a clean white apron and went to work. The cookhouse was back in full swing, so Juanita was no longer carrying out double duties. Lunch on the Sombrero was a casual affair, although some traditions held fast. Dinner was more formal with Juanita serving and then retreating to her kitchen. But at lunch time, everyone ate together. If the weather was congenial, they would, one by one, load their plates, carrying them to the table on the veranda where Juanita would join the newlyweds.

Cob discussed the rustling situation freely in front of Juanita, knowing she was completely trustworthy and carried a deep knowledge of cattle, country, and ranching, from her growing up in the area, and her time ranching with her beloved Ricardo.

Cob stumbled a bit trying to find his way around wanting to join in the manhunt, all the time knowing he wasn't going to be able to. During a gap in the conversation, Gwyneth surprised him when she smiled, saying, "No, you're not."

Hesitatingly, he said, "Not what?" Trying to sound innocent.

Continuing in her almost flippant approach to the situation, seeing it clearly and knowing the truth that Cob was simply not in good enough health to lead a manhunt, truths that were too obvious to ignore, she said, "Well, let's think. Let me list out some things, my love. First, your health may or may not improve to where you can again live as you once did. But you're not there yet. Second, we've just been married. I'm on my honeymoon. Traditionally, the honeymoon is to include the groom. Third, you're not needed. You have a more than adequate crew. They can be led by Louis or Tab, or your foreman, Trinity Castillo. And fourth, we're going into town this afternoon to inform the sheriff. You will remember that he's county, not just town, elected. He'll send a man along with the authority of the law. Now let's eat our lunch and we'll go to town."

Juanita, feeling motherly, advised, "You listen to wife."

"Am I to face the two of you ganging up on me from now on? Is that what it's come to?"

Cob harnessed a driving animal to the carriage and saddled Gwyneth's horse. Juanita was busy in the kitchen putting together a package for the sheriff. She hadn't been to town for several days. It was time to look in on Olaf. The stubborn man thought little of housekeeping. He had been known to wait until he had eaten off the last clean dish in the house and taken a meal or two directly from the frying pan before heating water to clean up. Juanita would see to his home and food pantry while he and Cob were talking. Gwyneth had plans to visit the clinic.

They arrived in town with Cob leaning back on the seat, as casual as he ever was, and with Juanita driving. Gwyneth peeled off at the edge of town, riding toward the clinic. The builders were still there, tidying up some last-minute details. And along the front, where the hitch post was now installed, were two horses plus a team and wagon. She dismounted, found a place for her own animal, and entered the building. The sight of three weeping people in the waiting room and the sounds of silence from Dr. Shultz's treatment room told the story. While a family wept in fear, Dr. Shultz was busy, deep in thought. Doing rather than saying. She would have to know more before there could be any comfort in her understanding of the situation.

As always, Gwyneth's first act was to wash her hands. On this occasion, because she had been around the ranch and ridden her horse to town, she lifted a clean white smock down from a shelf and put it on.

With a light, two-finger tap on the door, Gwyneth entered. Gabriel Shultz held his position, neither looking up nor speaking. Concentrating. Gwyneth looked quickly at the woman who stood silent, hands constantly wrapping around each other at shoulder height, a respectful distance outside the doctor's work area. Gwyneth, coming closer, finally saw the patient, a young girl of perhaps ten or twelve. It was difficult to judge, with most of her covered with a clean sheet, leaving only the area where Dr. Shultz was working exposed.

Summer was standing at the girl's head, administering a calculated amount of ether. She had become quite adept at that responsibility.

Gwyneth quietly asked, "*Appendix*?"

So quietly Gwyneth was forced to lean closer, Gariel Shultz said, "Their small ranch is a three-to-four-hour wagon trip from town. The girl reported being ill last evening. By midnight, she was throwing up and suffering much pain. Folks didn't know what to do. They wasted precious hours before they decided to bring her to town. I've come to think the appendix held together until just before they reached town.

You can see the pus pooling and spreading. I haven't gotten to cleaning up the peritonitis yet. I'm still dealing with the removal."

"I'll get some swabs and give you a hand."

Preparing to assist in the operation, Gwyneth thought it better if the mother would join the others in the waiting room.

"Ma'am, I know you're concerned, but there is nothing you can do to help. There's three of us here. Your girl is in good hands. Please join the others in the outer room. I'll come to you just as soon as there is anything to report."

The woman looked as if she was going to argue but finally gave in and left the doctors to their work.

One half hour later, Summer quietly said, "Signs of waking here."

"Let her wake up, Summer. We're done. Done all we can do. If infection doesn't set in, she has a good chance. You wrap it up, Gabriel. I'll talk to the family."

LATER, over dinner in the café, Cob, Gwyneth, and Summer were discussing the near future. Gwyneth said, "You first, Cob. What's the sheriff doing?"

"Mostly, he's whining because he thinks the doctors have ganged up on him. He's pretty sure he'd be able to lead a manhunt if he got advice from someone else. He's been talking about going to see Diego Esteban. But he finally decided that Diego is so enthralled with you, Gwyneth, that he would never go against your verdict. Then, after all that, I had to recruit help to get him loaded onto the buggy for the ride home. He was so struck by a sudden headache that he came near to collapsing. Juanita had a dinner ready for him, and the house looks like it's never been lived in, it's so clean. I expect he'll settle in and be all right with the situation. I'll pick Juanita up later for the trip home.

"What was decided was that a wire would be sent for the rangers. But in the meantime, one of the deputies would put a small posse together. I'm going to offer Moses the opportunity to represent the ranch since he was the one who spotted the trail. I'll send one other man along. Sometimes a small posse is better than a big group, making noise and rattling their way through the country.

"You know how I feel about my part, Gwyneth, and I know

how you feel about my going. I'll accept it, but that don't mean I'm happy about it."

"I'll be happy, my love, if no one gets shot."

"As long as it's a rustler, shot or hung. It's the same ending."

"Perhaps it's time to bring different thinking into the matter."

"Perhaps. But that's up to the lawyers and the politicians. And if ever you suggest you want to go back to school to become either one, it's going to put considerable pressure on our marriage."

Since the last comment was delivered with a smile, Gwyneth allowed the conversation to come to an end.

After a short verbal rest and an opportunity to start in on the hot dinner plates that were just delivered, Cob said, "I've been thinking about you, Summer."

The nurse smiled and replied, "And you so recently married and all."

"Girl, you do test a man's patience. I'm thinking what a blessing it would be if Tab would marry you and take you off to the south. Let the home folks figure it all out."

All Summer said in reply was, "This is really tasty beef. Probably rustled off the Sombrero and sold for a profit."

Cob tried again. "Seriously, Summer. I'm going to make you a suggestion I haven't even asked Gwyneth about yet. Listen. Then the two of you can decide.

"I can see that Gwyneth is needed in town. We talked about that earlier, but it kind of registered with me today when she was there to help save a little girl's life.

"I'd like if you would consider moving to the ranch while Gwyneth and I move to town. We can make do in the cabin while our house is being built. You can stay in the big house with Juanita. Tab will stay in the bunkhouse. You can make the ride in when the weather is good. Otherwise, the buggy is there for your use. It should only be maybe three months till the house is ready."

As in practiced unison, both women laid down their forks and studied Cob.

Finally, Summer spoke. "Don't hardly seem fair to Tab. I'm assuming you're mentioning him in that context means you've been talking with him again about taking over for you. Surely the big house comes along with the job. The big house and Juanita, and a bit of space between the boss and the crew."

"Living apart is the only way it would work, Summer, and you know it. Why your folks would hog tie you and drag you off home if there was any other way."

"My folks might not. Father would simply advise me to keep my weapon and enough ammunition close by. Mother would think that was good enough advice and let it go. But big brother. Now that would be a whole other situation. You'll remember, Gwyneth, how he rode along, ready to take on the entire Ute nation if there was any threat to his little sister. No telling what would happen if Tab and Charles locked horns. No matter the outcome, I wouldn't like it. If Gwyneth thinks your suggestions would work, I'll go along."

Cob turned his head to look directly at his new wife. She simply said, "One more week at the ranch unless something big comes up for Gabriel. Then we'll make the move."

SUMMER HAD the choice of three upstairs bedrooms or, if she wished to force more teasing onto Cob, she could take his big downstairs room. Tempted and smiling at the thought, she nonetheless moved upstairs. Tab took a wagon in for her trunks, hauling a couple of boxes to the cabin for Cob at the same time. Summer joined him on the wagon for the trip back to the ranch with her black gelding tied on behind.

Gwyneth returned to the clinic with competing thoughts fighting for dominance in her mind. She wished with all her being that people would remain healthy and safe. On the other hand, the clinic needed income to justify its existence.

At the end of the first week working closely with Gabriel Shultz, she was more than ever satisfied that the two could work successfully as individuals, or as a team when needed. Summer worked between the new clinic and Diego Esteban's modest operation. Dr. Esteban located a young boy who was willing to run errands between clinics, bringing Summer his way when needed. His business had picked up considerably after the treatment of Lupita, which he really had no part in. But the news had gone through the Mexican part of town that the doctor had a nurse on call who was very good with birthing, and that there was a lady doctor who could be called if needed. Suddenly, the small recovery room had been cleaned out and three cots installed. He didn't really expect to fill all three cots at once, but already the space had housed two new mothers and their infants.

Diego kept his fees low, but still, he had more coins in his pocket than ever before.

Chapter Thirty-One

Cob was unworried when the Ranger had taken more than a week to make his appearance. While it would seem as if the rustlers had gotten away with a sizable portion of the Top Up Pass herd, they had also trapped themselves. That was rough country up there. The terrain alone said the gang held the stolen cattle, but in reality, unless the rustlers had discovered a way through that Cob didn't know about, the terrain held them.

Trails open to horse travel would be inadequate for the movement of hundreds of cattle. Even if somehow they managed to move the cattle, there was just nowhere to go that didn't present an abundance of risk. South were miles of similar terrain, with limited grass and water to sustain a herd. To the west and north were established ranches. Crossing them with a Sombrero herd would bring more attention than was wanted and would not at all be promising for their hopes of a long life and career as cattle thieves.

As an additional backup, Cob had detailed Moses to select one rider to accompany him going directly to Top Up Pass. He had chosen Elmer Talkham to ride with, a tough, battle-worn rider who had come seeking a job the year before. Since then, he had shown his worth in knowledge of both cattle and men. They were to find the herd, stake out a safe position, and simply watch the rustlers until the posse arrived.

Thieves weren't always smart. Cob and Gwyneth had a rather one-sided conversation on the matter, with Gwyneth claiming the desire to live should override the thought of easy money. Cob came back with the suggestion that perhaps Gwyneth had been so long in the big eastern city that she had forgotten her former ranch life.

That moved Gwyneth to say, "Mister, I saw things in Chicago slums that would shake your last ounce of faith in humanity. I won't describe it all. I'm just saying that I have not become naive. But even the worst of city thugs seemed to know when they were fighting a lost battle. Perhaps when the posse locates the herd, they'll find it unattended, with the thieves having ridden for brighter possibilities."

With a loving smile, Cob replied, "Perhaps."

A FEW DAYS LATER, Cob and the sheriff were stationed at their regular boardwalk window in the café, taking their morning coffee, when the returning posse entered town from the northwest. Together and immediately, they noticed that one horse was burdened with a man lying head and feet down, over the saddle. Several others wore crude bandages. One of the townsmen was being helped out of the saddle. Cob said, "Don't recognize the horse or that one man, judging by clothing. Perhaps we should saunter over there."

The sheriff replied, "We'll do that, but we'll drink coffee until they get settled a bit. They'll have a story to tell, and I want to hear it. But I don't want a dozen versions, just the rangers. If any of ours are hurt, they'll let the clinic know soon enough."

"RAN that bunch all over creation up in those hills. Seems to be barely visible trails running off in all directions like a poorly planned cobweb. They simply abandoned the cattle and ran."

The trail-worn ranger was sitting with Cob and the sheriff. He hadn't simply taken a seat. He more or less melted into it, looking as if he just might stay there a while and then need help rising to his feet.

"Rustlers appeared to know every one of them trails. Couple of the townsmen wanted to forget it, and who could blame them? A twelve-man posse tracking riders on no end of single horse trails leading nowhere. Your deputy, sheriff, got the idea to follow a runoff trail that seemed to parallel the one the thieves were leading us on. Turned out to be a good guess. I kept the big bunch with me on the track we had been following.

"Hammond, your deputy, and one other fella called Blaze, they swung off to the north on the other trail. It apparently veered off for a while but came back together down the road a bit.

"Took two more days, but when the rustlers thought they were off and free, they found the deputy waiting for them, sheltered in a nice bunch of tumbled-down boulders.

"Deputy says he called them to a halt, but they chose otherwise. Everyone, rustlers and posse together, were worn down and tired. Edgy. Might have impacted their thinking. Anyway, seems as if they dove off their mounts and behind rocks on the opposite side of the trail. Blaze, he brought that first one down before they got to shelter. The others never got started. Deputy and his man poured enough lead after them, sending ricochets and shards of limestone off in every direction, to where they finally hollered for mercy. Deputy says this Blaze fella sure knows how and where to point the lead. Maybe I should recruit him for the rangers.

"Anyway, we hurried along with the sounds of shots ringing

across the hills. Still got there too late. Your boys had it all wrapped up, sheriff. Coup'la bullet nicks is the worst of it, except for that one draped over his saddle. The ones needing attention are over at the clinic now, under guard. Just the single dead man. Rustler thankfully. Always pains me to lose a posse man."

Cob said, "I don't see my men in that bunch."

"No, and you won't. I told them to take the cattle home. We helped them dig the bunch out of the hills and narrows and up over what your black rider, Moses, I believe he goes by, called Top Up Pass. From there, they were on their own."

Cob thanked the ranger and stood to his feet.

"Think I'll saunter over to the clinic. See if there's anyone there I know."

As he walked, Cob lifted his Colt from the holster and checked the charges. With Gwyneth and Summer busy patching up rustlers, there was no telling what might happen. What if the ranger had missed a holdout weapon on one of them? If escape appeared to be possible, he might take a hostage. Cob didn't even want to think about that.

The ranger was going to send for a judge and a couple more rangers. Until the trial was held and everyone was gone from their sleepy little town, Cob would be on the alert.

He got to the clinic and walked into turmoil. A careless townsman had let a rustler grab his weapon, lifting it right out of the exposed holster. Using the handgun as a threat, he was planning on disarming the other two guards, but Cob's entry changed his plans. He turned the weapon toward the door and, without even finding out who was entering, he squeezed the trigger. The shot missed Cob but took out a chunk of the door trim.

Ducking from the scattering slivers of recently cut oak, Cob was almost as upset at the damage done to the door as he was at the risk he was under. He lifted his own weapon and, with two shots, put the aggressor on the floor. Whether dead or alive,

Cob didn't care. The owner of the Colt quickly snatched it out of the man's hand and flashed it around the room, looking for more trouble before re-holstering it.

The inner door to the examination room eased open. It was Summer's eyes that peered out. When she saw Cob standing with his weapon in his hand, she opened the door wider and stepped out.

"What happened, Cob?"

"Something that shouldn't happen happened, that's what. But it's past and it don't matter any further. You might check that fella on the floor. Looks all dead to me, but I could be wrong."

"You want me to shoot him again if he's still alive?"

"I'd as soon shoot him again myself and these others along with him. But I guess the doctor may get upset supposing I should do that."

Summer got back to her feet after checking the man's pulse and breathing. She looked at Cob, saying, "Best get him out of here. There's no help for him. I know him though. He's one of the ones backing Carl Macon when he got himself shot a few weeks ago. Coward. Ran like a sissy, he did. Just as well he's gone. Now be quiet out here. The doctors are trying to work."

As the inner door reclosed, Cob said, "Couple of you boys take your old buddy there and tote him into the shade outside. We'll deal with him later. Another of you get a bucket and some water. Clean up this mess of blood and whatnot.

THE JUDGE CAME AND LEFT. The rangers escorted the surviving rustlers away to be dealt their due as the judge had determined. The town balked at the cost, but finally paid the bill rendered by the clinic for the treatment of prisoners. The clinic settled into the normal pattern of most small towns. Summer began keeping notes on all the foolish and careless ways folks managed to injure themselves. Gwyneth had begun the same ritual at Chicago General years before but finally gave it up, deciding there was a never-ending assortment of possibilities.

Summer's family decided they were needed at home. With hugs all around and promises to keep in touch, they mounted their borrowed Sombrero Ranch horses and buggy and rode south to the whistle-stop station. Tab escorted them and would bring the buggy back. Summer decided she had seen enough of her mother's tears and her brother's untrusting looks at Tab. To avoid more of the same, she claimed she was needed at the clinic.

A formal agreement between Tab and Cob was approved by Louis, who then headed for home, leaving his son in charge of the Sombrero and leading the remaining Hat riders.

Watching the last of the visitors ride from sight out past the Sombrero barn, Gwyneth turned to Cob, waiting for him to comment. With nothing to say, Cob simply put his arm around his wife's shoulder and walked to the big house. Juanita would have coffee hot. They would sit on the veranda for a bit, thinking it all through before heading back to town.

Chapter Thirty-Two

AN EVENING'S RIDE IN THE BUGGY SHOWED CAUSE FOR concern to Cob and Gwyneth. They hadn't been out to the flatland area for some weeks. It was time to make themselves acquainted. But they were startled to see a small tent-topped structure with a sign informing one and all that trade goods and general groceries were available. A short distance away was another tent-topped structure offering beds for the night.

Cob pulled the buggy horse to a stop, watching the movement of people. Although it was no land rush, there was certainly more activity than he had thought there might be.

Gwyneth brought both their thoughts to the surface. "It's like a town of its own. With the farms being small and each one housing a family, this could become serious competition to Sombrero."

Cob, deep in fearful thought, nodded but said nothing.

~

THE FOLLOWING DAY, with Gwyneth at her usual work in the clinic, Cob strolled down to Abe's general store. A warning of competition was in order, perhaps even a discussion on the entire situation with the small beginnings of a potential town center.

"Morn'n, Abe. Good to see you up and looking cheerful this morning. We haven't talked for a while. Thought it might be time we set aside a few minutes for a visit."

"Yes? Well, that's easy for you, having taken to your retirement and all. But Helen and me, we've got things to do."

"I don't see Helen. She taking a day off?"

"There's no such thing as a day off."

"Okay, partner, I'll talk while you work. Took a ride last evening. Gwyneth still won't let me mount a horse, so we were with the buggy. Drove out to the farmland area. Lots happening out there. Looks promising for the future of the area. You been out there lately?"

"Out there almost every day. That's where Helen is this morning."

Cob struggled to think that news through. Unable to make much sense of what he knew so far, he decided on the direct approach.

"Care to explain what you just said, Abe?"

"Nothing to explain really. Me and Helen, we learned this business the hard way, making mistakes and correcting as best as we could figure out. You saw a lot of that up in Kansas and Colorado. Should be no mystery to you."

"So, you know you have a bit of competition right in the farming area?"

"No competition I know of."

"Abe, there's a tent-topped shack out there advertising groceries and such."

"Sure is. That's where Helen spends her days."

Another pause brought clarity to Cob's mind. "You're saying that tent store is yours?"

"Sure enough. I wasn't about to let someone else be first on the ground. We got a start with Helen working the place, but we've got a grandson just coming into his adult years. We're working a deal with him to take on the running of it for us."

"Is the tent hotel yours too?"

"No. Got enough trouble and work with just the store. Make a wagon trip out there near enough every day, hauling stock to sell. Ordered in a load of farm supplies too. Well pumps, shovels, and such. Couple of windmills."

"You're amazing, Abe. We'll have to talk again."

Cob rigged out the buggy again the next morning. A long, slow drive through the farms, both operational and developing, drove home the thought that even the single mile separating the closest farms from the town of Sombrero may turn out to be an invitation for competition to spring up. He judged the furthest farm was near enough to ten miles from town. That was a long ride for a busy farmer when he found himself in need. It was a long ride too when a medical emergency arose. And the hard truth was that two towns a mile or two apart couldn't both thrive. They would either grow together as the country grew, or one would thrive and the other die out.

Cob stopped to talk with several people along the way. He talked mostly to women while the men were either building or working the farms, having no time to talk. One of his questions was whether or not the folks were aware of the new clinic in town. Some were, most were not. He arrived back in Sombrero with a thought brewing in his head. A thought that needed discussion with Gwyneth at the first opportunity. That opportunity came after dinner when they were discussing their day's events over coffee.

After listening to Cob and sorting out the details of his ride through the farming area, she asked, "So what are you saying?"

"I guess I'm asking more than saying. Is there some easy way to spread the news about the clinic and your better-than-usual training and experience?"

The question was not one easily answered. Gwyneth was silent for longer than Cob was comfortable with, but he had to acknowledge that dealing with men and cattle was a sight easier and less challenging than dealing with illness, injuries, and medical services. So, he waited through the long pause.

When Gwyneth lifted her eyes to his, she said, "I never once thought of advertising. But the truth is that I was successful in Pueblo largely because a couple of small, local newspapers noticed my presence and sang my praises to their readers. And going back to the beginning, the papers noticed me because when the small hospital couldn't deal with a man badly injured in the steel mill, he was brought to me. In fact, he was my first patient. So, you might say I enjoyed a degree of notoriety right from the start. After that, I was never without patients."

Again, there was silence, this time broken by Cob. "We could write up a single-page pass-out. Explain about the clinic and its services. We could cover one side with your story and the other side with Dr. Shultz's story. I could hand-deliver them all through that area out there. Even here in town, if you thought it necessary."

"There's no printer in town, nor any newspaper. What do we do about that?"

"We go to where there's a printer."

"And how do we find out where that is? Are you planning on riding all over the country until you find one?"

"No. I wouldn't want to be away from you for that long. In any case, it's not necessary. Now, to explain myself clearly, if you watch carefully the next time you're walking downtown, my dear doctor wife, you just might see a little building with a pole rising from the roof. On that pole is a wire that hangs in the air until it reaches another pole just like the first, and from there it disappears into the mysterious netherworld. Also mysterious are the little blips the man with a special key sends over that wire.

I've heard him call them dots and dashes. Anyway, it all somehow happens that someone far, far away in that netherworld hears those mysterious blips and sends back a series of his own blips. Then, for about sixty cents, the man sitting at that key will actually write out what those blips mean. And so, we contact the outer world."

Gwyneth was watching him intently as he rambled on. Answering with a bit of sarcastic storytelling of her own, she said, "Why, that's amazing, Cob. Do other folks know about this wonderful tool, or is it mostly your secret? But, of course, I'm looking at the one who wanted a letter delivered on horseback until a sprite of a girl rewrote it into dots and dashes and sent it off. She must have gone to that little building to do all of that."

"All right, enough of that. You stay with your doctoring, working on your write-up in your spare time. Have Gabriel write his up too. Leave the finding of a printer to me."

The sun had gone down while they drank their coffee. Rising from their porch seats together without so much as a suggestion that the day had been long and trying, Cob laid his hand on Gwyneth's shoulder, pulling her close, while she lay her head on his shoulder. The door squeaked just a bit as they entered and squeaked again as Cob closed it behind them.

THE NEW HOUSE was coming along. As anxious as Cob and Gwyneth were to have it completed, Summer was equally anxious to move into town. She loved her time on the ranch, and she couldn't imagine anyone not thriving on Juanita's cooking and care. Then there were the alone times with Tab. Clearly their relationship was growing in a direction that pleased Summer, but they were nowhere close to being more than serious friends. Her desire to return to the little cabin was simply the need to be released from her twice-daily rides between the ranch and town. And with winter coming on, as easy as Cob claimed their winters to be, the rides would lose their warm, early morning, magical appeal.

Cob and the sheriff were enjoying their mid-afternoon coffee, this time sitting outside to enjoy the lovely, cooling fall weather. The change was a welcome coolness after the summer's heat. Their conversation stopped when a lathered horse ridden by a boy of about ten years, by Cob's guess, rode up to the boardwalk in front of where they were seated.

"You men know where the doctor is?"

"What do you need a doctor for, young man?"

"Don't. It's for Pa and Ma and them others. Mighty sick. Sent me to fetch the doctor."

"That horse is about done in, boy. You've ridden him hard. Come some distance too, I'm guessing. You step down. Sheriff here will take your mount over to the livery. Get him a bait of oats and a rub down. Hostler's good at his job. You and me, we'll walk to the clinic. It's not far."

Cob found himself being gauged by the boy's untrusting eyes. But seeing no alternative, he swung his leg over and dropped to the ground. His knees buckled as his feet hit the road, and he dropped until he stopped the fall with his outstretched hands. Cob jumped to his feet and reached for the youngster, saying, "Whoa there, boy. You're about as done in as your animal. How far have you come?"

"Some distance. Don't know the miles. Come all the way like Pa said to do. Daren't stop."

"Well, come along. I'll get you to the doctors."

Dr. Shultz had a patient under care, but Gwyneth was sitting in the small kitchen area, enjoying a cup of tea. Cob led the youngster in saying, "Young man to see you, Doctor. Says his folks are mighty unwell. From a ranch somewhere far up into the hills."

Gwyneth stood and dipped the boy a cup of cool well water, setting it on the table. "Sit down, son. Tell me what this is all about."

The boy nearly choked on the water before he slowed down for a second swallow. Gwyneth waited patiently.

"Don't know what's wrong. Some sickness. Ma and Pa are both down. Two brothers and a sister, too. Gramps is all right, but Gram died yesterday. Gramps is too old to make the ride to here. Pa sent me. 'Get the lady doctor,' he said. I'm guessing that's you, ma'am."

The question didn't need an answer.

"Tell me how they're sick. Are they coughing? Feverish? Rash or blisters on the skin? Throwing up? What can you tell me, son? Tell me too, has anyone off the ranch been to some other town or just arrived from somewhere else?"

Cob broke in with, "Tell us your name, boy."

The boy was taking another big swallow of water. With a gulp, he drew in the last of it, caught his breath, and said, "Bennie Chalmers, sir."

"All right, Bennie, what can you tell the doctor?"

"Gramps, he rode down to the station some days ago. Met the train and brought up a man about my Pa's age. Said he was my uncle, Pa's brother. I don't know where he came from, but I never before saw him. Then, four days after, Gran took to her bed. Ain't like Gran to do so. She died maybe three days later."

"Did you see her, Bennie? Did she have blisters on her face? Any other signs that would say she was sick?"

"Folks hustled me and the other kids aside. Wouldn't let us come close. They buried her on the hillside above the house."

"And what signs do your folks have, Bennie?"

"Ma, she's all the time hot, thrashing in her sleep, throwing her blankets off. Says her head hurt something awful."

Gwyneth looked at Cob. "Smallpox. Brought in by the uncle, sure as shooting."

"Can you do anything for it?"

"I don't have any vaccine. Too late for those folks anyway. Vaccine doesn't help once the patient is ill. But there are things that can be done."

Gwyneth looked back at Bennie, "Tell me where your home is, Bennie. And how long it took you to ride to town."

"Ranch is near to the other side of that big hill you can see to the west. Only you don't go in that way. Folks don't have no clock 'cep't the sun. I suppose I got aboard ol' Hank bout breakfast time this morning. Never once stopped except to water the animal. Jest kep a-com'n."

Cob did the numbers in his head. "That's a good six hours, Gwyneth. More going uphill to get back."

"Bennie, can a buggy or a wagon get up the trail?"

"Folks got a wagon up a couple a times, but I ain't seen it used for quite a while. Lots of new growth on the two-track. Might need to chop out some small trees."

"All right, you men. Cob, you take Bennie and get him some food at the café. Have them pack a good lunch for three. Get the buggy out and our saddle horses. Put the saddles in the buggy to make it easier on the horses until we need them. If Bennie's animal isn't fit for the back trail, get him another from the livery. Leave his here. Take Summer's black. That's the best ride for you if you're coming along, Cob. He's steady and tough. I'll pack up some gear here and we'll get on our way."

Cob, wise to hill travel said, "You do realize it would be full dark long before we get to their ranch, if we ever do."

Gwyneth said, "Bennie, can you find the trail in the dark. Is it well enough broken out of the brush?"

"If I can't, ol' Hank can."

"All right. Let's move. You haven't ridden since the shooting, Cob. We'll ride the buggy as far as possible. Then you have to promise to tell me if you're not well."

A HALF HOUR LATER, with Gwyneth rushing home to slip into men's riding pants and grab a warm coat, they were leaving town, praying it wasn't too late.

The trail left Sombrero behind, heading mostly west, until just the trace of a two-track was seen on the left. Bennie, riding a rental animal the livery promised would be able to hold out for the distance, turned with no talk or explanation. Almost immediately, they started to climb. The hillside was lightly covered with shrubbery and small, native, semi-desert growth. Interspersed among the other plants were beds of prickly pear. Cob, knowing the country from birth, idly thought, *be more cactus the further we go.*

The slight hill leveled out after a mile or so, settling into a gravel-based canyon sided with rocky escarpments. The brush on the trail was rubbing on the bottom of the buggy. The horses were sidestepping around the multitude of prickly pear. Clearly, if the family were to live in these hills, they would need to spend some energy with an axe and a shovel, improving the passage.

The level reprieve from the climb was short, no more than another mile. Then the more serious climbing started. The trail wound around as the canyon bent, with the escarpments beginning to level out. Soon, the trail cleared the canyon, still climbing, but now out in the clear, as if they were riding on the top side of the hill. But with the return to clear daylight, unencumbered by the steep-sided canyon, came more growth, and more difficulty for the buggy horse. After a few hundred yards, Cob pulled the buggy to a halt, looking ahead. With the hand that was holding the reins, he pointed ahead, saying, "Tough going up ahead."

Calling out to Bennie, he asked, "Figure this might be about halfway, Bennie?"

"I'd guess it's some less than that. Good place to go to riding though."

"My thinking too, Bennie. We'll turn the buggy around, so we don't have to do it in the dark on the return ride. Then we'll swing over to the horses."

Gwyneth's black bag and another satchel of medicines and such were tied behind Bennie's saddle since he was much the lightest. His horse could handle that load without trouble. As Gwyneth was watching Cob and Bennie rig out, her eyes went to Bennie's slim form and gaunt look, and then to the uphill ranch they were headed for, wondering how they lived and what diet they managed to sustain. Certainly, Bennie showed no signs of overeating. He was strong though, from hard work, that was obvious, in spite of his thin arms and shoulders, demonstrated with the ease with which he handled the big stock saddle.

Underway again, they were able to move a bit faster than travel with the buggy had allowed. Cob moved with the horse as he always had, showing no signs of being grounded from riding for weeks. But it was his breathing Gwyneth was watching. That's where his trouble would arise if trouble there was to be.

The day was just short of full dark when the rough log buildings came into view. Gwyneth was struck by how beautiful the location was, even covered mostly by shadow and sunset glare. She immediately understood the choice the family had made. They had been walking their horses through several miles of grass, liberally interspersed with cactus and broken rock, but still good grazing. They had waded across several runs of water. All in all, a good ranching country for a small spread. But even with all of that, she suspected the final decision on location was a financial decision. If there had been funds available, most families would choose an easier setting, no matter the beauty around them.

As soon as they rode into the yard, they were noticed by an

old man sitting in the shade of a small shack, which turned out to be the home he and his wife had shared, up until her passing a couple of days before. The spry old grandpa—as rail thin as Bennie, but bigger in the bones, dressed in bib overalls with no shirt, wearing boots with no laces, and topped off with what appeared to be a home-wound straw hat—almost sprang to his feet. With a smile, he said, "Yer back, Bennie. And good on ya. Ye brought along some help. Well, step down, y'all. Yer welcome as the sunrise. I'll take yer animals. Bennie, you get some rest. Best ye go ta the loft, keep'n yerself off ta the side till the doctor sorts this all out."

Appreciating the old man's wisdom, Gwyneth smiled down from her saddle. "That's good advice, Bennie. I'll come and talk with you just as soon as there's anything to talk about."

"Name's Sol," the grandfather said. "Jest as easy as it sounds. Jest Sol."

Cob spoke for the first time since entering the yard. Still sitting his saddle, he said, "Good to meet you, Sol. That's a fine young grandson you've got there. Fine boy. I'm Cob. Cob Fleming, Sombrero Ranch. I'm not a medicine man. Just came along to escort my wife, Dr. Gwyneth Wycome. She'll do whatever is to be done here to help your family."

"I know who you are. Seen ya a time er two down ta the town. Know the doctor by sight too. Was in town when that posse returned after making a mess of things up here. Asked around when I seen her aid'n the wounded. That's why I told Bennie ta fetch her particular. Didn't want no other doc. Figured the family needs the best there is."

With nothing to add to that conversation, Cob stepped to the ground. Gwyneth dismounted too and passed her reins to Cob. Bennie had untied the medical bags and laid them where they were close to hand for Gwyneth.

Before heading to the house, Gwyneth addressed Sol again. "What's happened since Bennie rode out this morning?

"Noth'n far as I knows. I'm hold'n shy of the house, ya

understand. Bennie's folks, they be in the big house. Kids 'r in the barn, bedded down as far apart as I could git 'em. I check on the kids time ta time. Haven't been near the house, except ta prop the door open a while back ta let in some air."

"You're doing just fine, Sol. I'm glad you're here to help."

With that, she picked up her two bags and walked to the house. Beside the porch and just a safe distance away to protect the cabin from fire was a burning pit, complete with a rock enclosure and a metal slatted grill. Perhaps the family sometimes cooked outside to hold at least a bit of coolness inside. But really, it was more likely that this was the washstand where a tin boiler would lie over the fire while the clothing was stirred, mashed, and finally rinsed and wrung out on a line. But whatever it was, today it would be a water warming stand. She called Cob over and explained the need for hot water and left him to figure it out.

On the porch, typical of ranch layouts, was the wash bench. There was a bucket of water, a washbasin, homemade soap, and a semi-clean towel.

Gwyneth took advantage of the provisions before lifting a clean towel from the satchel, avoiding the used one. She buttoned her blouse to the top. She wanted as little skin available as possible. Her long sleeves hung just a bit past her wrists. She dug out a bottle of disinfectant and massaged it into her hands and all around her face and neck, being careful to avoid her eyes. With a mask tied tightly in place, she was ready to see to her patients.

The door propped open by the grandfather was letting flies in, but when Gwyneth stepped into the stifling heat of the kitchen, she told herself the old man had made the better of the two choices. Hot, dark, and rank. Put together, it presented a poor combination for the ill. On the table was a lamp. Gwyneth found a match on the cupboard shelf and lit it. The entire hilltop, including the small ranch, would soon be in full darkness. She would do as much as possible before that happened.

From the kitchen, she could see three doorways. Each had a blanket curtain separating her from whatever was hidden behind. Cringing a bit at the possibilities, she moved to the first door, elbowing the curtain aside. The doorway opened into a small bedroom, clean and with the bed made neatly, but empty. The room across the short hallway was its duplicate. These would be the children's rooms. Another door took up most of the end wall of the hallway. Holding the lamp ahead of her, Gwyneth stepped past the curtain into dimness and almost intolerable warmth.

On top of the blankets lay a man of perhaps thirty-five years, although Gwyneth wouldn't lay a bet on his age. He was unshaven and haggard. Sweat was the most prominent feature wherever there was exposed skin, which in this case was from the waist up. Two bleary and illness-shaded eyes studied her. Despite that signal of consciousness, there was no speaking, although the man's lips worked just a bit. The woman beside him wore her full nightdress, adding to the heat she was already enveloped in. Perspiration soaked through most of the nightdress. Her eyes were closed tightly, not in death, Gwyneth hoped.

She bent close to the man. "Can you see and hear me, sir?"

Just a slight head nod.

"My name is Dr. Wycome. Your son came to town and guided me up here. Can you move? Do you think you could stand up and walk just a bit?"

Again, there was a nod.

"All right. You stay here until I come for you."

Gwyneth went back outside and called for Cob. When he joined her, she explained about washing thoroughly, covering his skin, and treating himself with the disinfectant. He caught on to that and the mask immediately.

"All right. You get yourself ready. I'm going to need you in just a few minutes."

Back in the bedroom, she said, "Sir, I'm going to help you

stand now. But you have to help me too. You're too heavy for me to lift. We're going to get you as far as a kitchen chair. Do you think you can do that?"

The answer was the nod she expected.

~

AFTER A MAJOR STRUGGLE and a threatened collapse that, together, they managed to prevent, he was seated in the kitchen. With warnings not to fall off, Gwyneth left him there. She stepped outside and returned almost immediately with Cob.

"We're going to lift a mattress off one of these beds in the small room. Take it outside. Find a level spot to place it on and do what you can with the straw filling. Then we're moving the man out there. Ready?"

"Done," was all Cob said.

Moving the mattress was only the work of a couple of minutes. Finding a level spot to lay it and to flatten out the straw stuffing was a bigger task, but soon it was set, and they returned for the man. With total fatigue being close to the surface, the man came near to collapse again, but Cob took him under the arms and half-dragged him to his new bed. As gently as possible, they laid him down.

With a joking few words that almost appeared out of place in these dreary surroundings, Gwyneth said, "Perhaps I should train you to be my nurse. You show all the makings."

Cob came back with "Anything to help the woman I love." But neither believed what the other said.

When they had both caught their breath, Gwyneth said, "Now, we'll want another mattress. You can do that yourself while I deal with the woman. And I'll be wanting that warm water just as soon as possible too."

Gwyneth re-entered the house and closed in on the sick woman. Propping up the lamp carefully, as close as safely possible, she untied the strings that held the top of the nightdress tight and pushed it over one shoulder and then the other, pleased to see there were no markings or signs of a rash. There was, however, a rash on her face and neck, but no signs of red spots or sores. Since there were no vomit remains on the bed or floor, she assumed stomach distress hadn't yet been a problem. The woman would almost certainly be contagious, but so far, she could see no signs of anything leading to death, although the patient was most certainly experiencing discomfort enough.

Again, calling Cob, she instructed him on the moving of the woman. When she was finished, he said, "Just a suggestion, my love, since she's unconscious and certainly can't help by walking, why don't I simply pick her up and carry her out?"

"Now why didn't I think of that? There is a warning though. I believe you and I are about as protected as we can be, but there's still a slight possibility of us catching this awful thing."

"We're in this far, Gwyneth. And wasting time won't fix anything. Let's do it."

And they did.

WATCHING FROM AFAR, and sensing the need, Sol brought lit lanterns, setting one beside each outside bed, on chairs he brought from the kitchen. Then, wordlessly, he moved to the barn where he would check the children again, his self-assigned task. As Sol was turning to leave, Gwyneth stopped him with a question.

"Sol, Bennie said you had had a visitor recently, an uncle, brother to the patient here."

"And so, we did. My son. Lives down by the coast. Came for a short visit about two weeks ago. Only stayed a few days. Gone back home now."

"All right, Sol, thanks."

When the old man was out of hearing, Gwyneth said, "The

brother. Almost certainly the source of this plague. Brought it in with him."

Cob asked, "Wouldn't he have been sick himself then?"

"Not necessarily in the very early stages. He'd be a carrier though. Probably picked it up during his travels. And that means there's another plague going on right now, down south somewhere. He's probably sick enough by now. And there's no guessing how many he infected in his travels. We'll say nothing about that right now. Sol has enough on his mind."

With the parents laid out in the fresh air, it was time for Gwyneth to check on the children. Before leaving, she said, "Cob, I'm going to need you to tend to the fires. We're going to bathe both husband and wife. And since you're the closest I have to a nurse, you're going to help. Don't get squeamish. It's just a thing that has to be done. Provided the patients wake up and survive, we'll say nothing about it. The less they know, the better."

HOLDING a lantern so Gwyneth could kneel by each child, Sol walked her from one bed of straw to the next. They were all asleep, lulled by the occasional snort of a stalled horse or the shifting feet of the milk cow.

"Jest tired now, is all, I suspect. They was all awake not long ago. I fed them some beef broth soup. Heavy. Almost more a stew. Kids 'r tough. I'm hoping the strength God built inta them will pull them outa this."

"I'll hope and pray for that too, Sol, but in the meantime, I'll do the couple of small things I know to do. You will have to understand that not much is known about smallpox. There's a vaccine for it that's showing some promise. But once a person has the disease, it's too late for the vaccine. Anyway, they're all breathing easily, and none are showing signs of distress. We'll let them sleep while I deal with their folks. Have you checked Bennie?"

"Cain't hardly make the ladder to the loft anymore, but we talked. Says he's feel'n good, jest tired from that long ride."

WITH A STEADIER HAND than Gwyneth expected from him, and with nothing to say, Cob followed Gwyneth's instructions, cleaning the woman first and putting on a fresh nightdress found on a shelf in the bedroom. Showing his strength gained from a lifetime of hard work, Cob lifted and held the woman aloft while Gwyneth stripped the bedding and replaced it, again from a small supply in the bedroom.

The bedding and the nightdresses both husband and wife were wearing were bundled up and carried away, held for later burning. The mattress from their bed was added to the fire pile.

While Gwyneth was doing what she could for the patients, Cob went from room to room opening windows and folding back curtains.

Together, Gwyneth and Cob prepared tea from a supply of herbs brought from Colorado and warmed up the last of the soup/stew Sol had on hand. One by one, Cob lifted the patients to a sitting position, propping them against his knee while Gwyneth fed them, managing at the same time to get a bit of liquid past their closed lips. None of what they did held a cure. As far as medical science knew, there was no cure for smallpox. The best Gwyneth hoped to do was keep them somewhat comfortable while the stew and tea fed their bodies. If they were to survive, it would be their own inward strength fighting off the scourge that held a tight grip on them.

Cob found some clean blankets they used to cover the patients. When he was done and Gwyneth had done all she could for their comfort, she said, "Let's pray it doesn't rain. The night will be colder than we'll find comfortable, it might be warmer in the loft if we get a chance for some sleep."

TOGETHER, Cob and Gwyneth went from child to child, repeating what they had done for the parents. Sol stayed well past his bedtime, putting together another pot of soup/stew. His little cabin was warm and surprisingly comfortable. After making her rounds again, carrying a lantern, checking the patients, Gwyneth and Cob rolled out their bedding on Sol's floor and lay down. Cob lay awake long into the night, thankful his weary wife was able to sleep, and wondering what the day would bring.

The following morning, the rising sun showed a few blisters on the woman's mouth. Lifting the nightdress away from her shoulders revealed the beginning of a rash. There was no question, the disease was progressing. Again, Gwyneth knew there was no cure, only comfort from pain to be offered from the best medical care had to offer.

The husband was in better condition. He would undoubtedly follow the normal pattern well established by smallpox, but he was certainly stronger than his wife and perhaps had more internal resistance. He would be sick, there was no doubt of that, but possibly not quite so sick. When the sun moved across the sky far enough to peek around the corner of the cabin, swathing the two mattresses in light, he blinked his eyes, looked around, as if orienting himself, and pushed the blankets away. With some effort, he sat up, and glancing at his wife, and then at Gwyneth. He asked, "You the doctor?"

"I am, Mr. Chalmers. Gwyneth Wycome. My husband is with me. Cob, by name. He's checking on the children."

Glancing again at his still-prone wife, he asked, "What about Mona?"

"She's not as well as you appear to be. She has blisters

around her mouth this morning. And the beginning of a rash on her upper body."

"What does that mean?"

"It means the disease is progressing."

"And again, Doctor, what does that mean?"

"MONA, like you and the children, will almost undoubtedly follow the illness through to the conclusion. You will have mouth blisters and a chest rash. You may have a very high fever and vomiting. You will most likely feel very weak. And to be honest, there is a very good possibility that one or more of you could pass away. This is a very serious disease."

"And yet, you're here. You and your husband."

Gwyneth chose not to respond to the remark.

THOSE WHO COULD EAT WERE OFFERED a few spoonsful of Sol's stew. And all the water they could take in and hold down. The children were brought out into the light and treated as best Gwyneth could. Bennie climbed from the loft but was warned not to come anywhere close.

And so, the morning passed, with Gwyneth trying to find an answer to the problem of caring for patients in this very isolated location, and with seriously limited supplies. At noon, she had a thought and a proposal. She went to Sol.

"Sol. I see a sturdy wagon there beside the barn. Is it in good usable order?"

"Don't use it but to haul in cut hay, but it's never failed us."

"And I assume you have a strong team."

"Indeed, we do. Maybe the best we ever had."

"I have a suggestion, Sol. Cob and I can't stay here for the full time of the need. The disease could take another ten days or more to work its way through to the end. Even if we could stay, the work is too much, facing the circumstances, and what we have to work with."

"Tell me what I can do."

"You can hitch that team and wagon and throw on a foot or so of hay. When you're set, Cob will carry the children and place them in the wagon, as far apart as possible. Then we'll move the parents. You and Bennie will stay away. Cob and I will deal with the patients."

"You'll saddle horses for yourself and Bennie and put a couple of axes on the wagon. Then we're going to town. Cob will drive the team. You and Bennie will ride ahead, cutting out any brush that might stop the wagon. Move a rock or two that might have fallen from above. Smaller growth, we'll simply plow through. We're taking these patients where they can get more help. You and Bennie will return here. Stay away from the house. Burn that pile of bedding and such.

"It's best you leave the cabin windows and door open. It's asking a lot, Sol, but if it was my home, I would burn it to the ground. At the very least, all the clothing, bedding, and such must be hauled out and burned. But don't you do that. You would almost certainly be struck down with the malady. Just leave it as it is. In two or three months, it will be much safer to deal with it. When the family can return, they mustn't live in the cabin until that time has passed. Leave the doors and windows open.

"Now, Sol, you've seen how Cob and I covered ourselves up, including the masks. That's the only way you can move around the cabin, or even the straw in the kids' beds, without risking yourself and Bennie. Is that all understood, Sol?"

"Clear as a summer day, Doctor. Some time before I'm called home to Glory, I hope to find a way to show my thanks for all you've done."

"Just take care of yourself, Sol. You're one of a kind."

Chapter Thirty-Three

Taking the wagon down the rock-riddled, brush-smothered mountain trail was something Cob hoped to only have to do once. The team balked but continued pulling. The saddle horses, tied on behind, suffered when saplings would spring back from their forced bend as the wagon pushed them down, only to snap back, whapping the following animals on legs and chest. It was Bennie who came up with the solution. "Sir, I'm thinking we should cut those horses loose. I'll fall back and push them along, but they'd have no reason to stop or leave the trail. Be easier on them."

Cob replied, "That's a very good idea, Bennie. I'll hold the team if you can untie them."

Surprisingly, Dale, Bennie's father, rolled halfway over until he could reach the ropes. "Stay to your horse, Son, I can get it from here."

Sol and Bennie, as need dictated, cut some of the bigger trees, then stood aside, watching to see if the wagon could make it through. The ride was slow and tedious. An hour became four, then six. When they reached the abandoned buggy, Cob hauled the rig to a stop. He stepped down and gathered up the loose animals, unsaddling them and throwing the leather into the back of the buggy. With the buggy horse harnessed and all in readiness, Gwyneth took her place on the seat of the smaller conveyance. Cob retied the saddlers to the back of the wagon. Night was coming on, and there was little challenge to the rest of the downward trail. They would follow easily.

Together they bid Sol and Bennie well as they turned their horses for the ride back to the ranch and whooped the team into movement. They would arrive after full dark, which suited Gwyneth just fine. Driving through town with a wagon-load of smallpox patients could cause all kinds of misery and misunderstanding.

They eased around the town without drawing any serious inquiry and headed for the clinic. Surprisingly, there was a light in the window. Cob continued on with the wagon, past the clinic building, and into the total darkness of the hillside. Gwyneth turned aside. Wanting to attract no attention at all from the town, she drove to the back door and dismounted. A rap on the door brought Summer. As the light fell on Gwyneth, she warned, "Don't come near, Summer. Stay where you are."

"What's happening?"

A very brief explanation silenced the young nurse until she asked, "What can I do?"

"Why are you here this late, Summer?"

"A young woman, a girl really, had a difficult birth this afternoon. Dr. Shultz saw to it. I'm just here to watch over things till morning."

Gwyneth listed off several medications and most of the disinfectants stored in the clinic. When Summer rushed back to the door with those gathered in a sack, Gwyneth added, "And gather up some bandage material and a roll of cotton for mustard plasters."

Gwyneth laid the two sacks on the floor of the buggy and returned to the clinic door.

"Is your patient awake?"

"Yes."

"Tell her you will be gone for no longer than a quarter hour. Then run to Abe's home. Wake him up. Have him go to the store. I need at least a dozen warm blankets. As many ground sheets as he has in stock. Three changes of clothing for kids, and two for adults. Sleeping wear and day wear. Tell him to bring it right away to where he'll see lantern light on the hillside behind the clinic.

"Then he's to gather up the fixings and take them home for Helen. Tell him we need dinner for seven people and some plates and such. Sick folks won't be big eaters, so there's no need to do but partial fixings. We'll be wanting breakfast too. Be sure they both know not to come into camp. We've got a whole family out here on a big wagon. Smallpox. We have to keep them from town, and we can't infect the clinic. We're going to rig a covering of some sort, far from here."

ABE, with no certainty from the little that Summer was able to tell him, thought to himself, *Don't know what's going on, but if Gwyneth says she needs it, that's what's going to happen.*

Within one hour, Abe pulled his rig to where the lantern light directed him. A voice from the dark, Cob's voice, advised, "No closer, Abe. Sick folks here. Smallpox. Contagious. You don't want any part of it. If you could unload that gather, I'll wait till you're gone and then pick it up. You don't want to get close to either Gwyneth or me."

Cob carried the sacks stuffed with bedding and clothing to where a second lantern lit the hillside. There was one large, heavy bundle. As he watched from a safe distance, he asked, "What's that, Abe?"

"Happened to have a big tent. Thought you might use it."

"And you sure thought right. I'll thank you now, but I know Gwyneth will want to thank you special when she's got the time."

Abe had given a light slap on the horses' rumps and said, "Be back just as soon as Helen's got some grub cooked up for you."

~

THE SUN ROSE bright and clear, although there was a small showing of clouds off to the west. With the lateness of the season, there was a constant threat of rain. Cob walked beside Gwyneth as she checked each patient. Helen would soon be sending a small breakfast out, but other than the father, whatever food was taken in would be force-fed by Cob and Gwyneth.

Cob then went to look at the rolled canvas that Abe said would make a large tent when it was erected. He had stored it a distance from the wagon bearing the sick family. He had no idea how to erect it, but he'd figure it out, given time. He and Gwyneth had both enjoyed a night's sleep under the wagon, so with Helen's breakfast offering, they would be fit for the day. As Cob was just managing to get a start on the tent, Summer rode up on her gelding. Cob had turned the loose saddlers in at the livery, with instructions to keep them separate for at least one week. Summer had retrieved her black, first thing.

Staying a distance away, Summer addressed Gwyneth. "What can I do to help?"

"You're helping by keeping your distance. I know you've been up all night, but if you had strength enough left for a ride to the ranch, I'd ask you to ride out and bring Juanita in. Tell her we need a good cook. She can stay in our cabin until the crisis is over."

Cob hollered, "And bring in Moses and one or two others. Someone who might know something about big tents."

~

By noon, it was all in place. Suspended on fresh-cut poles, the tent was already occupied. They had no mattresses, so the hay was dragged in from the wagon. It would do, with the ground sheets protecting the family from the dampness of the earth.

After Juanita delivered her first offering of food, Gwyneth had to explain again how the patients were able to eat only small portions.

A week of busyness, with the work and care continually repeating itself, came near to wearing out both Cob and Gwyneth. And at the end of that week, there came a shout from town. Cob looked up to see just two riders herding a small bunch of perhaps five hundred cattle. Cob knew immediately who they were and guessed at the story.

Sol saw the tent on the hillside and spoke to Bennie. Bennie went back to holding the cattle in a tight bunch while Sol rode for the tent. He stopped far enough away that he had to holler to be heard. His first words were, "How are they? All still alive?"

"Still alive, Sol. Sick but improving, I believe. But what's with the cattle?"

"Decided we'd best give 'er up. Spent long enough up in the big lonesome with no folks around. Rode the hills till we found most of the stock and brought 'em down."

"What about the place, Sol?"

"Ain't no place no more. No more but ashes. Stacked the few keeper items. Hid 'em in the brush along with some tools. Touched a match to every piece of burnable wood. Burnt 'em and left. Need a place for the cattle."

Cob sent Sol up to the Sombrero with a message. Let Tab sort it out.

~

Time itself seemed to drag on. The Chalmers parents gradually improved until, with guidance from Gwyneth, they were able to manage for themselves. They had both been through the blister and rash phase, arriving at the point where the blisters dried up and eventually the scabs fell off, leaving a permanent scar to attest to them having been through it.

The children advanced through the stages of infection a bit more slowly, but within three weeks, they, too, were showing health. When Cob mentioned to Sol how fortunate the family was to have all survived, except the grandmother, the old man replied, "Ain't just so sure it was the smallpox that took her down. She'd been ail'n for some time. Anyway, she died just three days after her son was welcomed onto the place. The doctor explained the stages of the sickness, and hers don't fit. Anyways, you're right on this much. We have more reason than most to be thankful and to praise the Lord for his care."

One long month to the day after Bennie had ridden that long rocky trail to seek help, Gwyneth checked over the family for the last time. For several days, they had been doing mostly for themselves.

Hearts and lungs all seemed normal. They had not altogether regained their strength, but Gwyneth considered that to be acceptable. They each had scars they would carry for life, but there was no cure or prevention for that. The thanks at Gwyneth's parting from the family was emotional and sincere. Promises to keep in touch were typical but perhaps not altogether necessary or practical.

Cob pumped the last barrel of water he hoped to have to pump for a while and wagoned it up to the family. New clothing supplied by Abe was laid out for all of them. Cob walked to the cabin Juanita had taken over to tell her there was nothing more for her to do. He was going up to the ranch. He advised her to rent a horse or the livery buggy to keep a safe distance from him. The set schedule for smallpox said he was well into the safe period, but he wanted a bath and clean clothing before he mixed with anyone. Cob would use the ranch facilities to bathe, and he had adequate, clean clothing at the ranch. What clothing he removed would be burned.

Gwyneth would use her own cabin for her bath. She planned to soak off any remains of the disease. And while she soaked, she would go over in her mind every thought, every memory of the last month.

A few days later, Sol had found her just as she was leaving the clinic. "Doctor, I told Cob one time up on the hill that perhaps I would live long enough to someday thank you proper. That still holds true. But I know you missed a whole month of your normal work—Cob did too. And several of your friends pitched in to help. Abe and Juanita, especially. So again, I've come to say thank you."

"Sol, your thoughtfulness is much appreciated, but again, you must remember—there is very little medical science can do for smallpox. It's mostly the strength of the patients' already healthy bodies, the surrounding cleanliness, and the good food. That's what saved your family."

"I'm remembering you telling me that some time ago, but still, our thanks for your sacrifice stands."

Holding out a small bag Gwyneth could see held coins, he continued, "Until that better time, perhaps this will help pay for Abe's supplies and for your time, with a bit for Juanita."

Gwyneth allowed the old man to drop the small sack into her hand. It was much heavier than she had expected—only gold coins could be that heavy. She looked up but Sol was already walking away, his gratitude spoken, his debt quietly paid.

Chapter Thirty-Four

In the weeks following the defeat of the smallpox invasion, Cob seldom mentioned the month with the Chalmers family. Gwyneth was equally silent in public, but alone, her mind seemed to be in a constant whirl. She thought of goals dreamed but not yet realized. The clinic, unavailable to her for the full of that month, weighed heavily on her heart. She rocked between feelings of failure for her absence and thankfulness that Gabriel Shultz had been able to pick up the slack. Gabriel, in keeping with his nature, pushed a lot of the praise onto Summer.

The adobe being built for Cob and Gwyneth was completed. Furniture ordered through Abe and Helen from catalogs kept on display in the store was delivered on two large wagons. The cottage was turned back to Summer, who was more than happy to be relieved of the ride in from the ranch each morning and the return ride in the evening. As much as she had seen no cause for concern for her safety since the Carl Macon incident, the truth was that she was just a little bit frightened during the fall morning and evening rides, both of which were taken in the semi-dark.

Juanita, surprising no one at all, continued to make trips to the sheriff's small dwelling, leaving behind a thoroughly scrubbed and cleaned living space, and a larder weighted down with sufficient rations to keep Olaf contented until her next visit.

The closeness between Dr. Diego Esteban and the lovely Lupita appeared to be growing, although Lupita was never heard to comment, and the glowing recital of the doctor, although always entertaining, was not totally believable. What was true was that Lupita was back in her small Cafecito, and Diego's reports on the wonders of her kitchen were drawing new faces with new coins to her place of business.

Gwyneth and Dr. Shultz worked out a rotation schedule, giving each doctor one day in every week free of the clinic. The remaining five days, they would work as needed, moving between home calls and clinic patients. There would be no Sunday calls except in emergencies.

On one of her free days, Gwyneth decided to take another buggy ride through the rapidly developing farmlands. As an unchanging habit, when she traveled, her black medical bag traveled with her. Late fall or early winter, depending on the opinion of the speaker, had taken over the land. Although there were still signs of unharvested crops, the time for planting was over. It was time for clearing and preparing the land for the future. Well-drilling seemed to never stop. A few settlers, those with more time than money available, were hand-digging wells. Brutally hard work and somewhat dangerous, but except for the cost of lumber for cribbing, there was no expense to charge against the few dollars standing between the settler and a dim future.

She heard stories of a few dry holes, but for the most part, the wells were good. A few temporary shacks were being replaced with more substantial buildings, some of cut lumber, many of adobe.

As she was passing through a more heavily wooded section, where visibility was shrouded, she heard a shout of greeting. Pulling the horse to a stop, she looked around, seeking the shouter.

"Here, behind you, Doctor. It's Bennie. Bennie Chalmers."

With a smile for the young man, Gwyneth turned the rig and followed the voice. When she came beside an opening into the brush, she stopped. A rush of bodies, aroused by Bennie's shouts, greeted her.

"Well, good morning, Chalmers. All of you. So, you decided to hang around. I hope you are all still well."

Sol, always the leader of the pack, stepped forward. "We're well and thankful for it. It's good to see you well also, Doctor. We've been a bit concerned that you and Cob may have a delayed reaction after all your closeness to us during the really hard time."

"No, but thanks for your concerns. The Lord continues to protect and bless. But what are you doing here? I see no cattle."

Dale answered, "Figured Dad was right. Time to rejoin the world. We loved our bit of hilltop country, but it was lonesome. Mona often wished for other female people to visit with. Made another trip up to gather a few stragglers Dad and Bennie missed. Sent the whole lot off to market with some hands hired from the Sombrero crew. Did well on the sale. Decided to give milking a try. Kids need to be close to a school. Need folks around look'n to buy milk and cheese and butter, and such. Need a church and a community to call home. Decided this was as good as any, and better than most."

Mona, who rarely spoke, added, "There was some fear among the neighbors about the smallpox, but that's pretty well gone now. Good folks around. Good neighbors."

~

LATER, driving and studying the happenings on the flatlands, Gwyneth repeated in her mind the last of what Mona said, *Good folks around. Good neighbors.* She decided Mona had hit on the key to any good settlement. She thought of her early days in Colorado and how good the living was, in spite of its remoteness and periodic hardships. She then thought of *Big Beef* Bill Cameron and his intransigents, and how little it sometimes took to upset the whole area around.

With those thoughts, she found herself thinking of how seamlessly she had slipped into the Sombrero community, and how little objection there had been to having a woman offering medical treatments. The concept of a woman doctor was still new to most of the country. Perhaps it was the smallness of the community plus her connection to the ranch that made the difference. Whatever it was, she was thankful.

Describing her day's adventures to Cob that evening, she said, "It was good of the ranch to lend out a few men to drive the Chalmers' herd to market. I'm sure they paid for the men's wages, but still."

"Didn't know about that till you mentioned it just now. I'll check into it."

"Remember? You turned ranch affairs over to Tab."

"And I'm not going back on that. But remember, too, it's my pennies he's playing with. I figure it to be my right to count the pennies from time to time."

Gwyneth had no comment because she knew Cob was right, it was still his ranch. Or as Cob enjoyed reminding her, *"Our ranch."*

The evening drifted on with the conversation moving from subject to subject, none of them particularly important. Until Cob ventured into previously unplowed land. Determined to move ahead, clarifying a mystery of the past, he said, "Gwyneth, I'm remembering that stormy, wet evening I stepped onto your porch up in Pueblo. In the moment before you saw me, I registered the look on your face. You were deep in thought. I took it to be a sad or troubling thought. At least melancholy.

"You had progressed as a doctor better than most would ever dream of, and yet you were sad. I know now, because you've told me, that you had been unsuccessful at building the clinic you really wanted. Your big city cohorts from Chicago took a look at Pueblo and caught the first train home, leaving you to search elsewhere for the key to your dream.

"You were doing well in reputation and financially, but you had the undeniable urge inside to grow. I'm not sure if you ever really knew what you wanted to grow into. I've never seen Chicago, but I'm prepared to believe it's a long jump from a one-woman clinic in Pueblo, Colorado, to Chicago General, as you often refer to it. I doubt that it was one woman, or even one man, who built that big hospital. I'm thinking it took time and money, and the work of many hands to manage it. Perhaps partly it was the mystery of the urge that made you sad. Like as if you wanted something with all your heart, but you didn't quite know what that something was, or how to put it all together."

Cob stopped there, waiting. The wait was long for people who were more familiar with quick questions, quick decisions, and quick answers.

During surgeries with the incision already made and the patient's very life in the doctor's hands, he had to make decisions. And altogether too often, he had to make them alone. It was the same working cattle. The lone rider, coming upon a problem, had to decide, and decide quickly.

Over the years, Cob had ridden thousands of miles alone, with only the cattle or the cactus to talk with. Along with the ability to pull the sights and sounds of a situation together quickly and make a critical decision, he had also learned the art of patience, although he didn't always show it. Or practice it.

Finally, Gwyneth leaned forward and laid her coffee cup on the patio table. She then turned her whole body a quarter turn, with eyes burning into Cob's eyes, as if to wonder how to respond to him. She took three or four deep breaths, putting words together in her mind. Reminding herself who she was speaking with, she chose alternate words. When she finally spoke, her voice was low, almost inaudible.

"You have a way about you, Cob. I saw it way back, on the drive west, and many times on the ranch. When others were all set to speak, displaying their ignorance, you had a way of cutting through the issues with few words, and sometimes, letting your actions speak for you, with no words at all. Sometimes you saw right through a situation with such clarity that it frightened me. Frightened me only because I knew that if you spoke your thoughts, thoughts that would demonstrate the weakness in others' opinions, people's feelings could be hurt and friendships threatened. But that never happened. Thankfully, it never did.

"That evening on the veranda, I was facing the fact that I had sold a portion of my clinic under terms that, while they solved an immediate problem, I wasn't at all happy with. So, my clinic dream, while not completely dead, was certainly compromised. I'm sure that dreadful storm, and the pouring rain added to my melancholy. And the fact that I would soon be rising from my lovely wicker chair and returning to an empty house for another lonely night was also amplified by the storm."

Gwyneth paused, and again Cob waited.

She finally spoke—words that were unfamiliar to him, in that she had never said anything like them before. Words describing a situation he suspected existed. But he had never dreamed of the depth of feelings the situation dealt to this woman he had loved for so long.

"Some nights I thought the loneliness would kill me. Kill me dead and transport me into some sublime paradise, some quiet, almost sacred sanctum of peace. I often came close to wishing for it. And then, out of that dark night of my soul, soaked and dripping rain, you were standing there."

Gwyneth seemed to be finished talking. All Cob could think of to say was, "Let's go in. It's getting late."

Neither mentioned the dreams a young doctor had held in her heart or what had become of them since moving to Texas, perhaps modified, perhaps expanded, perhaps diminished. It all remained a mystery locked in Gwyneth's heart, not to be shared until the right time came.

Chapter Thirty-Five

GWYNETH AND THE CHALMERS FAMILY HAD celebrated their entry into the community, following the smallpox scare, but they were to find out that the acceptance wasn't total, including everyone in the community. Dr. Shultz, with Summer's assistance, was dealing with a broken leg on a boy who fell out of a tree. Gwyneth was delivering a baby. Once the baby decided it was time to enter the world and face whatever awaited him, she had two house calls to make. Another house call, a young girl with a serious case of what the messenger had called *"coughing and such,"* would be taken by Summer. The young nurse didn't offer more than cursory medical assistance. Anything more meant a call for one of the doctors or a trip to the clinic for the patient. The afternoon was normal, verging on common, when there was an outburst on the road, introduced by three pistol shots into the air.

Shouts of, "Git yerself out here, you so-called doctor. You got yerself some answer'n to do."

When the clinic door remained closed, the shouter got even louder and more demanding. "Git out here, else I'll put the next lead through yonder window."

Dr. Shultz said, "Summer, will you see what that's all about.

Be careful though. That very much sounds like a real gun carried by a very unhappy man."

Standing behind the adobe wall for her own safety, Summer opened the door just a crack.

"The doctors are busy. What's the problem?"

"Smallpox. That's the problem. It'll be ragin' up and down the valley next thing we know. And it was that so-called woman doctor let it loose in our town. Me and them with me come to see that woman rid out of town. And no fool'n about it. Git her out here."

Taking a chance, Summer opened the door wider and stepped out. "Dr. Wycome is delivering a baby. Now I'll ask you to go somewhere and keep the noise down. And if you shoot into the clinic, I'll guarantee to shoot back. And, mister, I'm a good shot. Now get gone with you."

The men sat where they were, but Summer ignored them and stepped back, closing the door.

She returned to Dr. Shultz's space to find the boy staring at his completed cast, moving his tear-filled eyes between his hovering mother and the doctor. Dr. Shultz was washing his hands and grinning at the boy. "I'm willing to bet you'll be the only boy in your school with a nice white cast to brag about. I'd be careful about kicking the ball at lunchtime though, until you've healed up some and we can get rid of the thing.

"Summer is going to give you the loan of a pair of crutches and show you how to use them. You come back in around two weeks from now so I can see how you're doing. And don't climb any more trees until that leg heals."

To Summer, he said, "I'll go see if I can tame the animals outside. How many did you see out there?"

"I counted eight. Only one had his pistol out though. A couple looked uncomfortable. As if they weren't sure exactly why they were there or why their leader had shot off his Colt."

"Well, we'll go take a look."

Just as Summer was about to warn the doctor to be careful,

he pulled a closet door open and lifted out a double-barreled shotgun. He checked the loads and went to the entry door. Leading with the shotgun to be sure the rioters understood the situation, he hollered, "You were told to leave. It saddens me to see that you're still here. Be sadder too if you were to do something foolish like pointing that gun at the clinic. The clinic or me, for that matter. Now state your case and be gone."

"There's smallpox brought into town by that woman, so-called doctor. Far as that goes, there ain't no such thing as a woman doctor. Ain't natural. Goes against the Word. Ain't no woman doctors in the Word. And now she's gone and infected the whole town. Whole valley. Be a miracle if any of us 'r standing come a week from now. We need her gone. Ain't no room here for such as her."

Gabriel Shultz answered, "Mister. That's about as plain ignorant a thing as I've ever heard anyone say. Dr. Wycome is the best doctor, the best trained, that I have ever met. You won't find another better anywhere around here. I'm proud to work with her."

Sensing their rider's unease, there was some nervous shuffling of horses' feet, scattering a bit of dust into the air. When Summer stepped back out with her hand at the front of her smock, holding her pouched weapon ready for use, there was further unease among the gathering.

"Now I want you gone, like Summer here has already told you. But first, listen to this. There was a family up in the hills with smallpox. Isolated. No one else anywhere nearby. They were very ill, but everyone survived. They were never brought into town. They were treated off by themselves, up on the hillside behind the clinic. Thankfully, they all survived. And now they're healed and back to normal. It is now perfectly safe for them to live here and work here, and for you to mix with them.

"The truth is that once a person has survived smallpox, it is impossible for them to get it again. Those good folks are no danger to anyone. And you men, don't listen to this loudmouth with the opinion and the revolver. Go about your business and leave the doctoring to us."

Three riders at the back of the bunch quietly turned their mounts and rode slowly away. Two more made motions to follow until they saw their loudmouth leader glance at them. Horses continued to shuffle their feet, and finally, one man said, "I'm leaving, Boxer. As usual, your mouth makes trouble for everyone else. Ain't got one single reason fer following you here. You can be sure I won't be doing it again."

When the leader, now identified as Boxer, found himself alone, he threw a final ugly look at the doctor and the brave nurse standing beside him, turned, and left.

Returning to the clinic, Summer completed cleaning up the debris left from building the cast and then went to see what progress Gwyneth was having with the birth. She found the doctor in the final steps of cleaning the baby of the birth leavings. After just a couple more wipes with a damp cloth and then one with a dry towel, she wrapped the little girl in a soft blanket and picked her up.

Holding the baby in one arm, she gently arranged the mother's coverings, lifting them aside so the baby would have access to the breast. As she lay the blanket-wrapped child in the mother's arms, she smiled at the woman, saying, I never have gotten over the magical, almost holy experience. You have a fine little girl. A beautiful girl. Treat her well through life."

As was the routine, Gwyneth went to clean up in preparation for her outcalls, leaving Summer to put the room in order and then swing her attention over to the baby and mom before making her own outcall.

~

On a dull, almost sunless October morning, Sombrero welcomed a flat-bottomed wagon, painted bright blue, with two-foot side rails. The driver was a man of about thirty, wearing a heavy wool coat and a flat-topped hat.

Beside him on the seat rested a black and white, medium-sized dog, the type folks were beginning to call the border collie. The breed was known to be faithful, gentle until aroused, and natural herders. The wagon was drawn by a matched pair of light bay animals with black manes and tails. Beautiful and rare horses of a breed not commonly seen.

Hauling to a stop at the livery, the driver grinned down at the man seated nonchalantly beside the door. "Morn'n, friend. I see you admiring my animals. Dog's name is Peaty. Horses are Troy and Dardania. Myself, I answer to Howard. Howard Kinsella. Is it possible, sir, that you could direct me to anyone around here that could offer care for a pair of carriage horses, without laming them in the process?"

The man dragged his pipe from his mouth, gently tapped the now cold dottle into the palm of his work-worn hand, spat a brown gob in the direction away from the wagon, looked at the man and said, "If yer meaning them there horses, no. Them are eastern animals. Like as not to come down lame fer no reason at all. Should have sold them off a few hundred miles back to the east. Took whatever the best offer come to and bought yerself some real animals. Texas animals. Caught in the high up country and broke to work."

Still grinning, the wagon driver said, "I take your meaning, sir, as uninformed as you obviously are, demonstrating your lack of knowledge on the subject. These are animals with royal lineage, as any knowledgeable man might guess from their names. Know anyone close by who might respond favorably to the layout of a few coins, with an offer of keep, if not care?"

"If that pair have the strength to shuffle another short way, you might find room in the back two stalls. Hate to have them lowering the overall grade of kept animals in my establishment, but it's not their fault they was born poorly. Hay and a mite of oats time to time. Dollar the day fer the pair of 'em."

"Thank you, brother. Am I to assume I may store the wagon under the shed roof?"

"You may make that assumption. Same cost as one animal, fifty cents the day."

"Thank you again, sir. Now, I'll be needing a small business shop to rent as well. Any chance you have insight on that?"

"Business, is it? What kind of business and how big a shop?"

"Printing's my game, friend. That's a small printing press under that oiled canvas sheet. The way I heard it, the town had become too big to exist any longer without a newspaper. Smaller print jobs always welcome as well, anywhere Howard Kinsella sets up his print shop."

"Most everything is full up. Folks mostly put up their own shops. But you might check down at the medical clinic. Doctor moved over there from town a short while back. Place he left might be available."

"I'll put the animals up and care for them. Then get right over to the clinic. And again, I thank you."

"You park the rig and leave the Clevelands to me."

Grinning again at the thought that the liveryman recognized the breed of horse, he said, "And what do folks call you, sir?"

"Ain't rightly my proper name, but folks call me Oscar. Some history to that, but I don't share that with strangers."

"And how long does it take in the town of Sombrero to shed the appellation of stranger?"

"We'll have to see how that goes."

"Right, you are, friend."

Howard Kinsella rubbed the noses of his two horses, saying a few words of nonsense about the amateur he was leaving them with, words he was well aware the liveryman could hear, grinned at Oscar, and walked across the road, focusing on a sign offering food. If pushed on the matter, he would admit to his lack of skill with pan and grill. There were days, as he traveled across country, when he would have gladly paid double for even a modest meal cooked by other hands.

As a treat, breakfast that morning had been more than adequate. He had chosen an out-of-the-way, wooded stream to camp beside. There was other camp smoke nearby, but that was not unusual. The entire flatland appeared to be alive with plowing and planting.

He had his fire lit that morning and coffee on, wondering if he would be better off with the leftovers he had set by the evening before, or to settle just for the coffee, when the brush parted and a tall old man on a big horse entered camp. He had heard the horse far off of course, but had little fear of whoever was approaching. He was well armed and adept with most kinds of weapons.

The old man's horse came to a stop and the rider leaned forward, the heels of both hands resting on the horn. His first words were, "Ain't mean'n no disrespect, sir, didn't go ta barge inta yer camp. If you'll pardon me, I'll jes skin past ye along this here creek an' be on my way."

"Welcome, stranger. 'Tis a dull morning, but fine for all of that, and a grand day for meeting new folks. Will you take time for a cup of coffee before you ride on?"

He saw a slight smile form on the man's face before he turned in the saddle to dismount. "Always seemed downright unfriendly to me, hav'n someone turn down an invitation fer coffee. Obliged."

Bringing his own crockery mug, the tall man held out his hand, saying, "Sol. Sol Chalmers. New here myself, me and the family. Family's upstream jest a bit. Mona, that's the daughter-in-law, she's putt'n the vittles together. Thought I'd take me a ride around, learn a bit more about the country, till I figure grub might be ready. Son and the kids 'r milk'n cows. I usually figure someth'n else ta be doin when milk'n times come. Not mean'n to poke ma nose in er noth'n but you appear ta be maybe a bit short on the breakfast fix'ns."

"My good sir, you have read the situation with envious clarity. I've come to believe, with all these folks I've been seeing as I came along, that there must be a town close by. I have targeted that town for this day's travels, wherever it may be."

"Mean'n, sir, that yer outa food."

"That would be another way of putting it, yes."

"We'll jest have this coffee and ye'll come along with me. Mona, she's a fright fer cook'n up more than what's rightly needed. Come along, there'll be a-plenty."

With coffee drank and the mugs dipped in the creek for cleaning, Howard rigged out his wagon and followed Sol. They arrived in a camp that was already taking on the looks of an established home and dairy business. It seemed to Howard that everything in the valley was new or near new. For this family to have progressed so far, so quickly, since their arrival, as Sol had outlined for him, was a credit to their ambitions and skill with tools.

Tying off well away from the camp, Howard walked in with his dog close by his feet. Sol walked beside him. Calling out, Sol said, "Brought ye a guest fer breakfast, Mona, hop'n ye might happen ta have an extra egg 'r two."

"Welcome, stranger."

The voice was that of a man. Mona, the woman addressed, had looked up from her work but had said nothing. The man who had spoken walked the few feet to meet the stranger. Shaking hands, he said, "Dale Chalmers. That's my wife Mona at the stove. A bit blackened and burned looking. The stove, I'm meaning, not Mona. Dug 'er outa a burned-down cabin. A bit damaged but still doin' the job. Young folks are just finishing up with the cows. We'll be seating ourselves shortly."

Howard accepted the handshake, saying, "Thank you, sir.

Howard Kinsella here. Heading for this Sombrero town. It would help if you could direct me."

With that agreed upon, the men casually strolled to the outdoor table. A holler for the kids to come to breakfast got a muttered response. Howard couldn't make out all the angry words, but the word cow came through clearly enough. Cow, and a few words that might get the boys a stroke of discipline when the family was alone again. Howard looked over that way and saw three young boys trying to gather up a dozen milk cows who appeared to be determined to each go their own way. Dale saw the grin on Howard's face. "Boys are likely to sour on the dairy business if I don't get some fencing up pretty soon."

Howard bent to the dog, pointing. "Peaty, go."

The three men watched the black and white animal flash across the distance, as if he were headed to an exciting challenge of some kind. Howard gently said, "Come away, boys, and watch."

Looking at their father for directions, Dale simply nodded and then watched in wonder as Peaty circled the widely spread herd. Within minutes, the cows formed a tight bunch and dropped their heads to graze, the urge to wander seemingly forgotten."

Dale, never taking his eyes from the black and white wonder, said, "I needed to see that to believe it."

Howard said, "The boys can leave the cows with Peaty and come in. You can trust the collie."

A leisurely breakfast led to questions about Howard's purpose in coming to Sombrero and his trade. Howard, in turn, remarked on the smallpox scars. That brought out a long tale of illness and survival. Just the kind of tale a printer and newsman look for. Howard took notes and asked questions, writing down names.

Howard finally took his leave with thanks for the meal and the visit. Peaty was rewarded with a small pile of leftovers from breakfast. They parted with both parties thinking it had been a profitable morning.

Howard entered the café, took a seat, and studied the handwritten menu on the chalkboard above the self-serve coffee counter. He took the steps necessary to pour a coffee and placed his lunch order with a young lady wearing an apron made of some flowered cotton cloth. It was probably a flour sack, but he couldn't be sure. He leaned back in his chair, looking out the window, in time to see Oscar returning from the water trough leading his two Cleveland Bays, expensive animals he had purchased as he was leaving his last business location. Peaty lay quietly at his feet.

"Don't worry about Oscar there, stranger. He'll do well by them horses. Knows his stuff, he does."

Howard turned his eyes to the next table. Four men sat there, all looking at him, two with their heads turned to the back so they could see him.

"Not worried, friend. Simply watching and wondering."

"Saw your wagon. Unusual. What brings you to Sombrero?"

"Oh, I suppose I could be a bank robber casing the possibilities. Or I could be a lawyer, come to help improve your town. Could be almost anything, I suppose."

"But what, actually, are you of them choices?"

"I'd have to know I could trust a man before I give out personal information, and so far, you haven't offered your name or your position."

"I'm not the sheriff, but I met him once. Does that hold any water for you?"

"Well now, why didn't you tell me. A man who knows folks is a man to know. My name is Howard Kinsella. And on that wagon you say you watched me come in on, is a printing press.

Reporter, newsman, and printer. That's me. Looking for a small space to rent to set up my business. Of course, I need to know a bit more of the town before I make the final decision."

"A printer. Why that's fine. Just the other day Cob was mentioning having sent out wires all over the country, inviting a newsman to set up here."

"And who is this Cob, sir?" He had heard that name mentioned by the Chalmers family, but he might learn more if he held back that information.

"He's the owner of the Sombrero Ranch and husband to the lady doctor. Lives over on the south end of town beside the clinic. He'll be happy to meet you."

"Here he comes now," offered another coffee drinker.

"And over there comes the sheriff. You could set your pocket watch, if you had a pocket watch, by them two."

The outer door opened and closed again, letting in a well-built but somewhat bulky man wearing a plaid wool coat and a gray range hat. This had to be the sheriff. If he had ever been a cowboy or rancher in his younger days, there was little sign of it left in his presence or bearing.

The second man had to be Cob. Jeans, riding boots, cowhide vest over a blue checked shirt, black flat-brimmed hat. Only their holstered Colts were a match in these dissimilar men.

Several voices rose into the air, voices of greeting and teasing.

"Catch anyone yet today, Olaf?"

"Juanita still bringing yer vittles down from the ranch fer ya sheriff?"

"You best get back to ranching there, Cob, I do believe this city living is making you soft. You've put on a coupla pounds."

Cob and the sheriff stood just inside the door, staring at the table they had been using for as long as memory served. For someone to have settled in there was as bad as some stranger taking your regular spot in church. It just wasn't done, unacceptable.

One of the four said, "Mr. Printer, I do believe you've overstepped the bounds on your first day in Sombrero. I probably should have warned you before. You're seated at the sheriff's table. Could be he'll up and shoot you just to get his proper seat back."

Howard smilingly looked up at Cob and the sheriff. "Sorry, sirs, I didn't know. But since I'm not in the habit of giving up what I've already claimed as mine, I plan to take my lunch right here. I'm good at sharing though. Why don't you join me? Could even be we'll find something in common to drag our thoughts away from café seating."

An hour later, the four men from the next table had long before taken their leave, while Howard, Cob, and the sheriff had tracked all through the happenings in Sombrero and district, and how a newspaper and printing services could indeed add positively to the growth and sophistication of the town.

By the following morning, Cob had arranged for Howard to use the space Dr. Shultz had left vacant, and the cleaning and small renovations needed were underway. Two days after that, the first printing of the Sombrero News Reader hit the streets. An introductory paper only. There would be another soon, offering advertising, items of interest, and an editorial. With the crowds of young families in town, it was a simple matter for Howard to arrange for two youngsters, a boy of eleven and a girl one year younger, to carry the printed page to the far corners of the settled area.

When Gwyneth heard there was a printer come to town, she immediately thought of the foolishness of the man named Boxer, who had attempted to rile up the citizens with claims of smallpox being spread throughout the area. But what Gwyneth and Cob failed to know was that Boxer was nowhere finished with his mischief.

Chapter Thirty-Six

Word came to the sheriff from Sol Chalmers himself. He had found the lawman at the small office this time. A deputy had jailed a couple of drunks. Olaf was playing jailer while the deputy was catching up on his sleep after a long night. Another deputy was out of town hunting down a horse thief. That left Olaf. When Sol Chalmers tied off in front of the jail and stepped toward the door, Olaf checked to be sure the loop was off his Colt and that the holster was free of the arm on the swivel chair. He didn't know the visitor. It could be anyone, with intentions unknown.

The door opened, letting the tall old man enter. Olaf held his position, leaning back in the chair, his one foot on the desktop, the other braced slightly back, ready to propel him away from danger.

"Something for you, sir?"

"Sol Chalmers, sheriff. Me and the family have settled a few miles to the east, just at the base of what I've heard folks refer to as Hobo Hill. Dairying. Milk, butter, cream, cheese to come soon. Got a good start. But come yesterday, trouble arrived."

The sheriff stopped him with a question. "Trouble? In what form, sir?"

"In the form of night riders. Guns, masks, and all. Thought they'd ketch us early in bed, I'm guessing, not understanding the nature of the milk'n business. Come a-whoop'n and a-shoot'n inta the air, and riding through the yard, terr'n up the garden spot I jest finished digg'n. Boys were down to the shelter doin' the milk'n, none of us armed, but my son and me. Swapped a coupla shots with neither them nor us any the worse for the effort. Rode off holler'n about smallpox and killer diseases and gett'n us run outa the country. That or bein' shot. Kilt."

Olaf dropped his foot to the floor and sat up straight.

"The whole territory is familiar with the smallpox story. That was your family?"

"Sure, as shoot'n. We was sick to death, all but me and one grandson, ranch'n in the up country. Dr. Wycome and her husband Cob set their other matters ta the side and near a month of their lives ta risk themselves to help us. They tell me there's no cure for smallpox, just good care till the body the good Lord gave us gains strength enough to fight off the disease. Couldn't a asked fer more from any doctor than what Gwyneth and Cob gave. Now someone's rankly'n up the folks around, tell'n that we're all still sick and anyone com'n near will git sick an' die. Threatn'n with guns to move us out. We'uns ain't got no plans to go nowhere. Thought y'all should know."

That last statement caught Olaf's attention. He saw the threat wrapped up in the simple comment. Studying on Sol, Olaf saw a determined old man. A man who had fought his way through life to arrive as a small but successful cattleman, before smallpox turned the situation around. His mind told him, *These types of men don't make idle threats nor run easily.*

"Do you have any names that might help me?"

"No, sir, I don't. Could maybe describe several horses and some clothing, but that ain't much help. All wore masks covering everything but their eyes. Was about ten or eleven riders in all."

"You go home and leave this to me. Keep a close watch around your place. But please don't do any shooting unless it comes to protecting home and family. I promise to stand by you. I know the smallpox story, and I know Dr. Wycome and Cob. The fact is, the doctor is well known and well thought of in Sombrero."

Olaf hoped a hard look would drive his message clear to Sol. Again, he said, "Leave it to me."

Olaf was sincere in all he said. He intended to bring an end to any uprising. The name Boxer, passed along by Cob after the attack on the clinic, was added to Sol's evidence, a name unfamiliar to the sheriff or either of his deputies.

~

IT HAPPENED that it was the day for Juanita's weekly visit. Olaf went home to keep her company while she cleaned and cooked. When she insisted on doing the sheriff's laundry, he laughed and said, "Juanita, you already do far too much for me. I've always let Chin Wah make a few pennies off me. I expect I'll keep on doing that."

"I enjoy coming to your house, Sheriff. Doing laundry is not too much work."

"You are my friend, Juanita, not my servant. And judging by the odors rising from the stove, my friend and I will soon be enjoying dinner together. Anyway, there is no time for more work. The days are getting shorter. You'll be wanting to get back to the ranch before dark."

"Maybe someday I stay."

Olaf studied her for just a moment before escaping to the woodpile, intending to replenish the indoor supply. But he couldn't help thinking, *What in the world did she mean by that?*

~

EVENING CAME and went with the fall sundowns becoming shorter, it seemed, every day. Except for a few lights along Main Street, the town was in darkness. Peace reigned. Until around midnight, a sleeper couldn't have asked for more. But the quietude of the night was broken when riders rode into town from the east, all wearing dark clothing and masks. They held their peace until they were close to the home of Cob and Gwyneth. Then, as if on a signal, they lifted their mounts into a run, circling the house and firing their revolvers into the air, with one or two shots purposely whanging off the rain barrel, the veranda support posts, the tile roof.

Both Cob and Gwyneth came awake instantly, sitting up in bed as if lifted by an irresistible machine of some sort. Cob leaped to his feet, stumbling in the darkened room and warning Gwyneth, "Get down. On the floor."

He grabbed up his carbine, which he always kept close to hand, and ran to the back door, bouncing off the wall in the dark just once. Opening the door a crack while using the adobe wall for protection, like Summer had done at the clinic not many days before, he eyed the darkness over the V-notch sight, waiting for movement that would bring a target into view. The riders had bunched up in their circular ride, becoming confused in the almost total darkness.

Suddenly, Cob's vision was blocked off by a moving target. He had no idea who he was about to shoot, but flashing the question through his mind in no more than a split second, he found he didn't care. These were raiders who had come to his home. It was his responsibility to protect Gwyneth, himself, and their home.

He squeezed off one shot, then, as the sight cleared and blanked out again, indicating a second rider, he squeezed off another. The shouting and shooting ceased immediately. The pounding of hoof indicated the gang had fled. All except the couple he believed he would find on the ground once he got a lantern lit.

Cob stood sideways at the bedroom door, watching the kitchen windows while speaking to Gwyneth. "You stay there. I'm going to light a lantern and see if I hit anything."

"Not alone, you're not. Wait, you, until I find a robe. Find my carbine and check the loads, although I'm sure it's loaded. I'll stand cover while you do a quick search. You might try to remember that you aren't exactly dressed for company too."

Cob emerged from the rear door onto the small, covered porch, holding the lantern to the side, the length of his arm from his body. The shaking lantern created strange shadows as it swung back and forth. He had gone about thirty or forty feet into the yard when he saw a form on the ground. It could only be a man. There was no sign of movement. There would be a second, he was sure, but before he could find it, voices called from the road. Voices warning not to shoot, that they were friends from town, including the night deputy.

Cob, still in a defensive posture and mood, hollered back, "Come. But you'd better be who you say you are."

"Deputy Hammond here, Cob. I know the others."

"Come then, Hammond. Just you. Tell the others to stand guard out front."

Cob and the deputy stood looking down at the second body. At first, he appeared to be dead, but Gwyneth had dressed as quickly as she ever had and rushed into the yard. After a quick examination pronounced the two men to be alive. Shot badly but alive. Gwyneth, from that point, took control.

"You men, Cob must stay here. A couple of you run down to the laundry. Chin Wah keeps a hand cart. Grab it and bring it on the run. We'll explain to Chin another time. Another of you get yourself as quickly as ever you can to wake up Dr. Diego Esteban. Dr. Shultz is away for a few days. Tell Diego that I need him. Now. Go!"

THE HANDCART WAS SOON on site, and the two injured men transferred to the clinic. As a last-minute thought, Cob had hurried to wake Summer. Diego arrived shortly after.

Gwyneth had done a preliminary examination, discovering that Cob had been aiming high, while a lower, full-body impact would have been easier and more likely to hit its target.

Both men had taken upper chest wounds. One man had been shot through the arm, causing serious damage to his upper arm deltoid muscles. The lead had penetrated the arm, traveling into the upper body and glancing off the collarbone before leaving the body. The impact would have resulted in unbelievable pain and momentary mental confusion.

The second patient had a shattered lower arm, plus some rib and lung damage toward his back. Both men had bled badly.

Gwyneth and Diego Esteban made a long night of it. In reality, there were four bullet holes in the one man, two as the lead passed through his deltoids and two more as it entered the upper body and exited again a few inches away after glancing off the collarbone and tearing flesh in his back. The angles of the entry and exit wounds indicated that Cob, the shooter, was kneeling in the doorway of the house while the patient was sitting high in his saddle, making a considerable height difference between the shooter and the target. Diego bent over that patient while Summer arranged a lamp as closely as possible. Although the arm would never be the same again, the doctor would be able to patch it up without too much trouble. But the shattered collarbone would test his knowledge and his surgical skills as they had seldom been tested.

As Gwyneth studied the second man, she saw that the bullet might have missed entirely, except when it glanced off the man's forearm, it struck his upper rib cage, shattering some bone and nicking the edge of one lung, before tumbling through flesh and disappearing into the night.

Thinking of leaving Diego with the shattered collarbone gave her pause. Diego had always been modest about his surgical skills, claiming he preferred to work with diseases rather than with scalpel and stitches. She momentarily considered exchanging patients. But a second thought told her that no one ever died from a broken collarbone, while it was very possible that one could die from rib and lung damage, especially if infection should take hold. She decided to leave matters as they were.

Having before witnessed the modesty of Dr. Esteban, she knew he would not be insulted if she could find a moment to lean over his shoulder and ask how things were going.

Both doctors were wishing for more light as they very carefully searched for and removed bits of shattered bone. In addition, the bleeding was a constant challenge. Summer, moving from patient to patient, did her best to be where she was needed most. And, as usual, and without unnecessary instructions, the young nurse was handling the ether matter. To say it was a busy night would be no exaggeration.

WHILE THE LAMPS burned as brightly as they were able at the clinic, the sheriff, his two deputies, and a few carefully chosen volunteers were scouring the area for the raiders. Neither of the patients were awake enough to identify themselves. No one among the few townsmen awake at the early hour was able to identify the night riders, meaning they were from the settlement area. Possibly farmers or small ranchers. Cob finally said, "Judging by the dirt under their fingernails, I'm guessing these are farmers."

The sheriff gave the fingers a long study and then nodded at Cob before turning and leaving the clinic.

They had one name. Boxer. He hadn't been singled out during the night raid, but he had led the daytime attack on the clinic and Gwyneth. So, who was Boxer, and where did he lie down at night?

THE NIGHT WAS FAR GONE when the first light fluttered to life in the café. The sheriff's posse were just returning from a search of the western edge of the farming area. They planned to gather and report to him. Since his gunshot wound on an earlier hunt, he had been unable to ride long distances without becoming dizzy and in danger of taking a fall from the saddle. The men tied off in front of the jail and office before following Olaf across the road to the café.

The report from the men confirmed that there was no sign of hard-ridden horses or of men who hadn't been home with wife and family.

By full morning, any sign of the raiders would be gone, and any hard-ridden horses tucked away in one of the many small barns dotting the eastern end of the territory. A somewhat discouraged Olaf said, "Boys, that was a good night's work regardless of the results. We'll take a different approach now. I'll work it out with the deputies. Y'all go to your homes, get an hour or so before your day's work calls. If you're needed again, I'll send word."

COB VOLUNTEERED to take on the hunt for anyone named Boxer. Gwyneth, just coming to the end of a long night, straightened her sore back, looked at him with a stare that silently said, *Listen up, mister*, then proceeded to explain life to this man who was still struggling with the reality of having been shot, and his lung damaged. When she turned to the sheriff, he was grinning.

"Shore hope to never have a dressing down like that there, Cob. Of course, I ain't got no wife so I'm free and easy"

Cob's answer was swift in coming. "You old fool. If you had the eyes to see, you'd be looking for a hiding spot where Juanita couldn't find you."

"Now what in the world do you mean..." As if a bright light had suddenly lit up the road ahead, he stopped talking so abruptly that everyone in the clinic started to laugh. Olaf had been holding his hat in his hands, placing it on his head, he said, "I'd best be leaving y'all."

Wide smiles followed him out the door. Diego said, "I think so the sheriff, he has much to think on."

That statement seemed to free Gwyneth to ask, "And how are matters with you and the lovely Lupita, Diego?"

"Ah. The Lupita, she is more beautiful each day. She made the Almuerzo, the lunch, I think you name it. Together we rode the buggy to the country after Mass, you know, church. We ate and talked together. Very fine day."

Sincerely, Gwyneth said, "I'm happy for you, Diego."

Gwyneth spoke again to Cob. "My dear, loving husband. I understand your wishes. But understand this too. We are all tired. Summer is going to her home to sleep out the day. Diego is going to where it is best for his patients and himself. I am going to lie down in the other room, hoping to get at least a few hours of sleep. I need to know that you will be here on guard. And if you can think of anyone who could spare the hours, we really should have a couple of other men on site as well. Now, if there is any sign the patients need attention, just call me. Otherwise, I'm going to rest."

THE SHERIFF CAME MID-AFTERNOON, when he thought the two patients should be awake. He had paper and pencil in hand. Showing no sign of sympathy for what the men had suffered, he looked at the first one. "Name."

He waited only a few seconds, and when the man didn't speak, he again said, "You're going to prison. For how long is up to you and how well you cooperate. Name. Now."

The hurting but seriously frightened man barely whispered the name. Olaf wrote it down.

"Where's your layout?"

He wrote that information down.

"Who is Boxer and where is he?"

That information was recorded.

By that time, the second man had become a fountain of information, capping it all off with a plea to understand that they all had family who were fearing for their lives with the threat of smallpox. And now to cap it all off, he was a virtual prisoner in the very clinic and with the very doctor where the smallpox was worst. He ended, saying, "Don't matter what you do to me. I'm a dead man anyway."

Gwyneth, freshly awakened from four hours of sleep, listened to all of this, appalled that anyone could be so ignorant. And so easily led. Patiently, she explained about smallpox to the two men. Still not sure they believed her, she turned to another patient who had been waiting in the other room.

THE SHERIFF GATHERED up Boxer and his followers, threatening them and making them promise to stay put until the judge could again be brought in. He had no intention of arresting them, nor anywhere to house them if he did. Privately, he hated the thought of ruining so many families over what amounted to stupidity and superstition. Perhaps he would suggest leniency to the judge. He had to think on that.

The matter was brought to the attention of the wider community and, in effect, solved, with a long editorial by Howard Kinsella where he quoted Gwyneth as well as members of the Chalmers family, at some length.

Within weeks, the matters of the lady doctor, smallpox, and the night riders were forgotten history. The sheriff allowed the threat of legal action to hang over the accused, although he had never called for the judge. The two wounded men survived and went back to their homesteads, and the entire matter was seldom mentioned again. Boxer had been encouraged to take up residence in some other town, or preferably, some other state, but without the court granting him the power, the sheriff had no authority to force such a decision by the troublemaker.

Chapter Thirty-Seven

Cob didn't bother finding out who started it, but a meeting had been called for all interested citizens of Sombrero. Howard Kinsella used the meeting as the focal point in his latest weekly paper, appealing to folks from all around to attend. The agenda to be discussed was, first and foremost, to elect a mayor and a town council. Following that was a proposal to change the name Sombrero to something more promising, more mature, more dignified, perhaps more genteel, speaking of the bright future awaiting the town. There were no names suggested. That would be left to the citizens to debate and decide. Following that, there would be an open session where people could bring up their thoughts and wishes.

When Cob announced his intention to attend, Gwyneth advised him not to go.

"Now, Gwyneth, my love. How would it look if no representative of the biggest brand in the area, and the one that began the town and named it, didn't attend? No, I think there's an obligation to be there. Anyway, what harm can come of it?"

"Oh, none, I'm sure."

That sounded a bit sarcastic to Cob, but he let it go.

Following dinner, Gwyneth, who had no intention of going anywhere near the meeting, saddled her gelding and rode out, with no destination in mind, saying a friendly *good evening* to a few folks along the way. She circled the town and rode a few miles into the territory. The farming progress had always surprised and pleased her. Even as late as it was in the year, the energy of the settlers was pushing changes ahead. On the return ride, still with no destination except home in mind, she rode past Summer's cottage. Summer waved to her from the tiny veranda and invited her in.

Dismounted, Gwyneth joined her friend, settling into the second chair. Summer brought fresh coffee, and the two talked of this and that, nothing of substance.

During a break in the conversation, Gwyneth said, "I was past here a few days ago. You had a guest in this chair. I was across the road and a distance away, but it sure looked like the new newspaperman."

"Howard. He walked over with Peaty, his wonderful little dog, and knocked on my door. You know I have a hard rule against letting men into the house, so we sat out here. Nice man."

"Does his welcome cast some kind of a dim light on Tab?"

"Oh, I don't know about that. I haven't seen Tab for a couple of weeks."

That was such a change from Tab's almost overwhelming interest in Summer not long before, she couldn't find anything appropriate to say. Giving in to what she hoped was wisdom, she chose to let the subject end.

When Gwyneth was home and the gelding settled into

the little, newly built four-horse barn for the night, Cob was waiting for her in the kitchen.

"I see a message in both your eyes and your posture, Cob. You might just as well tell me, although I suspect I already know."

"It all seemed to happen awful fast. I had trouble keeping up with everything. There were a few suggested names, but for now, we'll still be known as Sombrero. A town council was chosen."

"And you were named as mayor."

"Did someone come by and tell you?"

"No one needed to tell me. I knew before you left the house. Who else could they possibly choose?"

"I don't think there's much work to it. I hope you're not upset with me."

"There may not be much work now, but the job will surely grow. I don't think you and Olaf will be able to handle all that comes your way from your seats in the café window."

"I'm certainly not going to neglect you or the ranch. If mayoring becomes too much, I'll simply resign."

"Sure, you will. And just in case you want to sound more professional or more knowledgeable of the language, I don't believe mayoring is a word."

"Yes, dear. Now tell me where you've been on your ride."

Gwyneth explained her constant fascination with the farming area, saying she had enjoyed a good ride before the sun began to disappear, and then about her visit with Summer. At the mention of the newsman visiting Summer, Cob looked troubled.

"None of my business really, but if Tab's not careful, he's going to lose out on a good woman. Probably the best this territory offers."

"You're correct, Cob, it's none of your business, or mine either. But what is our business is the clinic. I want to make some changes."

"The mud in the adobe is barely dry, and you want changes."

"I've been sketching. Let me get my drawings and show you."

Gwyneth laid out a large sheet of paper, holding the corners down with the salt and pepper shakers and a couple of coffee mugs.

On the paper she had laid out with pencil and ruler, the outline of the clinic was drawn to scale. At the back and side of the structure were outlines of a proposed addition, all in all, larger than the original building.

"What in all the world are you proposing? You planning on renting rooms out too, like a health hotel?"

"No, Cob. Those small rooms are patient isolation rooms. For communicable diseases like smallpox, measles, whooping cough, and so many others. Two beds to a room, maximum. Isolated from the clinic itself by solid doors and this hallway. And from the population of the town by distance."

She dragged her pencil along to point at each area as she spoke. "And here's the kitchen. Here's the bathing room. Right outside the bathing room wall is a wood-fired boiler. It will provide hot water for general cleanliness of the facility as well as bathing water for the patients. And right beside it is the laundry.

"And here is a larger room that can be a ward holding more beds for those who are either not ill with a communicable disease or who have recovered and just need to regain their strength.

"Over here are the doctors' and nurses' dressing rooms. And at the other end, isolated from the large wing, is a recovery room for surgical patients, maternity, or non-communicable diseases."

"Well, my ambitious doctor wife, you seem to have thought of everything. Have you thought of where all the patients will come from and who's going to pay for all of this?"

"The short answer is yes, I've thought of all that. The longer answer, the answer that includes the details, is also yes, I have thought of it, but I don't yet have all the answers."

"Gwyneth, I have always understood that you feel the need to offer a large clinic or even a hospital to your community. I admire you for that. But right now, your two-doctor clinic is easily handling everything coming its way. It could be years before we need anything approaching what you've drawn here."

"I agree, my love. But we should also be considering the needs of the farming area as well as other communities. Especially with the communicable disease services. I spent some time down at the telegraph station. There's a large map on the wall there. It includes all of Texas and much of the surrounding area. It also shows the railway lines as they existed when the map was drawn, just a couple of years ago. There are two lines easily accessible, one to the north of us and one to the east. They are both spur lines, but they connect to the main lines. Given time, connecting Sombrero to one of them will connect us to the entire outside world with just a couple of hours' travel once the rails are laid. So, the answer to your question is, we need a railway."

Cob studied his wife for a long time, the smile on his lips growing as he pondered on her vision. Finally, he said. "Just a railway. If that's all, I'll get a note off to the railway head office first thing in the morning."

"Are you not the mayor of the booming town of Sombrero, Texas, my dear husband?"

Cob simply grinned and shook his head. But Gwyneth wasn't finished with the conversation.

"Perhaps you're not including the ranching industry in your thinking Cob. Or perhaps you're thinking only of the ranching industry. Either way, it's not a complete picture. In just the time I've been here, there have been several large herds pushed to Fort Worth. Several besides the Sombrero. And there are large ranches west of here that would use the rails. Any railway would be interested in that business. And look at all these settlers. Many of them would have happily paid for rail freight for their machinery and livestock to move it out here, had it been available. Then there's the matter of getting their crops to market."

"You really have given thought to this."

Gwyneth answered with a nod.

For the next few days, the clinic kept both doctors on their toes, partly at the clinic itself but mostly with outcalls. As Gwyneth had said several times over the years, there appeared to be no end to the creative ways working men could find to injure themselves. From a serious axe cut that nearly cost a young boy his leg, to having a log roll off a scaffold while a man was building a cabin, to a horse kick that broke a man's leg, Gwyneth had seen them all in a single week—Dr. Shultz's treatment room welcomed a similar range of patients. Thankfully, there were no new gunshot victims presenting themselves for treatment.

On the outcalls, Gwyneth delivered two babies, treated a woman's badly scalded arm—splashed with boiling water during the garden produce preserving process—and cared for a child with a serious cough. With the remembrance of whooping cough in her mind, it was that which concerned her most. She had the family isolate the girl, which was difficult in their small cabin, but by having the other children sleep outside—well bundled up for the cold nights—they had managed.

Gwyneth checked on the child each day for four days, applying mild mustard plasters on each visit. On the fourth visit, she smiled at the patient and said, "Young lady, I do believe you're getting better. What I had feared has not come to pass. Another day of rest and your mother's good cooking, and you'll be up and raring to go. I'll check on you again in a couple of days just to be sure."

GWYNETH WOULD PREFER to sit a-saddle than go to the trouble of harnessing the horse for the buggy. She could make better time and wend her way through the semi-desert scrub and roughly plowed fields to reach settlers' cabins better on horseback. With the help and guidance of the town cobbler, who did the sewing for him, Cob had cut and shaped a large piece of leather to accommodate Gwyneth's two medical bags behind the saddle, securing it in place with leather thongs.

As it had sometimes been in Pueblo and Bessie Creek, receiving payment for her services was sometimes a problem. In private conversation, she and Cob had joked about some of the offers for payment and decided they would prefer to wait for cash. Chickens, a sack of corn, or a gallon of milk held no interest for them. Some who couldn't pay apologized sincerely, with promises to make the debt right just as soon as possible. Gwyneth always smiled and trusted them.

While Gwyneth was busy with her medical practice, Cob was working over the building plans. He met with the builder they had used before, sketching, scratching out, and sketching again. Cob was becoming more interested each time he took out the rolled plan. When he presented Gwyneth with his or the builder's suggestions, he sounded truly enthusiastic. But always the costs involved lay at the front of his thinking. That, and the matter of the railroad.

Gwyneth had decided the better approach with Cob was to let him think it all through, confident that he would then act. It was certainly true that Cob knew what hard work and planning were, but at the end of it, ranching was, for the most part, a simple matter. So long as the cows birthed good calves, had access to grass and water, and his animals could be found come roundup time, the large acreage rancher had covered all the bases, except for the supply of coffee. That was a critical element beyond the others. No rancher she knew of had ever been successful without the addictive beverage.

A new eating house opened its doors in Sombrero—a restaurant more than a simple café. There were some tables and chairs in the center of the big room, but along the two sides were booths, built with high-backed bench seating, providing almost total privacy to a couple who would speak in lower tones. Eating out was a seldom thing for Cob and Gwyneth, but they decided to try the new place at the end of a busy week. They were shown to a booth and presented with printed menus. Gwyneth knew she would be ordering a beef dish if one was on offer, but she read the entire menu to familiarize herself with the choices. Cob took a quick look and laid the paper back on the table.

Gwyneth grinned at him. "Let me guess, steak and fried potatoes."

"Fair enough, but now let me guess for you, roast beef, boiled and mashed potatoes, and a vegetable. Or perhaps a baked potato if they had some."

They grinned, looking at each other, and leaned back, relaxing.

Gwyneth said, "To keep you from asking me about my patients, tell me what you and Olaf saw today in your study of the town through the café window, and what new ventures have come your way as you were mayoring."

"Remember, my dear, mayoring is not really a word. You told me so yourself."

"Right."

"However, if you insist on me repeating all the town's gossip and exciting news, the first thing would be that the Chalmers family dairy is now delivering milk and dairy products into town every second day. Abe and Helen are reselling it for them in both their stores. Abe is already complaining that the Chalmers are unable to keep up with the demand for butter. Chalmers' dairy, as the family have named their enterprise, has built a springhouse over the stream that winds through their land. They set the milk cans right into the water. The butter and cream and the bit of cheese they've managed to make goes on a low shelf just above the cool water. Very ingenious. And effective. They'll do all right, that family. A credit to themselves and to the community. Howard's doing a write-up on them for next week's paper."

Gwyneth replied, "As picturesque as their hilltop ranch was, I'm thinking they'll have a better life here."

"I agree. The other thing is that Howard had a batch of out-of-town newspapers delivered by stage. Says he'll have a batch each week from now on. I borrowed several for you to read. They're on the table beside your chair in the parlor."

"That's not enough to have filled your entire week. Come on, fess up."

"Tomorrow, after church, I'll show you. That's easier than telling you. Now here come our dinners. We'll talk later."

IF GWYNETH WAS WALKING MORE QUICKLY than normal on their way home from church, it would be because of her curiosity. It was not like Cob to hold back on something of importance.

As Gwyneth went to the hall closet to hang up her coat, Cob rolled out the big sheet of paper, weighting it down as usual with whatever was present. Gwyneth bent over, studying it for a moment before saying, "That's not my drawing. What is this?"

"This, my dear, is what I have come up with, after several hours with the builder. We moved a few things around and added some square footage. We also added another examination and treatment room because as sure as we're standing here you will be looking for another doctor soon enough.

"And to prove how forward-looking your mayor is, you'll want to take note of these rooms. We're a little ahead of ourselves on this, but the day will come. And not too long from now, if I'm reading the stars correctly. These are known by a variety of names, but we'll just call them the bathrooms. Here, there's one for the male and another for the female staff. And back-to-back with those, to make the job of running pipes easier, is another, larger space for the patients. I'm figuring the patients will want bathtubs, but the staff won't need them, figuring they'll have homes to return to.

"In the other wing, where you have your communicable patients, I've left space for three rooms, thinking you may not want to mix the patients with different illnesses. We'll have to do some research to find out exactly how much space to set aside and when the bathroom equipment might become available.

"Oh, and I almost forgot, here's a basin with running water in the kitchen. I'd like to be able to say hot running water, but I haven't yet figured that out."

Gwyneth was momentarily stunned by the drawing and all it meant. She daren't say anything for fear of embarrassing Cob. Among all the additions and changes in the planning was the evidence that Cob was now onside. To her, nothing was more important.

Instead of overplaying her hand, she said, "Show me what else you've planned."

Cob had space for equipment and supply storage, stables for a team and a boxed-in wagon he called an ambulance. He had added a few more rooms with doors separating three or four rooms from each other. He had a building outside marked *machinery*.

"That's for the unknown. You'll need some kind of heat, and we can't put a wood stove in each space. And someway or somehow, we're going to heat water, but I don't know how yet. Understand, Gwyneth, all these things are already being done in the big cities. We have to find out what they're doing and copy it is all."

"Cob, I don't know what to say. You haven't quite designed an entire hospital, but you've come close. Oh, Cob, you say this is mayoring as if it were a joke, but it's not. This would be the greatest thing you could ever do for Sombrero. This alone would separate Sombrero from any other town of its size and from many small cities. It would mean the mayor has put the health and well-being of the people ahead of everything else."

Becoming self-consciously uncomfortable, Cob rolled up the paper. "Enough of that. What's for lunch?"

Chapter Thirty-Eight

"You're taking the stage to where? And why?" Gwyneth sounded just a bit exasperated.

"That's two questions there, my love. In mayoring school, we're taught to only answer one question at a time."

"It's only two, Cob. Go for whichever you want first."

"Well then, I'll answer the easiest one. The why I'm taking the stage is because you won't allow me to ride my horse. So that's simple. The only alternative is the stage." Cob appeared to be content with the simple answer, but Gwyneth had not yet let up on her severe stare.

As it was clear that Gwyneth was going to hold out longer than him, Cob said, "The truth is, my beautiful doctor, that I have an appointment with a man at the end of the stage run. Mayoring, don't you know?"

He was met with continuing silence.

"Doctor Wife, I know you watch over me, but my lung injury was months ago. I'm doing great with my breathing. And with the periodic fall rains, there should be little dust on the trails.

"All right, here's how it all came together. From the telegrapher, I found out the name of the manager of the spur line to the east you mentioned as being a possible source of an extension spur into Sombrero. I wired the man. Introduced myself as the mayor of Sombrero and asked for a meeting. He wired right back with time and date, and location. He'll meet the stage two days from now. I leave in the morning. It's a two-day stage trip. Shouldn't be gone more than a week."

Gwyneth was equal parts surprised and delighted.

"I can't help being a wife and a doctor, Cob. You will be careful, won't you?"

"As careful as I always have been."

"That's not really much assurance, but I guess it's all I'm going to get."

"Rest assured, my love. I very much wish to return to you hale and hearty. I shall do everything within my power to see to that. But now I must dig out my *go-to-meeting costume*. Colonel Winthrop Percival Harrington would expect no less, judging from the handle he continues to burden himself with."

"Colonel Winthrop Percival Harrington? Oh my. Perhaps you will need to shave and have a haircut, as well, if your mayoring is to lead you into such auspicious company."

Cob had predicted rightly about the fall rains wetting the roads and settling the dust. That he missed the part about the passengers having to walk to lighten the load while the jehu worked the stage through hub-deep mud was forgivable. The stage arrived at the depot that was still called *End of the line*, where a canvas topped sleeping tent offered beds, a sawn-lumber built store offered about anything a traveler or settler might want, from packaged camp food to shovel handles, to rough frontier clothing, and, along one wall, a short wooden bar where a warm beer or a harder drink could be purchased. There was also a livery where the stage company held rented space for their teams and where a rider could wait out of the changeable weather for a stage heading further east or for the return run to Sombrero and points west.

With its wheels blocked firmly in place sat a small railcar—the home and office of Col. Winthrop Percival Harrington, Division Manager of Central Texas Rail.

The mud-splattered stage hauled to a stop at the livery. As the jehu stepped wearily to the ground, the three passengers, Cob, plus two peddlers, one a general goods salesman and farm implement man, the second, a menswear representative, who would be continuing east, alighted.

The liveryman spotted Cob. Identifying him as the one to watch for, he said, "I'm expecting you're the one hoping to meet up with Percy. If you'll lift yer eyes toward the railcar over yonder, you'll see him heading this way."

Cob turned to look. What he saw was a western-dressed man, perhaps mid-forty-ish, broadcloth pants, riding boots without spurs, a dark blue corduroy shirt, not commonly seen in the west, and a semi-clean western hat. He was sucking on a cold pipe, as if it were some kind of soother used to distract him from more serious happenings. His walk was purposeful. Judging by name and rank, Cob guessed the straight back and marching-like stride were the product of a strict New England upbringing, along with military service that earned him the Colonel rank. His present dress and manner would indicate that the man had managed to leave most of that behind as he settled into the west, leaving him with just the straight-backed walk, a habit that isolated him from the normally relaxed, almost lazy appearance of the western rider.

As Cob and the colonel closed the distance between them, the railway man was the first to hold out his hand in greeting, saying in his Boston accent, "Mr. Mayor, is it? It isn't like Marty to be a half day late with that conveyance of his, but from what I'm seeing on those animals as well as on the undercarriage of the stage, I'm guessing you ran into a rough patch of weather."

Shaking hands, Cob replied. "You might say that twice,

Colonel, and still have room before exaggeration could be claimed. It's just plain Cob, sir. Cob Fleming. You call me Mr. Mayor, I'm likely as not to turn around to see who you're talking to."

"Right, you are, Cob. I, as well, have long ago dropped the lengthy appellation the railway insists on using, for whatever reason is best known to themselves. It's Percy, plain and simple."

"In any case, Percy, it was good of you to agree to meet. I won't be needing much of your time. I'm sure you're kept on your toes with all that's happening with Texas railways."

"Busy enough, Cob, but we always have time to listen to reasonable proposals. I was about to see what's in the pot today, over at the store. Stella, that's the store man's wife, sets up for a few of us for lunch and dinner. Breakfast, we're on our own."

"I've taken my sustenance in places and in ways most folks wouldn't believe, Percy. Compared, the store looks almost refined. Lead on, my friend."

TAKING a seat at one of three small tables at the back of the store, Percy said, "Two of the best you've got, Stella, my love. We have the mayor of Sombrero, Texas, gracing our table today."

"Two it is. And if you're curious, I baked bread this morning, so we're offering warmed -over beef sandwiches. With that comes a choice. I opened a quart canning jar of my own sauerkraut. I can give you a nice taste of that in the sandwich. Or leave it out."

Cob answered, "Sauerkraut for me, please."

Percy grinned and said, "The mayor has spoken. So be it, my dear."

While they waited, Percy was anxious to get on with the purpose of the meeting. "Our normal run comes in here this evening, Cob. Depending on cargo to be loaded and unloaded, it is common to be heading back north within the hour. I intend to be on it. If it's all the same to you, I would invite you to explain the purpose of the meeting."

"Yes. And I'm hoping to be on the westbound in the morning. Wishing for the mud holes to be dried up is asking too much, but my intention is to be home as soon as possible. You will already know I wish to talk of railways. There would be no other purpose, given our roles in life."

Cob bent to lift his satchel onto his knee. He opened it and retrieved a folded paper. He laid that on the table between them.

"I will confess, Percy, to being a thief. I have little experience in that direction, so I thought, right off the top, it would be best to admit that I borrowed, without asking permission from the telegrapher, the map from your telegraph shack in Sombrero. I promise I will return it undamaged. Well, undamaged except for a few pencil lines and some fold creases. I have folded it so that our home area is seen. Just to help in our discussions, you understand."

Percy didn't seem to be too overwrought about the map, so Cob carried on.

"This area I have outlined gently with a pencil is the district of Sombrero. Understand, though, that the district I outlined is not the entire county, only the portion of immediate interest to our discussion. This dot is the town itself. On the south, to both east and west are grassed hills and ranches, including my own. On the north, beginning virtually within the town itself, are farms, small cattle outfits, a thriving dairy, and many irrigated holdings. Irrigation wells are being drilled faster than I can count them.

"All the ranches, including my own, ship beef twice each year. Currently, we get together and drive the herds to Fort Worth. But that's a long drive, time-consuming, and, with the land being taken up for farming, becoming more difficult with each year. We spend days finding routes past and around the farms. That's all business a smart railroad could pick up."

With that, Cob lifted his eyes off the map to look Percy in the eyes. Their short staredown was interrupted when Stella approached with their lunch.

"Looks mighty fine, Stella, my love," Percy said with a smile. "Mighty fine."

As soon as Stella was safely out of earshot Cob whispered, "That's a fine-looking woman, but with her being married, I'd think discretion would be the order of the day."

"Oh, I am being very discreet."

If you say so, thought Cob.

The empty plates were replaced by steaming coffee mugs while Percy studied the map, his finger tracing out the route of the telegraph line. Without lifting his head, he asked, "How many miles did you say this was?"

"I don't exactly remember saying, but now that you ask, I'm thinking about fifty miles. Mind you, we, in the west, content ourselves with counting by country miles. And that measurement can vary some depending on who's doing the measuring."

"You're pretty close. The contractor who ran the wire for us charged for fifty-five miles. But he went around some obstacles that the rails would burrow through, so to speak, meaning we would move a few hills and fill in a depression or two. I'll call it fifty miles in my report to the family."

The comment about family caught Cob's attention. "Family? Do others in your family work for the railway?"

"Not so much work. They pretend they're working while they take their ease at the club. But mostly they talk. Actually, the family holds majority ownership of the line. I'm the only one who actually left Boston to work on the development of the company. My recommendation holds considerable weight in decisions."

With a smile, Cob said, "Great. And how would your recommendation be worded after just this short meeting?"

"I'll tell you what I'll do, Cob. Mr. Mayor. Just as soon as I can get away again, I'll come down here with our planning engineer. We'll risk the stage ride. Or hire wagon transport of our own, depending on what approach the engineer wishes to take. The stage can't make stops just for us as we study the terrain. The engineer will judge the terrain. I'll just explore the town and surrounding area for possible business. That's how it's done. That system has always worked for us in the past."

"When do you think that may happen, Percy?"

"That's a difficult question to pin me down on."

"All right. Let me ask another question. As I told you earlier, Percy, I'm new at this mayoring thing. I know something about grass, water, weather, and the well-being of cattle. But I'm stumbling a bit in this new post of mine. But the thing is, as I'm sure you know, there's another line just to the north of us. How long would you recommend that I wait for you before I contact that northern line?"

Percy studied Cob so long that Cob began to feel uneasy. Perhaps he was applying too much pressure. But then he thought, *No, I'll just let him answer the question.*

The answer came. But only slowly. "I predict a long and successful mayorship for you, Cob. You didn't threaten. And yet you very much threatened. Can you give me two weeks?"

"Done and done, my eastern friend. I'll watch closely for a wire from you advising of your travels. And thank you."

As Percy was walking away, he suddenly stopped, turned, looked at Cob, and said, "Put that map back on the wall where it came from."

The two men smiled and parted.

Chapter Thirty-Nine

Cob arrived back on the stage to find considerable excitement and a few questioning looks passed from friend to friend. Seeing the sheriff sitting in his normal window seat, Cob decided to have a coffee. As much as he wished to go to the clinic to advise Gwyneth that he was home, he also wanted to catch up on the town gossip. He was, after all, the mayor.

Cob entered the small café and took the seat across from the sheriff.

"So, Olaf, my friend. With the mayoring job calling me to far-off lands, I'm left with no choice but to ask you what's been happening in town. I've seen a few smiles where normally there would be sober expressions. I can't help but be curious."

Olaf had little chance or time to answer before the waitress came to their table with a big smile on her face.

"Welcome back, Cob, or should I say Mr. Mayor? So very much has happened in the few days of your absence, it's good to have you back to kind of bring matters under control again."

"That all sounds a bit ominous, Ruby. How about you lay my curious mind to rest. What are you referring to?"

"Why, just the biggest news to hit town since that newspaper man arrived weeks ago. The news is that the sheriff, the very one who sits across from you and who is now staring poison arrows at me, has announced his intent to be married. And a happy announcement it is, him being so miserable and cranky most times. A woman at home might mellow him some."

Cob turned his eyes away from Stella, toward his friend, and waited. Olaf was twisting his fingers in knots and untwisting them, only to repeat the action. Minutes seemed to pass before he lifted his eyes from the table. Still not looking directly at Cob, but more or less past Cob, to stare out the window, he said quietly, "Not much to tell."

Taking pity now on his suffering friend, Cob said, "Would I be correct to guess that you and Juanita have come to an understanding?"

"That's putting it as clearly as any other explanation."

"You do understand, don't you, Olaf, that this puts me and the ranch in a difficult situation?"

"I'm getting married. Giving up my freedom. And all you can think of is the ranch. Fine friend you turned out to be."

"You really aren't giving up anything except badly cooked food and nights alone. You're asking me to give up our ranch cook."

"Nothing of the kind. Juanita already has a new house matron in place. Tab seems happy enough with her, so expect your life won't change over much."

"Seriously, Olaf, I'm very happy for you. Juanita is a fine woman. But she must have often been lonely out on the ranch. I'll be praying that the two of you have many years together to bring happiness into each of your lives."

"Thank you. Now, can we talk about something else?"

"Like railroads and such?"

"For a start."

~

Cob ended his visit with Olaf and headed to the clinic. The treatment room doors were both closed, but Summer came from the small kitchen, saying, "They're both busy, Cob. No injuries this time, illnesses. Both serious but not contagious."

"Tell Gwyneth I'll be at home. Might take me a rest. There's just nothing at all restful about that stage."

"I'll tell her."

Chapter Forty

Two days later Cob announced that he was intending to ride up to the ranch. Gwyneth lifted her head from the breakfast she was preparing, all set to suggest he take the wagon. Cob caught the look, responding before the words were out of her mouth. "Gwyneth, you turn men out of your clinic who've had more serious ailments than I've had. They all went back to work. If any died, I haven't heard of it. I've agreed from the start that I wouldn't ride roundups or long trail drives, but a ride from town to the ranch isn't about to lay me under the sod.

"I suggested to Tab that he should look for some replacement heifers, perhaps five hundred or so. He sent word down while I was away that he'd located a likely looking bunch. He bought them and drove them to the corrals a few days ago. I'm going up for a look-see. There's no more to it than that."

"Summer has the day off. Why don't you see if she wants to ride along?"

"To protect me or to put her in front of Tab again, since he's not been seen in town for a worrying length of time. Worrying, that is, to those who are playing cupid, which does not include me."

Gwyneth smiled as she placed a plate before him. "Just ask her. Leave the rest to her."

Cob and Summer rode under the big gate at mid-morning. Trinity Castillo was the first to see them. He turned from his path to the barn to welcome them, inviting them to coffee in the cookhouse.

"Ain't that just something now. Being invited to coffee in my own cookhouse. I believe it might be time I spent a little more effort in keeping track of things up here."

Summer giggled, saying, "No one will ever forget you, Cob, or forget who's the boss, either one."

"Well, let's take a look. Might be a piece of pie lying around. I'll be wanting to meet this new *doña*, too. Juanita left big shoes to fill."

As they stepped up on the cookhouse porch, there was a holler from the big house. They turned in unison, seeing Tab hurrying across the yard.

"No other two people I'd rather see this morning. Glad you could make it up."

Sitting over coffee, after being told there was no pie, Cob said, "Came to see those heifers. And to meet the new house *doña*. I'm thinking to see the calves first and talk some business."

Summer smiled, saying, "And since I'm here to protect Cob from the dangers of sitting a horse, I'd just best tag along."

Tab replied. "I was kind of hoping there might be another reason for your being here."

"There might be. We'll just have to wait and see."

Tab looked at her as if he was having trouble deciphering the meaning of her words.

Cob and Summer, both standing on the raised platform to see over the corral railings, looked at the heifers long enough to make Tab think they might be weighing their value one by one. The first words from Cob were, "What's the final count?"

"Four hundred and eighty-two. I turned back the rest."

"They look good. You going to turn them out this fall or give them another year's growth?"

"They've got good growth now. I figure they're ready. I'll put them in the close-in fenced field with the young bulls. The sizes will match. And I can keep a close eye on them."

"You want my suggestion, Tab? Assign Moses to that job. You'll need more pasture come spring. I've got another suggestion." From that point, Cob explained about the land given up by the Chalmers family.

"At one point up there, I could look down and see our big log gate. Couldn't see the buildings, but the gate stood out clear. Have a couple of the boys ride up there on the trail. See if they can find a way down. A way cattle might manage. Tell them to stay away from the old building site. It's all apparently burned to the ground. Should be safe enough, but stay away anyway. I'll check with the Chalmers to see if they still hold to a claim."

Tab agreed, then suggested that they go to the house to meet Amelia.

"She's been anxious to meet you. She apparently worked for a White rancher one time who was a bit of a tyrant. She's a good cook and a good housekeeper, but serious. I've not tried to joke with her or anything like that. I'd advise against it."

The meeting at the house was brief but fine. Everyone parted smiling. As they were walking back to the cookhouse, knowing the lunch triangle could sound at any time, Tab quietly spoke to Summer. "There's a newborn in the horse barn. Cutest little thing you ever did see. Come, I'll show you. We can catch lunch later."

On the ride back downhill to town, Summer asked. "However did you get that big carved log to sit on top of the gate posts?"

"Blacksmith from a ranch over east of here had been a sailor. A genius with forge and steel, knew how to work around rope and pulleys, a sheave they're called. After we set the two uprights and tamped them in solid, that blacksmith showed us how to rig a tripod hoist. He formed the metal bands to fasten on each end of the carved log, once it was in place. Put that tripod all together on the ground in such a way that when we hoisted it upright, it was long enough to draw that big log right to the top. He had tied the double rope sheave and run the ropes through it so that, when we got it upright, it all hung in place, ready to do the job. You can still see the angled support posts we left in place. They're notched on top, like I'm told the Indians did to reach their stone houses out in Arizona. Never seen them stone ruins myself. Like to see them someday.

"Moses hot-footed it up one notched post, and I, more slowly, climbed the other. The boys worked the ropes, hoisting that big log till it was above the vertical posts. With me and Moses guiding it, they lowered the log right onto the posts. Moses and me, we hammered spikes into the upright to hold the metal strap in place. The hard part was climbing higher, then leaning over the top to hammer the spikes in on the other side. I was sure glad to have that done. I dropped the hammer so it wouldn't be in my way crawling down, then waved my foot around until I contacted a notch. When my boot finally settled onto that good Texas caliche soil, I heaved a great sigh of relief. And there she still stands, proud after so many years."

Chapter Forty-One

Cob walked in the back door of their home, seeing Gwyneth putting a stick of wood in the big iron kitchen range. He said, "Never you mind with the stove, Doctor. Your husband is in a celebrating mood today."

"Oh? And how and where are we planning on celebrating? And what, exactly, are we celebrating?"

"We have a reservation at Sombrero's finest restaurant. There's good news to share and good food to share it over."

"You're serious!"

"Of course I'm serious. You have about fifteen minutes to get yourself ready."

Gwyneth, liking the sounds of both the good food and the good news, went first to the back porch, cleaning herself as well as she could, using only the small washstand. There was no time for heating a tub of water for a bath. Cob dawdled the waiting time away with a fancy pair of spurs he had purchased one time and had never worn. With a can of metal polish at his side and a soft rag torn from an old towel, he worked over the spurs until they glistened. He still wasn't quite satisfied, but the footsteps sounded out Gwyneth's return, so he laid his project aside and rose to meet her.

"Your carriage awaits, my love. If you would come this way, please."

With exaggerated pomp, he held out his arm as an aid in rising to the buggy seat. The drive to town took only a few minutes. They were soon seated in the restaurant with the horse tethered at the railing outside.

"It's not really top of the agenda this evening, but I've wondered all afternoon if you managed to save that fella's foot, the one who somehow managed to get tangled up in his own sickle mower."

"Very sad situation. On the other hand, he's fortunate to be alive, considering the damage he did and the amount of blood he lost. I had to trim almost half his foot away, all of one side, and two toes. The healing will take months, and he'll always limp and most likely always experience some pain. But, thinking positively, he's alive and he'll be able to walk."

"You're a marvel, my love. A credit to yourself and to the town of Sombrero. And for all of that, I believe it's time to build that larger clinic. I've talked costs with the builder. It's a fair chunk of change, but manageable. I'll be wanting both you and Gabriel Shultz to go over the plans very carefully. If there's something you believe you'll be needing, even if it's not possible right away, make a note of it for me. There's new equipment coming on the market all the time. I've glanced through a couple of those medical journals of yours and I see the advertisements. You need to consider what will be available in the near future and plan for it now. As soon as you tell me the plans are complete, we'll get started."

"What are the costs? I have funds, but I'll want to know I have enough before we start."

"There will be no cost to you. The ranch has done well these past few years. I've decided building a full clinic is a good way to return something to the town. Mind you, now, the building of the clinic will just sort of happen, so far as anyone knows. There'll be no talk of costs or of who's paying. Can we agree on that, so we never have to mention it again? I've never wanted notoriety of any sort, and neither does the ranch."

Gwyneth, with a bit of a troubled look on her face, responded, "But it's me pushing you and Gabriel Shultz into the risk. And we could still fail. It's really my call to pay."

"The answer is no, Gwyneth, and that's final. And if we can move on, I have other news."

Dinner interrupted the flow of conversation, but such was Cob's enthusiasm that he managed to talk and eat at the same time. "I got a wire today. Colonel Winthrop Percival Harrington, otherwise known as Percy, will be leaving end of track tomorrow, with his engineer, in a rented wagon, exploring and measuring their way west. He expects to be here in less than one week. He added that the family was all for the track extension as long as the engineer didn't find any serious problems with the route. I'm taking that to mean that you're going to get your railway. Construction can be slow with such a project, but eventually, my dear, eventually, you will delight as a grand steam whistle announces to the world that because of Dr. Gwyneth's persistence, the project is complete."

They finished their meals in silence, both of them wondering what was still to come. Gwyneth was reasonably sure she had news to share too, but she chose to wait. Cob hadn't yet run out of enthusiasm or news.

They were nearing the end of the meal when Gyneth said, "I'm still listening, Cob. If you don't spill it pretty soon, you're liable to come apart at the seams."

"I do have more to talk about, but it's not in the category of the new and expanded clinic. It's more along the mundane lines. Just things that come together to make life easier and tick a couple of goals off the list.

"Somehow, Howard Kinsella got wind of the need for an ambulance. He came to the café this morning while Olaf and I were having coffee. Hardly taking time for a greeting, he said, 'I heard about the ambulance the clinic wants to have available. I like it here. The town of Sombrero has grown on me. I've decided the town and surrounding area are just right for me. At least for the foreseeable future. I find myself wanting to stay and watch it grow. And perhaps have a small part in the growing.

"'That means that special-built wagon of mine will get almost no use, and my Cleveland Bays will lack for exercise. You tell the doctor that she's welcome to the team and wagon whenever there's a need. I'm not giving the set to the clinic, you understand, only to use until I feel the need to move on. But, repeating myself, I'm content here for now.

"'She's welcome to arrange a hooped canvas top if that would make for a better ambulance. And she really should employ a qualified teamster. I'd hate to lose one of my horses.'

"While I was thanking him, Olaf was staring out the window. I could see a question forming. When his thinking was all done, Olaf said, 'You mentioned special built. What did you mean by that?'

"Proudly, Howard answered, 'There are a number of things, but four main items. First, you will notice that the wheels are smaller than usual. And they're spaced further apart than what is normal. That means the wagon bottom is wider. And a bit closer to the ground.

"'Then, I had special suspension worked into it. I feared damaging my press, so I wanted a gentler ride. I'm sure ill patients will appreciate that. Lastly, the frame and axles are much sturdier than normal, giving the unit great strength.'

"Of course, both Olaf and I acknowledged the usefulness of the wagon, thanking the man again. That's when he dropped another bit of news on the table. In a way, he came for coffee mostly to seek council's blessing, but in another way, it was just giving notice of what he's planning. And for me, being new to this mayoring thing, I have no idea if I have any power to object anyway. So, I just nodded, assuring him that I had heard his news." Cob paused to finish the apple pie that lay before him.

Gwyneth laid her pie-fork on the edge of the dish and said,

"Do I have to ask what he's planning, or do you intend to eventually finish the story?"

"He's got it all set up to run in tomorrow's paper to begin a town renaming contest. He figures that since council intends to apply to the state to name Sombrero as county seat, it really deserves a more appropriate name. More distinguished. A name that will sound solid and prosperous in folk's minds. You'll recall we talked of this some time ago but did nothing. So, I really couldn't get too worked up about the contest, one way or another."

"Sounds harmless to me, Mr. Mayor. It might even be fun. Perhaps council could offer some kind of an award or tribute if someone's suggestion ends up being the name. It's all kind of a package, isn't it? Town name, county seat, post office, clinic or hospital. Court house, rail depot. Cattle shipping point. If you and Olaf put your minds to it, there's no limits to the future."

Cob grinned and nodded. "Sounds like fun when you say it that way. And speaking of Olaf, he and Juanita have announced their wedding date for one week, Saturday. They'll be married in the little church and then have a bit of an outdoor celebration if the weather cooperates. He's asked me to stand up with him."

"I'm very happy for both of them, Cob. A lot of folks stand against mixed-race marriages, but they're both strong enough to ignore the chatter. And that reminds me of your ride up to the ranch with Summer. The second trip, not the first, when you went to look at the new heifers. You didn't tell me you came back alone. I only caught on when Summer was late to the clinic the next morning."

"Wasn't none of my business to get involved in. My business that day was to look over the new trail the men had found leading up to the Chalmers holdings. I talked to the Chalmers too. They never did own the land and have no further interest in their claim. It's good graze for the ranch, and with the new trail, we have access.

"I left Summer visiting with Amelia, the new *doña*. When

we got back off the hill, she and Tab shared lunch on a table in the corner, away from the others. When I was ready to leave, they were nowhere in sight. Turns out they were busy looking at newborn foals.

"Summer is an adult, Gwyneth, and Tab is an honorable man. And I believe we've had this conversation before. Anyway, what Tab told me after was that when darkness fell and Summer decided to stay the night, Amelia brought her into the house and told Tab to go sleep in the bunkhouse. Apparently, the boys all had a good laugh when he laid out his bedroll and had nothing to say."

Gwyneth yawned and leaned against the back of the booth, looking as if she was feeling the effects of the long day.

"Come, Mrs. Fleming. Let's get you home."

"No more startling news?"

"It will keep for another time."

Chapter Forty-Two

Olaf and Juanita had a small, but happy wedding in the town's little church. Only a few Mexican guests showed up for the ceremony, but when the newly married couple stepped outside onto the plaza, most of the town was there, Mexicans and Texans alike. With the Mexican genius for arranging a celebration, from almost nothing it seemed, the small, planned celebration, intending to include coffee and sweetcakes only, soon spread onto the dirt plaza in front of the church, taking on the sounds and food odors of a fandango.

To Cob's and Gwyneth's surprise, Dr. Diego Esteban, with Lupita walking close, as if she was glued to his side, arrived. Both were carrying large paper boxes filled with sweet treats Lupita had prepared in her little *cafecito*.

Three Texans brought their guitars and one, his fiddle, joining the Mexicans' Mariachi band with their guitarron, guitars, and trumpet. There was some laughter and many inquiring looks, and a few false starts before the two groups melded into one. Once they settled into playing, with the Texans adding a strong western beat to the lively strumming of the Mariachi players, the music could be heard all over town. People who had not danced for years somehow found their feet tapping to the rhythm. A few brave souls stepped out, whirling their wives in a long, almost forgotten display of celebration. Mexicans danced to their own rhythms, and somehow, it all fit together.

The formalities were nowhere near as prescribed as they had been for Cob and Gwyneth, but it was all done in great fun and celebration. When the September skies began to cloud over, the food was quickly laid out, with everyone helping themselves.

Cob found Gwyneth, offering her a plate of some kind of rice dish, heavily laden with spices. She turned it down on the pretense of not really being hungry. Cob gave her a studied look before turning to find someone to offer the plate to.

The threat of rain turned into reality. As folks began gathering up young ones and scurrying for shelter, Olaf hollered out, "I don't even know who to thank for this food and all, but thank you anyway. Best y'all get inside now."

With that, the newlyweds stepped into a waiting top-buggy and were soon home. The wood stove that was left burning before the wedding would hold the cottage to a comfortable temperature, while the heavy fall of rain on the tile roof would play out a rhythm of contentment.

The small house that had once known married happiness would know it again. The long, lonely nights were over.

THE TOWN of Sombrero returned to its natural rhythm after the sheriff married the former Sombrero Ranch house matron. Cob now often sat alone, staring out the café window, as Olaf was coming downtown only when his sheriff's duties demanded attention.

The *name-this-town* contest was bringing out far more suggestions than Cob ever thought possible. As mayor, he got to see the suggestions before the next newspaper was published. Some were sappy, some were humorous, but many were serious and worthy of consideration. He repeated them for Gwyneth during their evening meals.

As fall was turning into the typical Texas hill country winter with crisp, cool mornings, occasional rains bringing out the soft browns and faded greens of the leaf stripped trees, and, from time to time, a cloudy sky, more time was being spent indoors. People went to town mainly when they had some shopping to do.

Cob now took his traditional place in the café window, mostly to talk away an hour with the newsman. It was on one of those days that Howard Kinsella laid a few eastern papers on the table, passing them along to Cob.

"I don't know how thoroughly you read these, Cob, but there's one article in this first paper you should read and pass along. I've circled it with a pencil. And now, Mr. Mayor, my composing table has too little that requires composing. I need some news."

"I might have a couple of things for you. You'll have to pay for the coffee to get them though."

"Can't do that. I vowed to never offer a bribe to a news source. It's too easy to get fed bad information if I'm paying for it."

Cob's humorously sad look moved Howard to add, "But what I can do is buy you a coffee as two friends taking turns paying."

He turned his head toward the serving counter. "Ruby, would you come take this payment for our coffees, please."

When Ruby picked up the two dimes, Howard said, "There. I'm comforted now, knowing it's honest and impartial news scoops I'm receiving from the mayor."

Cob smiled. "Seems like a lot of fuss to reach the same ending. But for publication, I can confirm that the rail company has approved the extension into Sombrero. Don't talk of that until tomorrow. I owe it to Gwyneth to tell her before it becomes public.

"The second bit of news is that Abe and Helen have formally been awarded the post office franchise. One or two more items will have to wait."

"Can I release both of these tomorrow?"

"Yes. Tomorrow they will still be new. And you will have gotten your ten cents' worth."

As they stared from the café window, enjoying the late fall sunshine, Tab and Summer, riding Cob's black gelding, rode past. There was no avoiding the sight.

Howard seemed to hesitate and then said, "I heard that Summer and Tab, your ranch manager, have announced their engagement."

Both men were uncomfortable. It was well known that Howard had been seeing Summer on occasion, but Cob had never known how serious the two were. Tab was kept so busy on the ranch that his trips to town had grown fewer as the fall roundup had come upon them. That appeared to leave a door open for Howard.

As much as they had concerns, Cob and Gwyneth determined it was none of their business. But some days, holding their silence had been a challenge.

"I don't know what to say in answer, Howard. Summer is an excellent nurse and a great help to Gwyneth in the clinic. But our relationship really goes little further. We're friends, but not so close as to enter in where privacy seems more the order of the day."

"I'll admit to being disappointed, Cob, perhaps even a bit hurt. But as a seeker of truth in publishing, it falls upon me to also be a seeker of truth in personal matters. Summer is an exciting, vivacious, energetic woman. A ranch-raised woman. I've recognized from the start that, truthfully, I'm too quiet to keep her satisfied for long. But sometimes a man lives on hopes. Your ranch manager is much more her type of person. I wish them well."

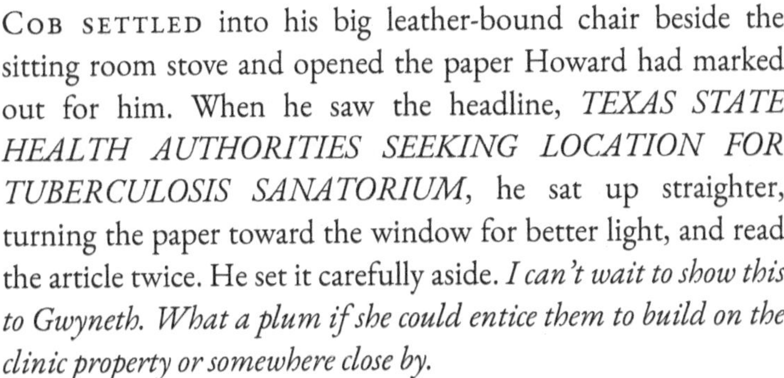

Cob settled into his big leather-bound chair beside the sitting room stove and opened the paper Howard had marked out for him. When he saw the headline, *TEXAS STATE HEALTH AUTHORITIES SEEKING LOCATION FOR TUBERCULOSIS SANATORIUM*, he sat up straighter, turning the paper toward the window for better light, and read the article twice. He set it carefully aside. *I can't wait to show this to Gwyneth. What a plum if she could entice them to build on the clinic property or somewhere close by.*

Cob reheated a cup of lunchtime coffee, placed his booted feet on the small stool, leaned back, and closed his eyes. For a few pleasant minutes he allowed his mind to wander through the many happenings leading up to his train ride to Pueblo, Colorado in search of Gwyneth—and everything that followed.

Into the gathering of memories, he added some that he hadn't lived himself, but were passed along as incidents Gwyneth had lived and told him about—trail driving cowboy and best friend, Trent, meeting and marrying a lovely nurse in a small Kansas town. The newlyweds leading a group of like-minded folks west. Settling onto new land in western Colorado. A rank horse taking Trent's life. Gwyneth, now a rancher and a widow, offering nursing to neighbors and townsfolk. Selling out and signing on at medical college, becoming a doctor, her one remaining dream—although she still suffered through the heartache of having been married to Trent and yet was childless.

Opening her own clinic in Colorado. Successfully expanding her medical services. How she responded positively when Cob, who had always loved her, even as he stood by while she married Trent, found her in Pueblo and persuaded her to follow him back to Texas. And, oh, so much had happened since they reached Sombrero.

The longer he sat in that comfortable posture, the dreamier his mind became. The more memories that passed through his mind, the deeper he breathed, and the closer he came to sleep. Feeling too mellow to even bother with the coffee, he dozed off. An hour later, he awoke with just enough time to put on his coat and walk across to the clinic to escort Gwyneth home.

~

AT THE CLINIC, he found her washing up after caring for yet another birth.

Announcing his arrival, he said, "I'm looking for a doctor who may be ready to walk home and put all of this behind her for a few hours."

Three heads turned to look, seeking the unexpected voice. Gwyneth said, "Good timing."

Summer smiled, saying, "Take her away. It's been a busy day. She can't help but be tired."

The new mother smiled but added nothing to the somewhat private conversation.

Gwyneth's footsteps seemed to Cob to be shorter and slower than normal, the walk taking a few more minutes than it did most evenings. As Gwyneth entered the back door of their home, Cob slipped the coat off her shoulders and hung it on a peg in the little porch. Gwyneth immediately dipped hot water from the stove's reservoir and cleaned her hands and face thoroughly. She then went to the bedroom to change into home clothing, leaving the medical smock in a wicker basket ready to add to the wash.

Together, and mostly in silence, Cob and Gwyneth put their dinner on the stove. Before he left to escort her home, Cob had started a pot of water heating for Gwyneth's one cup of tea she loved after her day's work was done. It was just coming to a boil. Following their in-home routine, Gwyneth settled into her favorite chair while Cob made the tea.

Gwyneth held the steaming teacup close to her nose, inhaling and enjoying the hot, scented aroma. In Cob's planning, he had anticipated showing her the write-up in the newspaper at this time, bolstering her hopes for their future.

Instead, he said, "I was sitting just about as you are now, before I came for you. Old memories slid through my mind like living dreams. I thought of ranching together. Of all the adventures. Of your working so hard to get your medical degree. Your clinic. Your successes. How your hard work and intelligence brought so much into your life and into the lives of those around you."

Without turning her head to look at Cob, she said very quietly, "But there was always one thing missing."

Cob was sensible enough to hold his silence.

Before he had the chance to say anything, Gwyneth continued, "How would you feel about becoming a father, Cob?"

For Cob, the world stopped turning. No sound existed in all of creation. His mind couldn't form a single word out of those available to him. His ears heard no sound. Just that one lasting word. The one he had reconciled himself to never hearing. *Father*. It can't be true, can it?

Gwyneth could wait no longer. "Did you hear me, Cob?"

"Were you speaking? All I heard was an angel, saying the impossible had become the possible. Was that really you and not an angel? And are you serious?"

"Oh, I am serious, my love. Serious and surprised. After all the years. After all the years of blaming myself for not being able to conceive. It's a miracle of love, Cob. God has blessed again. At my age, I'm feeling almost like Sarah must have felt when she presented her news to Abraham."

Cob rose from his chair and kneeled by Gwyneth, taking her two hands in his. Looking deeply into her eyes, he said, "I'm sure Abraham was overjoyed. As I am. And there's no fault or blame for the past. This is a new day, a new time. Your news is wonderful. Marvelous. There could be nothing better to brighten our futures."

They sat together in quiet contemplation as the tea cooled and the steam ceased rising, while dinner was forgotten and the future, not with a shout, but with a whisper, eased itself into their minds.

If You Liked This, You Might Like:

A GOOD MAN COMES AROUND: A CHRISTIAN HISTORICAL ROMANCE

Oliver Martin is done—with hope, with God, and most especially with women. When his well-meaning friend sends for a wife on his behalf, Oliver makes it clear he's not husband material. Abigail Holt agrees. The last thing she wants is another bitter, drunk, and spiritually lost man anywhere near her or her young sons.

But when a tragic loss leaves Oliver staring down the mess he's made of his life, a single, soul-deep question arises: Can a man who's fallen so far ever rise again?

As grief turns to grace and harsh judgments shift to healing, Abigail begins to see what her heart never dared to hope for: a good man worth loving—if she can only trust again.

Based on a true story of a gold strike that changed everything, this Western Romance offers a powerful tale of second chances, stirring faith, and the kind of love that doesn't just heal—but transforms.

Can a broken man become the blessing he was meant to be? And can a guarded heart learn to love again—without losing everything?

AVAILABLE NOW

Thank You

Thank you for taking the time to read *Gwyneth Finally*. If you enjoyed it, please consider telling your friends or posting a short review. Word of mouth is an author's best friend and much appreciated.

Thank you,
Reg Quist

About the Author

Reg Quist's pioneer heritage includes sod shacks, prairie fires, home births, and children's graves under the prairie sod, all working together in the lives of people creating their own space in a new land.

Out of that early generation came farmers, ranchers, business men and women, builders, military graves in faraway lands, Sunday Schools that grew to become churches, plus story tellers, musicians, and much more.

Hard work and self-reliance were the hallmark of those previous great generations, attributes that were absorbed by the following generation.

Quist's career choice took him into the construction world. From heavy industrial work, to construction camps in the remote northern bush, the author emulated his grandfathers, who were both builders, as well as pioneer farmers and ranchers.

It is with deep thankfulness that Quist says, "I am a part of the first generation to truly enjoy the benefits of the labors of the pioneers. My parents and their parents worked incredibly hard, and it is well for us to remember".

www.ingramcontent.com/pod-product-compliance
Lightning Source LLC
LaVergne TN
LVHW100519110826
845146LV00002B/706

* 9 7 9 8 8 9 5 6 7 8 6 9 5 *